# SACRIFICES

∞

## Alan D. Jones

A RISING SUN GROUP PUBLICATION
www.AlanDJones.com
Atlanta, Georgia, USA

# SACRIFICES
By Alan D. Jones

Rising Sun Group Publishing
Copyright © 2013 Alan D. Jones

ISBN-13: 978-0-9666679-6-7
Library of Congress Control Number: 2013914421

All rights reserved. No part of this publication may be reproduced or transmitted in any form or by any means, electronic or mechanical, including photocopy, recording, or any information storage or retrieval system, without permission in writing from the publisher or author.

This book is a work of fiction. Names, characters, places and incidents are products of the author's imagination or are used fictitiously. Any resemblance to actual events or locales or persons living or dead is entirely coincidental.

Cover Image: Mshindo
Editing Services: Wilma Jenkins, Cynthia Coles and Michele Beard
Interior Page Layout & Design: Abena Muhammad for DetailsCount
Front & Back Cover Design: Abena Muhammad for DetailsCount

Thanks to the following whose support and understanding helped to bring this work to life:

        Anika A. Jones
        Lesley "Tafiti" Grady
        Wilma Jenkins
        Joshua Dickson
        Eva Bird

# Contents

| | | |
|---|---|---|
| Prologue | Prologue | 9 |
| Chapter 1 | To Trap a Demon | 17 |
| Chapter 2 | Homecoming | 21 |
| Chapter 3 | False Gods | 35 |
| Chapter 4 | Fallen Saints | 43 |
| Chapter 5 | Echoes from Birmingham | 51 |
| Chapter 6 | The Trouble with Grubs | 59 |
| Chapter 7 | Tipping Point | 69 |
| Chapter 8 | Sad Conception | 79 |
| Chapter 9 | Slipping Away | 95 |
| Chapter 10 | Old Wounds | 117 |
| Chapter 11 | New Day, Old Nightmares | 125 |
| Chapter 12 | The Truth of Things | 133 |
| Chapter 13 | Star Fall | 141 |
| Chapter 14 | Vipers | 151 |
| Chapter 15 | In Bloom | 157 |
| Chapter 16 | Summer Harvest | 169 |
| Chapter 17 | The Sum of Things | 175 |
| Chapter 18 | What Should Never Be | 189 |
| Chapter 19 | Sisterhood | 199 |
| Chapter 20 | The Nor'easter | 209 |
| Chapter 21 | Chasing Ghosts | 221 |
| Chapter 22 | The Cost | 231 |
| Chapter 23 | Oblivion | 263 |
| Chapter 24 | Repast | 281 |
| Chapter 25 | A Kind of Peace | 285 |
| Chapter 26 | Revelation | 289 |
| Addendum | The Secret Sorrow of Saints | 295 |
| Epilogue | Eternal Prayers | 299 |

*"It's all energy...
our thoughts, our time and our
tears... all of it."*

*Genesis 6:4*

*The Nephilim were on the earth at that time (and also immediately afterward), when those divine beings were having sexual relations with those human women, who gave birth to children for them. These children became the heroes and legendary figures of ancient times.*

*International Standard Version 2012*

*"One to guide, one to create, one to protect, and one to destroy ... and a child to tell the story."*

*"Everything has a price.
The universe is resolved in this."*

# Prologue

*Do not walk with anger, for this is the path to ruin. Nor sleep with anger, for it is the death of dreams. Neither sow anger, lest you reap a harvest of destruction.*

*October, 1980*

Gasping and wounded, Rob rambled through the thicket towards the highway a mile away, his attackers still in pursuit. He'd played this game with them many times before. Today, no longer young, as he'd been for hundreds of years, his moves were not as sharp as they once were and his sight not as clear.

A dark voice that seemed to come from every direction whispered, "Why do you run Rob? You know your time has come."

It was Matasis, the leader of the Council of Nob. He was the shape-shifting, spell-casting demon from Hell with awful breath. Rob looked up just in time to see the demon close his eyes as he released a deadly bolt of ethereal energy. The bolt passed Rob's head. As he spun, Rob raised his hand toward his opponents. As he did, the ground rose to form a ten-foot barrier. It wouldn't stop his enemy but, perhaps, could gain him another two or three seconds lead time. Maybe it would be enough time for him to find the nearest underground passage. Or, maybe not. A rocket-launched grenade went off not fifteen feet away from Rob knocking him off his feet and stunning him. Lying on his back, Rob lifted a hand again toward this aerial combatant and fire erupted from his fingertips.

His second opponent, Destry, dodged the flames and hovered above him laughing, "You're losing your timing, old man."

Rob, stumbling to his feet and raising his arms and spreading them wide, exclaimed, "That may be, but my aim need not be true all the time."

At Rob's command, a mighty wind disturbed the trees and rushed towards Destry driving him and his warhorse into the bristling foliage. The wind swirled down and around Rob forming a mini tornado. This would have been a formidable barrier for most attackers, but not for his third attacker, Chase the Saint Killer. The pale, thin and intangible assassin easily walked through the rumbling debris towards Rob. From ten feet away, Chase cast two glowing green globes from his hands which affixed themselves to Rob's left and right wrists holding them fast. Chase smiled. He knew that this time, at last, they had their prey. The Council had been trying for generations to destroy Rob, a former Circle Knight. Now that he was no longer under their protection and had grown old, they'd finally succeeded.

Rob struggled to no avail against the glowing green bands that held him aloft. The bands not only bound him. They also prevented him from opening the ground beneath him as he had done the last time these villains had him cornered. As the winds he'd stirred died down, he could see Matasis the Deformer stepping through the thicket.

"Ah, Matasis, where are the others? Did they not think enough of me to attend my party?"

Matasis gave a mock sigh, "Oh, I'm sure they are rushing to be here even now, but I think they're going to be too late."

Unlike the rest of his troop, Destry was not in a good mood. He rushed towards Rob yelling, "That little wind storm of yours damaged my chariot!"

Rob smiled, "What? You don't have that death machine insured?"

Enraged, Destry pulled a weapon from his waist and pointed it at Rob, but Chase pushed his comrade's arm aside telling him, "Relax. I landed the telling move. The death strike belongs to me."

"I guess I should be flattered by your bickering, but...," Rob quipped.

The dead-eyed Chase, seldom one to respond to banter, extracted his sword and moved towards Rob.

Chase had not taken two steps before Matasis, the self-proclaimed destroyer of dreams and lord of chaos, stepped between Rob and him, "Hold on. This day has been so long in coming. Let us savor it just a bit more."

He then turned towards his captured foe, "I've always wondered. How is it that you're an outcast among the Circle Knights and yet hunted by our side as well?"

Rob smiled, "Guess I just got a knack for pissing people off. It's a gift really."

"Not a healthy one," Destry remarked.

"No," Rob agreed, "but, then again, on the bright side, I won't have to see any of your ugly mugs again. Or smell Matasis' breath for that matter.

"You can take on all manner of form but every one of them has terrible breath. Can't you do something about that? Hey, there's a mint in my front left pocket. Take it, please."

Matasis said nothing. Instead, he lifted his right hand towards Rob, closed his eyes and unleashed another wave of ethereal energy that caused Rob's body to writhe in pain. Rob cried out. Then, oddly, he began to laugh as he reflected on the course of his own life.

"Abandoned by my own and surrounded by mortal enemies with my arms bound and stretched out. Many endings I had imagined, but not this one."

Seeing Matasis turn away, Chase took another step towards Rob, but this time it was Destry who halted the assassin.

Destry, noticing the gray hair now in Rob's head for the first time, couldn't help but ask, "How did you lose your immortality?"

Rob, now barely able to lift his head, replied simply "Immortality?" He smiled one last time.

Matasis motioned to Chase to proceed. Blade in hand, Chase launched himself into the air towards Rob. His sword punctured Rob's chest and lower abdomen and blood began to flow to the ground.

Just as Chase finished wiping his blade, a light appeared in the darkness and through it stepped the stunning Elisa the Enchantress. Looking up, she saw Rob suspended several feet off the ground. She froze for a heartbeat and instinctively grabbed her left arm with her right hand as though to scratch it.

"What's wrong, my lady?" Matasis inquired of the pensive-looking woman.

"This one was mine. You were supposed wait for the rest of us to arrive."

"No need, my lady. His head will still fit just as well on your mantle," Matasis answered.

A now jovial Destry interjected, "What he means is that he got tired of hearing Rob's lip."

A nearly unconscious Rob smiled, but most his words were inaudible as he gurgled on his own blood.

Elisa, a mind reader, knew well what he was trying to say. Rob's last words were, "For the days to come."

"Release him," Elisa said.

Chase obliged as Elisa ascended into air and floated towards the nearly lifeless Rob. Taking his body from the air, she lowered him slowly to the ground as she whispered in his ear. Elisa then stood and turned towards the others, "Okay, let's go."

"What about him?" Matasis asked Elisa gesturing towards Rob's limp body.

Elisa stood still, indecisive for a moment as if she were choosing between two equally lovely floral arrangements. She replied, "Put him in the cooler for now. I'll deal with him after we finish the portal."

Matasis grinned a devilish smile, "Now, that sounds like a plan."

$$\infty$$

It is said that we are the remnants of those undefined by time and the substance of legends. Some say this with a certainty that I cannot claim as my own. Thus, I will focus on what I do know. I'm not like any I know. Most every night, I am haunted by dreams. Not my own, but the dreams of those long gone and those yet to be. While other gifts have been granted to me over the years, this one true gift has remained with me across time and space. This one true gift affords me the opportunity to share their stories through their own dreams.

One such story is that of my mother, Sarah, and her sisters Lucille, Deborah and Ruth.

# SACRIFICES • *Alan D. Jones*

# THE BOOK OF LUCILLE

## SACRIFICES • *Alan D. Jones*

# 1:
# TO TRAP A DEMON

*April, 1981*

*"God and Science are both true, but our inability to understand either fully is the basis of both our confusion and discontent. For if we truly understood and accepted where God resides, we would never doubt, never be afraid or ever feel lost, not even for a moment." Lucille Johnson*

*"If you tell it all, you'll have nothing left to say." Lucille Johnson*

Born Lucille Abilene Johnson, but known to her family and friends as Cil, my Aunt Cil was an amazing woman. A dark brown-skinned woman, standing about five-foot ten, and built like an Amazon, Cil taught physics at Spelman College. Simply dressed and often stoic, she appeared monolithic to me as I grew up in her shadow like a sentry guarding the gates of Hell which, in fact, she was. As the Gatekeeper, her job was to cast demons back into their own world. Suffice it to say, Cil had her complexities and secrets, the depth of which, even today, I'm still discovering. Her detractors called her "Cil the Fanatic." I, too, thought she was a bit intense when I was younger. Yet, the longer I live, the more like her I become.

One day about a year before my birth, Cil was on the northern end of the Baffin Bay, Canada, right below the Arctic Circle, one hundred miles from any human life. She was digging. Seemingly mad, she landscaped and sculpted the icy terrain for some unimaginable arctic vineyard. Her six foot staff drove through the snow and ice, time and time again. And that same staff swept way the debris.

And while she was unbothered by anything human, it was the non-humans she found to be a nuisance. That day she was literally being chased by demons. Before she could see or hear them, she knew they were there. Then, from behind her she heard, "Gatekeeper!"

Cil turned to face her accusers saying nothing. The four arctic demons appeared before her as half man, half polar bear beasts. The biggest of them spoke again, "Are you here to banish us?"

Cil was a beautiful woman. Statuesque and athletic, her brown skin was flawless and her beauty not fully appreciated in her time. She removed the knit covering from her mouth, revealing dark brown lips which spoke through the cutting wind a simple reply, "No."

The beasts, as was their nature, did not believe her. They bared their teeth. As the foursome began to circle her, Cil's gaze remained steady and straight ahead. The smallest of the behemoths spoke in agitation, "We have not tasted a human spirit in ten years and still you pursue us here?"

Cil replied, "Truly? Might it be that it is your own past that haunts you. Surely, by now, you know that there is a price for everything. Whatever this day is, your own sad existence has led you here."

The biggest demon growled in disapproval and leaned in towards Cil's right side, opening his foul mouth to unleash a torrent of arctic air cold enough to freeze a normal person in seconds. Cil leapt into the air with a back flip that carried her outside of their circle of doom. In quick succession, she swung her staff into the knee of one middle-sized bear, severing its leg, and into the snout of the other bear to her left, breaking it as well. Before either hit the ground, she ran three steps and slid beneath the legs of the biggest bear and sprung up upon his shoulder, her staff pulled tight across his neck. She accomplished all of this before that largest beast could release a second breath. Within another second, his neck was snapped and he too was falling to the ice. This left the smallest demon aghast and bewildered. He turned to run but, before he could take a step, Cil's staff pierced his right hind leg felling him as well.

She walked over to retrieve her weapon. As she removed it, she said to the departing evil spirit, "You could have just walked away. Go now and do not return."

It turned Cil's stomach to let that one demon go, but it was a part of the plan. Then, she returned to her icy garden. At last, Cil completed her task and stood to survey her work. Looking around the harbor, there was no obvious purpose to Cil's labors which is exactly as she wanted it.

She looked over her right shoulder and called to her sister, "Deborah, can you see it?"

The recently-wed Deborah, made herself visible and then affirmed "Yes, I can see it. But you know that little one will alert Matasis and the council that we were here digging?"

Cil smirked for a second, "I'm counting on it." She reflected on Rob's death last Fall. It had brought a sense of urgency for her and her sisters. They had realized for some time that something had to be done if any of them wanted to live and raise families in some semblance of peace. Rob had kept the four of them safe all those years, moving them from place to place around the world until they were old enough to fend for themselves. Now Rob, the most daring of saints, was gone. With his death there was no turning back. This was simply the first move in a series that Cil had planned. Cil took her sister's hand and smiled at what her handiwork revealed.

# 2: HOMECOMING

*August, 1963*

*The hardest thing to learn in life is that love does not come with a receipt. We certainly wish that it did, but how many times do we give love and do not receive an acknowledgement in return, much less a written one. But we are reminded that love, by its very nature, does not keep an account. In fact, when it comes to love, who among us is able to maintain a balanced ledger?*

*Oh, what a day when you realize that all you ever hoped for is already inside of you. Some people go an entire lifetime never realizing such a day.*

Deborah the Deceiver, as she would come to be known, was a precocious little girl with the curse of a jealous heart. Her big sister, Cil, was the target of most of her jealousy, but she had enough to go around.

On this particular day, the soon to be eleven Deborah sat quietly in an empty stall in a West End stable at one of the carriage companies still operating in 1963 Atlanta. Her father, Hosea, had punished her for not getting home the previous night before the street lights came on. She had to assist him with caring for the horses after school. He stood in the next stall with one of the horses. Hosea wasn't aware that Deborah was nearby since she could not be seen. She wanted the quiet time to finish reading the Ebony magazine she'd picked up from Miss Elizabeth's house. When asked about why she was late, she would tell her father that she'd missed her bus. Today, her deception had an added, unexpected benefit.

"Hosea, you crusty old man!" an all too familiar voice called out.

It was Deborah's mother, Lola. Though she'd spoken with her on the phone at Christmas, as she did most years, Deborah couldn't remember the last time she'd actually seen her mother. She could not help but sneak a peek at Lola strutting, her hips swaying as she proceeded down the path towards Hosea. Deborah longed to see her, but she was frightened. She remembered the ice cream cone Lola bought her one time, but she also remembered the more frequent screaming and yelling.

Hosea looked up from his horse grooming to respond, "Hello, Lola. I'm surprised to see you here given how you hate horses."

Lola, a beautiful cinnamon-colored woman, tip-toed a bit closer and said, "I grew up on a farm and, when I left, I said I'd never go back. Then, I married a man who's intent on bringing the farm to town."

Hosea smiled, "Babe, it's just a side time hustle to keep food on the table and just walking distance from the house. See. If you look out the front, you can see our mailbox. Being a substitute math teacher just isn't enough."

"And, the church isn't paying you?" Lola asked as she flicked her lighter.

"Oh, I'm still on staff part time at..."

Lola lit her cigarette, "No, not that church."

Hosea responded with a glance that said it all.

"So, why don't you quit?"

"Babe, you know I can't quit. Once you're called...," Hosea began.

"...you're called. Yes, I know. But, back in New Orleans, you made money. You were the hot new pastor. And now look at you?" Lola frowned.

Hosea stopped brushing for a second to consider his response but, before he could reply, Elisa arrived and injected, "That's because, dear sister, your antics in New Orleans got him run out of town. Don't you remember?"

Elisa was a striking, tall, dark-haired woman with soft freckles that only close observation revealed. The world mistook her for a white woman, but she didn't deny her black roots. This fact earned her a lot of respect.

Lola fired back, "Hey, you got that fancy car out there and nice clothes, but you've done your share of dirt too. You ain't no better than me."

"No, I'm not," Elisa conceded, "but, see, I know I'm no good. You, on the other-hand, are always making excuses for your behavior. I think these days I think they call that triflin'. But I do love your triflin' butt."

Lola smiled at her and admitted, "Yes, I did act a fool down in New Orleans. But, oh what fun I had! Still, that don't explain this fool here cleaning out horse stalls."

Elisa stroked the mare's neck "Well, a fifty-something year-old man who has to start over in a new city and can no longer work in his chosen profession doesn't have a lot of choices."

The still youthful looking Lola tilted her head at her husband "Yes, he has gotten old. Hasn't he? He looks like Matasis must have touched him. When I met him he was such a fine piece of dark chocolate and so gifted that I just knew he was going places. Known all over the world, yet, here you are grooming horses in a stable. While we're on the subject of things that don't make sense, how come you haven't tried to divorce me? You know them kids ain't yours, right, except maybe that first one?"

Deborah, standing in plain sight but hidden from them all, gasped. Elisa raised her brow slightly.

Hosea, who had continued to work while Lola rambled on, spoke up, "So, darling how's your treatment going?"

"Treatment?" Lola replied indignantly.

"Ok," Hosea continued, "so are you at least staying clean?" Deborah stewed. She always believed that her dad's strict ways had driven her mother away.

Lola's only reply was an incredulous look so Elisa answered for her, "Yes, at least in the couple of days that we've been together. I don't let her do that crap around me."

Lola interrupted, "I don't like where this conversation is going. Tell me about the girls. Do any of them have the gift? What about the prize?"

In our family we referred to special abilities as "gifts" and we were happy when any child began to display his or her gift. The prize was even more selective and more desired, for it was eternal youth. The prize didn't mean you would never die, but it did mean that you'd never grow old. Some family members got just a "touch of the prize." That meant that they aged very slowly. Elisa and Lola were both blessed with the gift and the prize. Unfortunately, Lola also possessed the third attribute regularly found in the family. Mental illness was known as "the curse." Sometime during the 1950's Lola complicated matters even more by taking a liking to heroin which was popular in the artsy crowd in New Orleans back then.

Hosea stopped tending the horse and smiled as he often did when speaking about his daughters. "Of course, it's too soon to know about the prize, but Cil definitely has the gift and I'm seeing things in Deborah that have me wondering."

Elisa smiled warmly, "Oh, I'd say that Deborah definitely has the gift!" as she looked towards where Deborah had been hiding.

The realization that Elisa knew where she was shook Deborah so much that she almost lost the concentration needed to remain invisible. Her memories of Aunt Elisa from New Orleans were vague at best. She knew that she was "gifted" but up to that point she had no idea how. Her mind raced with possibilities. When she contemplated telepathy, Elisa's quick wink confirmed it.

Hosea was puzzled for a second by Elisa's response, but then he quickly pieced together the clues he'd noticed before with Elisa's smile to conclude that Deborah was present with them in the stable. Hosea gave an easy smile, "I bet she's somewhere reading a magazine and dreaming of trading in her hot comb for a perm kit."

Lola didn't quite catch what they were inferring, but quickly her mind was on to the next thing. "Hosea, you're not still caught up in this civil rights foolishness, are you? 'Cause you know ain't nothing gonna change. I've been around a long time and it's the same as it's always been. It got a new name, but it's the same pig poop today as it was yesterday."

Hosea turned his head but held his tongue which he often did around Lola.

Just then, a car full of people with bubbles streaming out of the rear window pulled up. The back door swung open and out popped Deborah's seven-year-old little sister, Ruth Ann.

She ran towards her father screaming in delight, "Daddy, Daddy!" About three feet from him she leapt into the air and he caught her. "Daddy, the Caballeros are here!"

The Caballeros family also was gifted. In the early 60's, they were possibly a more powerful force for good than the Johnson family. They had a little girl named Gabriella who was the same age as Ruth. The two little girls fell in love with one another the first day they met. When the Caballeros visited, it was impossible to separate the two of them. The family was visiting from Mexico.

"Daddy, can Gabby and I go to get ice cream?" a smiling Ruth asked.

Gabriella's mother, Alejanda, motioned to the little girls and said to Hosea, "I will take them so that you and my husband can talk."

Hosea nodded and she began to lead the laughing little girls away. Ruth looked back at her father and waved.

Ruth jumped for joy and then grabbed Gabriella's hand, "Oh, and I have to show you the clapping game."

My mother and her sisters often played the clapping game as children. They'd sit in a circle and one of them would start a pattern, clapping their hands, banging on the table, or whatever. Then, the next sister would repeat the pattern and add one more component. Round and round they'd go until one of them messed up. That game had taught the four of them how to work together as a unit.

Lola called to Ruth, "Ruth-Ann!"

Ruth broke away from her girlfriend just long enough to run to her mother's waiting arms. "I'm glad you're back, mommy."

Lola held onto Ruth for a few lingering moments before releasing her. Lola wanted to be a good mother but always seemed to mess it up. Unlike her other daughters, little Ruth Ann never seemed to hold it against her. Lola could always reel Ruth back into her web of chaos.

Jorge Caballeros, the leader of his clan, said to his good friend, Hosea, "Can we take a walk?"

Hosea nodded and excused himself, "Sorry, ladies. I'll meet you all back at the house."

Lola shouted to her husband, "If we see you, we see you. We got places to go and things to do. Can't be waiting on you."

Deb thought to herself that her daddy just didn't get it. While she was no big fan of her mother, she also felt like her father was clueless at times when it came to women. She wondered how he and Lola had ever gotten together.

Elisa gave a half smile as she glanced down the road towards Hosea and Jorge. Then, she called out, "Deborah, you can come out now."

Deborah revealed herself to her mother and Elisa.

"I'm sorry. I was just hiding from Daddy so that I could finish reading my magazine before helping him with the horses."

An elated Lola reached for her daughter and pulled her close.

"Oh, darling, that's fine. I'm just so happy to see that you have a gift! Besides, I don't blame you for not wanting to clean these old stinky stables."

Actually, Deborah did not mind her stable visits so much. Certainly, she hated the dirty work of helping her father clean the stables, but she loved the reward of getting to ride and groom the horses.

Lola released her daughter from her long embrace and held Deborah at arm's length. "Oh, my gosh. Has your daddy finally learned to do hair?"

Deb smiled a bit and said, "No, Cil did my hair. She does all of our hair now, except for Daddy, of course."

Lola gave her a doubtful look. "I don't know...," Lola said.

She thought about Miss Elizabeth, her husband's fellow church member and single neighbor down the street. Lola didn't want her husband anymore but she didn't want anyone else to have him either. This ironic jealous streak had her thinking that Miss Elizabeth, who happened to be a beautician by trade, was using her talents to woo her husband and her children.

Elisa stepped in. "Deb, I think your sister has done a wonderful job with your hair. Just remember to wrap it up before you come down here after school. I'm sure Cil would appreciate that."

Deb nodded and proceeded to follow her mother and auntie back home.

Lola glanced at her husband and Jorge and asked Elisa, "What do you think they're talking about back there?"

"You know what they're talking about. But, what do you care? You're a noncombatant, remember? Unless you're ready to take a side?" Elisa asked.

"Oh, no!" Lola exclaimed, "I like breathing too much to get caught up in that foolishness."

There were guidelines to this calling. One of them was an out clause for any gifted individual who wished to stay on the sidelines. At least, that's how it was supposed to work. Those who served the darkness violated this accord whenever it suited them. By not taking sides, you had to agree to live a modest life seeking neither fame nor fortune.

Lola agreed to these terms. Around the family, she often crowed about her "independence" from either side. In truth, because of her mental instability and drug problem, neither side particularly wanted her on their team. Elisa knew this but, to protect Lola's fragile psyche, she allowed Lola to believe that she was indeed in high demand.

As the ladies entered the wrought iron gate at the house, they saw Lucille, the oldest of the Johnson sisters. She was already well into her gifted years. Lucille stood silently observing, as though she knew exactly where they'd been and what they'd done.

Cil nodded ever so slightly and spoke tersely, "Mama." Stoic, she stretched out her right arm towards Deborah. saying, "Deb, please, come get Sarah ready for dinner." Unsmiling, she added, "Mama and Auntie Elisa, you're welcome to join us for dinner."

Both of the women froze for a moment. Lola was given pause at the sheer power she sensed in her oldest daughter. Elisa was stunned by the realization of just how much Cil and Lola's relationship had devolved.

At last, Lola breathed and announced, "I'm gonna stay out here and take a smoke. I'll be in, in a bit."

Elisa looked at Lola and said to her telepathically, "You need to come in with me."

To which Lola replied audibly, "No, I don't. Not right now. And, stay out of my head!"

Elisa entered the house and was immediately met by a smiling Deborah and a giggling Sarah. Before she could even sit down, Cil entered the dining room carrying a piping hot plate of pork chops, which she sat on the table between the green beans and mashed potatoes. Elisa's eyes opened wide, "When do you have time to make such wonderful meals?"

Cil replied without looking up, "I make time."

Elisa narrowed her eyes and tilted her head slightly before asking, "And, no time for your mother?"

"She's a drug addict. She sleeps around on daddy. And, she refuses to work in or out of the house," the fourteen year old added, "Even I don't have time for that."

Falling into her New Orleans drawl, Elisa said sternly, "I know all too well who she is. I also know what she's been through and the challenges she faces. By the time she was your age, she'd already suffered terribly."

Just then, a jubilant Ruth Ann flew into the room dragging a reluctant Lola behind her and singing, "I had ice cream, ice cream, chocolate ice cream!"

Ruth raced to Cil and they held each other. Suddenly teary-eyed, Cil motioned towards her sisters before forcing out, "How long..."

Elisa who, upon seeing the weariness in the young girl's eyes, shared a tear as well answered, "Darling, love doesn't ask the cost. Love simply pays."

Lola entered the room looking confused, trying to figure out what she missed. Before she could inquire, Gabriella and her mother came in behind her. So, she changed her focus to the place settings.

"Cil, why do you have eleven place settings out?"

"Mother, we're going to have an extra guest," Cil stated wiping a tear from her eye.

Surveying the serving plate and noticing only ten pork chops, Lola inquired, "So, why do you only have ten chops in the plate? You need to cut up one of them."

"No, Mother, our eleventh guest won't want one," Cil replied as she bowed her head to bless the food.

Elisa smiled at the fact that Cil had set the table perfectly for a series of uninvited guests, herself included. It was evident that the child could predict the future to some degree. She also noticed that Cil's sisters had become so accustomed to Cil's ways that they failed to realize why their elder sister was right all the time.

Right on time, about ten minutes after Cil's blessing, Jorge and Hosea marched through the front door and into the dining room. Jorge sat at the head of the table on one end and Hosea on the other near his wife and Elisa. The table was packed, but one place setting remained unused.

About five minutes later there was a knock on the door. Before anyone could move, the door swung open and in stepped Hosea's friend and neighbor, Miss Elizabeth, announcing herself, "Hello!"

She had seen Hosea arrive home from her own front porch and knew he had a guest, but when she stepped into the foyer, she was surprised to see that the dining room was actually full of guests. After her gaze left Hosea, it fell upon Lola.

"Oh, you have company."

The full-figured Elizabeth adjusted herself and fixed her face through a nervous smile.

"Well, I saw you come home with Jorge and I thought you might like a pie. I baked two of them today."

Cil noticed that Miss Elizabeth was anxious, so she reached out to her. "Miss Elizabeth, would you like to join us?" Cil motioned towards the open chair.

Elizabeth smiled and shook her head slightly, "Oh, no. I had an early dinner and I've got an early morning tomorrow."

Hosea motioned to her as well, "Elizabeth, have a seat. You can at least have some pie with us."

"Well, if you insist...," Miss Elizabeth smiled.

Lola, who had been sitting motionless with her mouth hanging open during the exchange, spoke up, "What? Does she just walk into this house anytime she wants? Look at this!"

Lola began digging through her purse for something. Moments later she found her wedding band and slipped the ring onto her finger.

"You see this? This means we're still married and I'm still his wife!"

Miss Elizabeth laid her napkin in her lap before looking up to respond, "Yes, you are his wife. But, you have many husbands, don't you?"

Lola erupted from the table and tried to move towards Elizabeth, "Heifer, don't you know I will kill you if you don't get out of my house right now!"

Miss Elizabeth, still seated, calmly replied, "Oh, I have no doubt that you could kill me. But, that don't mean I'm afraid of you. I'm no more afraid of you than I am of these folks walking around here talking about where I can sit, eat, or even have a drink of water. But, see, I'll be in the picket line again this weekend and I'll be right back here until such time that Hosea or these girls tell me otherwise or you actually move into this place and become the woman of the house."

Hosea tried to inject a word of calm into the room, but neither of the ladies was listening. At last, Elisa, who was already holding Lola back, suggested, "Hey, why don't we just go outside for a while? Maybe go shopping?"

Lola fired off, "I'm not leaving my house while that home-wrecking hussy is still here!"

Miss Elizabeth stood up and announced, "Oh, I'm leaving…"

She said this with an intentional inflection that conveyed she could have said more, but chose to stop. She grabbed her purse, apologized to the Caballeros and blew kisses to the girls as she rose from the table. All the while, Lola continued to run her mouth.

After Miss Elizabeth left, Elisa was able to get Lola moving towards the door although, by this time, she was venting her anger towards Hosea. Elisa could have used her gift on Lola to quiet her, but refrained from doing so. As she turned Lola towards the exit, Elisa glanced back at the table and noticed that Cil had set out eight dessert saucers. The child had known every detail. She even knew that they would not be staying for dessert.

After dinner, Gabriella watched as Cil helped Ruth and Sara with their homework. Hosea worked with Deborah who struggled with her math homework. Hosea was patient and Deb enjoyed her time studying with her father. All of the girls were excited about spending the next day at the lake, even Ruth who was deathly afraid of the water. The fact that her friend Gabriella was also going filled her with enough joy to overcome her fears.

Later that night, after everyone had gone to sleep, Deborah awoke to notice that her big sister was no longer in the bed they shared. Deborah looked around for a moment and then sensed motion outside her window. She pulled the shade back a bit to peep outside. The empty swing on the back porch swung back and forth lazily, its former occupant now standing barefoot in the small backyard, her white cotton gown moving ever so gently in the soft evening breeze. Cil stood facing the brick wall which lined the back yard, saying nothing.

Deborah thought to call out to her sister but, before she could fully draw in a breath, a second figure entered the backyard. The person glowed a little and had not entered through the gate but, instead, passed through the wall like a ghost. This new girl, who appeared to be nineteen or twenty, with skin as dark as her daddy's and hers, wore her hair in an afro like some of the college girls over at Clark and Spelman College.

The girl, who was named Akina, and Cil hugged briefly. Akina asked, "Are you aware?"

Cil answered, "Yes, I am."

The unknown woman's name was Akina, a time traveler and relative from nearly forty years in the future. Her question was an inquiry into a state of being, and not limited to an awareness of any particular event, although there was a pending event that lead Akina to feel the need to make an appearance.

"Tomorrow will be a challenge," Akina stated so quietly that Deborah could not hear her.

Softly spoken, too, was Cil's reply, "I know." Cil hugged Akina and whispered into her ear, "Just the first of many."

In response, Akina held her tighter.

After a long moment, Akina released Cil, turned and walked into some other place and time. After Akina departed, Cil returned to the back porch and fell to her knees. Deborah was afraid for her sister. Had the woman bewitched her somehow? Had she poisoned her sister? Deborah rushed out of the bedroom and out the back door to see her sister on her knees looking up at her.

"Come here, Deborah. Join me."

Deborah stepped quickly to her sister and extended her hand before also falling to her knees. Deborah had questions and she was not one to easily hold her tongue; so, it took all her focus to submit to her sister's need to pray rather than her desire to know more about the mystery woman.

When they finished praying, Deborah peppered Cil with questions, "Who was that lady? Is she a friend of yours? Was she a ghost?"

Cil told Deborah that the young lady was special, like them, but that she had lost her way and needed directions. Cil hated to mislead her sister, but she knew that she could not tell her what would await them the next day at the lake.

# 3: FALSE GODS

*August, 1963*

*Hoping that others know your heart is like wishing on a star. Better to know your own heart and take comfort therein.*

Ruth was curious child, often so lost in her own world that the movements of this world passed her by. Many thought that she was odd. But thankfully, Ruth rarely cared much about what other people thought of her.

Riding down I-20 in the back seat of the Caballeros' Buick with Gabby, Ruth Ann, her pink ribbon flickering in the wind, made faces and waved at her sisters every time the two cars passed one another.

Looking over at her sister, Deb asked, "Why does Bubbles always have to be so childish?"

Cil responded to Deb, "Because she's a child. Let her be."

Sarah, who was six years old at the time, played along with Ruth Ann's game, giggling and playing peek-a-boo with her sister in the other lane.

Hosea drove Miss Elizabeth's car. Sarah, Cil, and Deb sat in the back seat. Cil rode in the front passenger seat while Deb and Sarah rode in the back seat. It was a warm day and neither car had air conditioning, so all the windows were either down or at least cracked.

Miss Elizabeth was supposed to go on the picnic with everyone else, but when Lola showed up unexpectedly, Miss Elizabeth thought it best that she not go. The attraction between Hosea and Miss Elizabeth was clear to everyone around them. Yet, they resisted and were always careful not to cross that line of no return.

Hosea had moved the family to Atlanta to start over after things fell apart in New Orleans. Lola never took a liking to Atlanta and was back in New Orleans before the close of that year. In the nearly five years since, she seldom visited although she often promised to. Rightly or wrongly, that was just fine with her daughters because Lola always brought drama. Miss Elizabeth, who had relocated to the neighborhood less than six months after Lola departed, stepped right in to help Hosea with his girls just as she had done in New Orleans. When Elizabeth first started helping Hosea with the girls, it was more a case of just trying to do the right thing but it became much more. Sarah spent so little time in Lola's care that she had no real attachment to her as a mother. The only mother Sarah would ever claim was Miss Elizabeth. But Ruth on the other hand, even though she too loved Miss Elizabeth, longed for her mother to take her place as her mama. She believed every story, every lie her mother told – even the ones she told to herself.

The two families arrived at the state park just after ten in the morning. They found a fairly secluded beach and set up camp. Setting up in an isolated section of the lake was not by chance. Jorge looked every bit like what one would expect a Mexican to look, albeit bigger than one might expect. His wife did not. Alejanda's pale skin, next to her husband's dark tan flesh, often raised an eyebrow or two when they traveled in the States. The fact that Hosea was there as well gave them even more reason to be cautious in the rural south.

The two big girls, Cil and Deborah were allowed to row their small inflatable rafts into the lake. Gabby was busy trying to teach the plastic sunglass wearing Sarah some Latin variation of "paddy cake". The adults sat at the picnic table discussing the matters of the day and the events of the previous evening. Ruth Ann was in her own little world, blowing bubbles out over the water and making her dolls fall in and out of love. Each bubble she blew would fall softly upon the lake and rest there for a moment shimmering in the sunlight.

Jorge, Alejanda, and Hosea surveyed their children and smiled. Finally, Jorge spoke up, in English, although they often conversed in Spanish. "What a beautiful day. Almost makes you want to forget about last night. Man, what happened?"

Hosea, who was fluent in English, Spanish, French and Creole, answered, "Lola just popped up. I didn't know she was coming, but that's what she does, pop up."

"That's got to be hard on the kids," Jorge offered.

Hosea took a breath before replying, "I think they're all dealing with it just fine, thankfully."

"What about that one?" Jorge's wife Alejanda asked and nodded towards Ruth who sat alone on the beach blowing bubbles out and over the water.

Hosea smiled, "Yes, I think she is the most affected. Look at her. She's in her own little world. I'm sure it's a much more beautiful world than this one often is."

"On that note," Jorge leaned in so that he might lower his voice, "what are you going to do about your wife?"

Alejanda leaned in, "What is he going to do? I think it's already been done. She's left him. She just visits from time to time when she sobers up and feels guilty. Then after a day or so she gets bored and leaves again for who knows where. And where does she get the money to buy these drugs she uses? She has no job and hasn't in years. Think about it. You don't want to hear it, but you know what she's doing. You should divorce her, wait six months and a day, and then marry Elizabeth."

Hosea grimaced as he massaged his salt and pepper goatee, and then he shared, "You both know that I have prayed on this matter a lot. But you don't know how many times I've asked the Lord to release me from this marriage. Each time He has said no, reminding me that drug addicts need love, too. Yet lately, it seems that He does not reply at all. Perhaps our Lord has grown weary of me and my petitions."

Alejanda shook her head and answered Hosea, "Hosea, what are you talking about? You're known as 'the one to whom God listens'. Certainly you have His ear in this matter as well."

Jorge added, "She's right, God not only hears you when He calls you to cast out demons, but also when you cry out during your own trials. Even more so, I would argue."

"Oh, I know, my brother. I know God hears me, but…," Hosea's voice trailed off.

"What is it brother?" Jorge asked.

"It's more than just an issue with my marriage. For the first time since I entered the ministry I am unsure about the future. Up until now, I've always been able to remove myself and my own desires from the conversation, so that I might hear God's voice. And, while not explicitly knowing the future, I always got a sense of it, a real oneness with what shall be. But, not now. Now, all I see is darkness."

The three of them sat in silence listening to the brisling treetops. Suddenly, as the wind slowed, Hosea focused his attention on the lake. There, he saw a blue-tinted man floating in the water. The man had a white beard and large sparkling crystals wrapped around his neck. He was speaking to Hosea's oldest two daughters. Hosea raised a brow and stood up for a better look.

The man began to move away from the two older girls, but in his wake, the waters began to swirl and the wind began to whip. Hosea then jumped when he heard the worst thing any father could hear, the frightened calls of his daughters crying out

"Daddy!" Hosea ran towards the beach to see a whirlpool forming in the lake around his two oldest girls.

The man rose up out of the water, grinning as he floated skyward. "I am Poseidon, god of the seas. Consider these two an initial offering unto me. I will be back for the others later. Meanwhile, I leave you a gift to remind you of me until I return." With that one of the jewels around his neck glowed brightly for a second. Then two serpents sprung from the veins in his arms and fell into the lake. Once in the lake the water snakes grew to monstrous proportions. While Hosea tried to make his way to the water, Jorge ripped the wooden top off of the picnic table and hurled it like a saucer at the neck of one of the raging serpents slicing its head clean off. Before he could move on to the second beast, Jorge noticed the first beast was not dead. Where he'd sliced off the creature's head, two new heads replaced the first one.

Jorge cried out, "Señor!"

Hosea amazingly managed to dodge the sniping head of the second hydra as he made his way towards Cil and Deborah. As he waded out into the fast-moving water, he saw little Ruth Ann walking across the water towards her sisters. Although the raging winds threatened to dislodge her from her glowing blue walkway, she stayed steady on her course and on her pace. Unlike her three sisters, Ruth-Ann had never liked the water, yet there she was running across the lake on a nearly invisible, shimmering pathway. Once she was above her two older sisters, who were hanging on to their rafts for dear life, Ruth stretched out her hands. Two blue bubbles floated from them encircling her lake-bound sisters. Each bubble held a sister and some lake water, and each one slowly rose into the air and followed Ruth as she walked briskly back to shore. All of this took place while the two hydras where focused on Hosea and Jorge.

Hosea, no longer speechless, began running towards the girls as they reached shore yelling, "Run!" over and over as he motioned towards the car. Then, panic hit him as he realized that the baby, Sarah, was missing. Hosea stopped in his tracks as everyone else raced on and in frenzy he called out, "Sarah, Sarah!"

Suddenly, there was a burst of light as though someone flipped on a 150 watt bulb in a totally dark room. For a moment, they were all blinded and the air filled with smoke. A smiling six-year-old Sarah walked out of that smoke as though nothing had happened. As the smoke began to clear, the group could see the hydras lying across the beach behind her. Every ounce of flesh of both beasts was smoldering as their ashes rose to the sky.

Jorge, mouth agape, asked Hosea, "What just happened here?"

A relived Hosea replied as he scurried his last little one along, "I don't know and at the moment, I don't much care. Let's just get out of here!"

Once in the car and headed back to I-20 for the ride home, Hosea engaged in a litany of commands to his daughters as he tried to calm down, "When I tell you to run, you run! That not only goes for Sarah, but for all of you. Do y'all hear me?"

"Yes, Daddy," the girls all said in chorus.

"That there was Poseidon, with his alien, would be demon self. He's a real…," Hosea, almost cursed. But, he caught himself.

The girls would sometimes, for fun, imitate their dad. They'd pretend to work themselves up to the verge of cursing, like their father. So, they looked at each other as Hosea searched for a word, wondering if this would be the time they'd finally hear their father curse.

"He's a real jerk, a bad man, or whatever he is."

Hosea in his work for the church had faced many demons, but by his faith, he was able to cast them out. However, Poseidon wasn't a demon but an alien from another world who had aligned himself with other dark forces who sought to rule over the earth.

Hosea continued to remind his girls about the need to take cover and the need to not leave your sister alone. As he ranted, Cil gave Deborah a look. At first she just stared as the still panting Deborah gazed back at her. Once she had Deborah's full attention, Cil raised one eyebrow ever so slightly. Deborah's eyes and mouth flew open in astonishment. Cil then nodded her head in confirmation. Through a series of glances and the hint of a smile, Cil had conveyed to Deborah that everything that had happened was according to plan.

The stress of the events had created such an emotional response in Ruth and Sarah that they, too, now had access to their gifts. Cil knew that dark days and many threats lay in front of them and that the little sisters would need to be able to defend themselves. Deborah looked over to her two younger sisters sitting in the back seat with her and shook her head. Then she looked back at Cil. Cil smiled slightly. All four girls rode all the way home in silence except for the repeated chorus of "Yes, Sir" to their father's requests.

SACRIFICES • *Alan D. Jones*

# 4: FALLEN SAINTS

*April, 1981*

*Wisdom is less about being right or wrong, than knowing when to speak and when to remain silent.*

A horrified Ruth floated to the ground in the Yucatan village of the Caballeros or, more accurately, what remained of it. Some of the cabins still smoldered and the air was soiled by the putrid smell of burning human flesh. Ruth walked quickly towards the several charred structures that were still standing in hopes of finding survivors. Mostly she was consumed with thoughts of her childhood girlfriend Gabriella and her family. She tried her best to follow protocol, but the thought of them being among the remains, shook Ruth and led her to rush from house to house without being as attentive to her surroundings as she should have been. She reviewed each body that she found looking for clues to their identity. With each face she recognized, her heart sank a little more.

Ruth exited the last cabin and reentered the courtyard. There she caught a glimpse of a figure laying prone in the dirt and partially covered in mud. She thought that she recognized the chain around his neck. As she knelt down to verify her suspicions, a burst of energy erupted out of the jungle towards Ruth, knocking her to the ground. Had it not been for her personal protective shield she would have been sliced in half. As it was she was knocked up and over the body she was inspecting. As she tried to stand, an artillery shell exploded not ten feet in front of her and she was blown into one of the cabins.

Destry emerged from the tree line exclaiming to his compatriot Chase "See, I told you I didn't need any help to take her down, just like I toasted that tostada she was looking at. I'm not like the last Destry you guys had."

The Council of Nob, of which they were a part, had a standing membership seat for the current Destry. The Destry represented a war mongering clan of murderers whose only goal was to obtain and use the deadliest weaponry. In this particular time period, much of it originated from worlds other than Earth. The previous Destry had accidently blown himself up about a year before this incident, although, there was suspicion in the group that he had some help. The rest of the Nob council members looked down on the Destry du jour. They merely tolerated them for the vast resources at their disposal. Matasis often said that, in times of war, it is sometimes good to have a rabid dog on your side.

Chase the Saint Killer, nearly translucent and completely bald, looked around searching for a second sister, since the sisters always worked in pairs. He stepped through a crumbling wall. Without looking at Destry he answered, "No, you're not like him. He was smarter."

As if on cue, the home into which Ruth had been blown began to glow in an ambient blue haze. Transfixed, the two killers saw a shadowy figure standing in the doorway of the ravaged cabin. All they could see clearly was one pink lock of hair. Illuminated by a thin beam of sunlight, it hung across Ruth's forehead.

The only thing they heard was a soft but determined "Do you realize what you've done?"

Immediately, a solid blue force beam extended from Ruth's left hand and into Destry knocking him back nearly fifty feet.

More loudly Ruth cried "You killed one of the nicest men I've ever known! And, you laugh and mock him?"

A second force beam erupted from Ruth's right hand and into the ground beneath Chase, tossing him into the air.

The battle suited Destry. Now back on his feet, he fired his alien particle beam cannon at Ruth again but, this time, she was ready. She had erected a blue shield around herself causing the deadly beam to disburse in a blue and red glow around her. A stunned Destry took a couple of steps back, before realizing that he still had his bazooka strapped to his back. He quickly loaded a shell into it as Ruth marched towards him. He fired the armor piercing round at Ruth from less than sixty feet away. The shell exploded on impact with Ruth's shield and kicked up so much dust and debris that Destry, knocked to the ground by the proximity of the explosion, could no longer see Ruth. The scruffy, short, squat man smiled, that is, until he saw Ruth continuing to march through the dusty cloud towards him.

The typically soft spoken Ruth shouted at Destry, "On your feet worm!"

A frightened Destry scampered backwards as he looked to the woods to see just how far away his warhorse and others weapons were stashed. He wondered if he could make a run for it. He stood, but before he could take a step Ruth was upon him. Ruth who, like her sisters was trained in the martial arts, side-kicked Destry in his back, knocking him to the ground again.

"On your feet!" Ruth yelled again.

Rage was building within Ruth and Destry was her outlet. However, before Destry could rise, Ruth caught a glimpse of Chase behind her. Somehow he'd penetrated her outer shield.

Chase smiled as he continued towards her, sword drawn, "Oh, child, you didn't expect that you could stop me so easily did you?"

In truth, no one on the Council of Nob feared Ruth. Not because she lacked power, she had plenty of that. No, they didn't fear her because they all knew that she was not a killer. In fact, at this point she'd never killed a mortal in battle. Ruth was and always had been kind. Therefore, her enemies would take liberties with her that they would not with her sisters.

Ruth quickly projected a second field. Chase engaged it and, for a moment, it held him. Then, slowly, he began to phase through it as well. In response, Ruth floated upwards and away from the two tyrants. In his ethereal state, Chase could float to the ground or even catch and float along on a breeze. But, he could not really fly. Chase could not pursue Ruth once she took to the air.

He called out to Destry, "Quick, go bring your sky chariot before she gets away!"

Before either of the villains could take a second step, a red hot beam came down between them and the forest. The beam blazed a line in the dirt. Finally, Chase had his answer as to which sister was providing backup on this mission. It was Sarah, the sister Chase feared most. He feared her because he was unsure if his ability to pass through matter would save him from her righteous fire.

Chase uttered the name Sarah's enemies often called her, "Black Sarah."

"Damn! Sarah!" exclaimed Destry. "I've got some toys on my chariot I'd like to try out on her." The sociopath began to move quickly towards the forest.

Chase motioned to his compatriot, "I know you don't value your life but if you value your warhorse you'll keep it on the ground."

Chase also knew that during the daylight, they had little chance of finding Sarah in the sky. It would be like trying to pick out a star in the sky at high noon.

Destry conceded the point and then yelled, "Where is our back up? Can't she do something?"

Zi the Sorceress emerged from the brush, "Sure, I could do something, but are you really ready to abandon our plan and have a battle to the death with them here, today, without Matasis or the space god?"

Destry conceded again, "No, but where were you when Ruth had me back peddling?"

Zi's only reply was a mischievous, wavering half-smile.

Destry yelled at Chase, "You see this? You see this?"

Meanwhile, up in the clouds Ruth rendezvoused not only with Sarah, but also with the young Mavis Few. Mavis had, among other talents, the gift of healing. She often tagged along just in case anyone was injured. Mavis, age thirteen, was the daughter of the family rogue, Uncle Paul. No one actually knew Paul's age. At the very least, he was many centuries old and a direct ancestor of every member of the family.

Over the centuries, Uncle Paul had become increasingly unstable. His inter-dimensional traveling had diminished both his mental capacity and his ability to stay in this dimension. At seemingly random times, he would simply disappear. In the past, he'd been able to recluse himself to regain some sense of balance. But, this was a difficult time to simply walk off the battlefield. With Mavis' father, Paul degrading and her mother a practitioner of black magic, Cil and her sisters had taken Mavis in to rear her.

Mavis' gift came in handy at times. Now, she sat quietly floating alongside Sarah in a blue half shell that Ruth had created earlier.

Ruth, a little out of breath, in part due to the altitude but mostly from the events below, spoke quickly to her sister, "I didn't see Gabby, but I found Uncle Jorge. They killed him.

They killed him, slaughtered him, and left him in the street like a dog.

Ruth began to weep softly, "I'm so upset and I don't know what to do."

Now that Ruth was closer to her, Mavis could see the tears streaming down her face. Mavis could not remember ever seeing one of the Aunties crying. She'd seen them upset many times but this was a first. Seeing actual tears on the face of an Auntie frightened her.

Sarah spoke softly to her sister, "I know. I saw it all from up here. I've never seen anything so horrible. But, I was so proud of you. You really kept it together down there. I don't know if I could have."

In truth, Ruth's sisters had varying levels of concern about Ruth's toughness. Though it pained her greatly, after receiving the distress call from the Caballeros' camp, Cil sent Ruth on this mission as a live training exercise. Ruth's sisters knew that she could be the alpha level resource the Elders deemed her to be but until Ruth knew it she never would be. Sarah realized that Cil had full knowledge of what Ruth would find here. Still she sent her with specific instructions that Ruth Ann take the lead and for Sarah to be her backup. This knowledge caused a shiver to run down Sarah's spine.

Sarah wanted to hug her sister, but she could not while in the star-like state that she needed to maintain to stay aloft. She landed on the platform her sister had formed in the sky and became fully mortal so that she could embrace her. Silently, she held Ruth, saying everything without whispering a word.

Mavis tried to stand on her floating half shell as she reached out to the Aunties. Seeing her, Ruth brought her to them, and the three of them embraced. Finally, Ruth said, "Let's go home." Sarah gave a reassuring smile to Ruth although she realized that Ruth would have to become tougher still to overcome the storm headed their way.

# 5:
# ECHOES FROM BIRMINGHAM

*September, 1963*

*Some are born teachers, some healers, and still others judges. Each knows their role and finds contentment once realized. But if you're born a sword, what then? Perhaps your whole life becomes a question unto God, one which you are deftly afraid to have answered.*

Sarah had an easy way about her and an easy smile. Even as a little girl, like a ray of sunshine, she would warm any room simply by entering it. Her favorite word was "Why" and her favorite two words were "Why Not." In her younger days, Sarah questioned everything. She even questioned the need for the family business or at least the need for her to be a part of it. Like so many black folks who grew up in the South during the Civil Rights movement, she had a deep desire to leave it all behind, including the "Call" as Cil called it, to wage this holy war against the darkness.

On this particular day in 1963, Sarah and her sisters were dressed for choir practice. They were waiting at the house for Miss Elizabeth to pick them up when they received a call from her to come to the church immediately. The four of them marched in staircase order with Cil, dressed in black, leading the way, while Sarah, adorned in red, brought up the rear.

Deborah, wearing a yellow polka-dotted dress and walking right behind Cil looked back at her little sisters, Ruth and

Sarah, and commanded, "Keep up. Cil says that Daddy needs us."

The girls burst through the door calling out to their father and Miss Elizabeth as they marched down the center aisle. Hosea was the associate pastor at that time and Miss Elizabeth was the choir director. As the girls approached the pulpit, their steps slowed when they saw their father sitting with his head in his hands. Miss Elizabeth sat beside him, trying to comfort him.

Sarah was the first to speak to him. "What's wrong, Daddy?"

Hosea, seeing his daughters around him, opened up his arms and reached out to his girls. They entered his arms and he hugged them all as best he could as he wept.

A blue-adorned Ruth Ann asked Hosea for a second time, "What's wrong, Daddy?"

He could not speak. All he could do was to hold them tighter.

None of the girls had ever seen their daddy cry before and this frightened them. In fact, Deborah, who was becoming increasingly upset, began to ask her father the same question for a third time when Miss Elizabeth interrupted.

"There was a bombing today in Birmingham, at a Baptist church. Four little girls were killed," she said.

Hosea wept and held his children even tighter. Sarah's plastic sunshades fell from her face and onto the floor. Tragedy was nothing new to Hosea or to anyone truly involved in the movement but this was different. Hosea knew the pastor and had fellowshipped with the families after church when he visited. He knew that it was only by the grace of God that it wasn't his four little girls who had been murdered on that dark day. Again, it crossed his mind to leave this place, to leave this battle for civil rights to someone else. He was a college graduate and held a master's degree in a time when this could seldom be said about a black man. Outside of the South, he had options. He could gather up his girls and move away from the madness of this civil and spiritual warfare. It could be so simple, if he would just allow it to be so. Yet he knew that he'd been called to this battle as surely as he'd been called to preach and to cast out demons.

In a rare display of open affection between the two, Miss Elizabeth reached over and rubbed the back of Hosea's head and neck as she whispered words of comfort to him. He had always been there for her as he had been for everyone else. He visited her in jail. He put up collateral to bail her out. He did the same for her siblings back in New Orleans who served time for less noble reasons than she did. Hosea was always faithful. Thus, she was sickened by how few of those he helped were there for him when he was no longer one of the most popular pastors in New Orleans.

Moments later, there was a knock at the door of the church. Hosea wiped the tears from his eyes and rose to answer it. He found it odd that anyone would knock, given that the door was unlocked. When he opened the door he saw a silver haired man and an olive skinned woman. A strange pair indeed, but neither was a stranger to Hosea.

"Matasis, I see that you've taken on a new host and seeing you with Isadora, I also see that the rumors are true."

Matasis grinned, "What? That I've formed a new Council of Nob? Yes, that is a fact. And I now see with my own eyes that you survived my touch, back in New Orleans. So far, at least."

A slightly agitated Isadora stood behind Matasis uncomfortable with the fact that she was standing outside of a house of light and that Hosea was, indeed, still alive.

Hosea teased, "I would invite you in except that you're not welcome here."

Matasis parried back, "Oh, and I don't want to enter your house of the poor and pathetic. What kind of life is that?"

Watch your tongue, demon," Hosea interrupted, "You cannot enter, so why are you here?"

Hosea glanced beyond the pair in front of him to see several forms standing along the rooftops across the street staring blankly down at the three of them.

Matasis glanced at Isadora before speaking to Hosea, "A new age is upon you and I come here to offer you an opportunity at freedom. I offer you the opportunity to gather up your belongings and to leave this place and this life of constant conflict. This is chance to move somewhere, where your children will be safe and you can live out the rest of your days in peace. A place where they are safe from random acts of violence from rogue space gods."

Hosea realized that Poseidon's attack was at Matasis' direction. His nostrils flared and, for the briefest moment, he thought he might take a swing at the smiling, demon-filled vessel. But, his years of experience had taught him restraint when dealing with demons. Instead, he stilled himself and resolved to confront Matasis and the other members of the Council of Nob at a time of his choosing.

Matasis and Isadora smiled wryly at each another before Matasis spoke again, "That's right. We don't want to cross this threshold but neither do you. And, be you mindful in the days to come. We have other team members that have no problem stepping across this line."

By this Matasis meant that the others — Chase, Destry, Poseidon, and Zi the Sorceress as mortal beings of free will — could enter the church as they pleased.

Matasis continued, "And, understand, too, this is an arrangement that has been worked out by others on your behalf. That incident at the lake was merely a taste of what awaits you and yours if you do not leave town."

Isadora the Soul Snatcher chimed in, "I still don't like the deal. We should just kill them all and be done with it." She scowled and Hosea could see the Gates of Hell in her eyes.

Matasis continued, "As you can see, I cannot guarantee your safety if you remain here."

Hosea coldly replied, "So, that's it? We just leave town?"

"Well, no, not exactly. But, I'll let Paul tell you about that. However, there is one thing which could turn this whole conversation around. What do you know of this Dream Box of which lesser demons speak? The prophecies say that your family has possession of it. Tell me where it is and you can remain here in peace."

Hosea knew of the prophecies regarding his wife's family too, but he grimaced before replying to the despots at his door, "Those stories have been around for centuries. But if I did indeed have the Dream Box, do you think we'd be having this conversation?" Neither party was forthcoming with all they knew on the matter.

Matasis smiled, "I figured as much but I had to ask." He then looked around Hosea to his children gathered around the pulpit, who were staring back at him, "So, those are your babies. Nice. You've provided a good life for them, all things considered. I hope things stay that way for them. Take the deal, Hosea, and leave this town to us."

With that, Matasis and Isadora laughed and turned to walk away. As they did, the six men standing along the rooftop all jumped to the unforgiving pavement below. Hosea could literally feel their lost souls depart their flesh and flow into Isadora in route to Oblivion, the realm she ruled. The Queen of the Dead wiped the corner of her mouth with a handkerchief she had pulled from her purse and winked at Hosea as she and Matasis walked off.

Hosea's fury could barely be contained as he walked back down the aisle towards the pulpit.

Miss Elizabeth asked him, "Who was that?"

Hosea answered, "That was Matasis and Isadora, two evil spirits."

A startled Elizabeth held her hand to her mouth before replying, "Here, in Atlanta? Lord…"

"Where's the phone?" Hosea asked.

Elizabeth replied, "They moved it last week to the phone jack on the side wall."

Hosea marched from behind the pulpit to the side wall, picked up the phone, and began to dial.

"I know you're upset," Elizabeth continued trying to calm Hosea.

Hosea was upset but not for the reasons that Elizabeth thought. Finally, someone on the other end of the line picked up.

Elizabeth and the girls heard a muted, "Hello."

"Paul, what have you done?" Hosea yelled into the phone.

Uncle Paul tried to explain himself. Hosea listened for a bit shaking his head all the while.

"Man, where is your faith?" Hosea asked Paul.

Harsh words were exchanged between the two until Hosea ended the call with, "You can't win in a deal with the devil. Don't you know that by now?"

Slamming the phone down, Hosea walked back towards his family. With a confounded look on his face, Hosea sat down next to Elizabeth and said softly, "For every action, there is a price, whether you're the one paying it or not. Everything has a price; the universe is resolved in this. And, this action by Paul will extract a price, a heavy one."

Elizabeth, still trying to put the pieces together asked Hosea, "What did Paul agree to?"

Hosea looked up and answered, "He convinced Elisa to serve the Council of Nob in exchange for the Council not harming my girls."

Miss Elizabeth who had developed a deep affection for Elisa shook her head as she called out, "No, no, no..."

# SACRIFICES • *Alan D. Jones*

# 6:
# THE TROUBLE WITH GRUBS

*May, 1981*

One by one, four black horses, exploded out of nothingness into the white pristine snowfall of a Scandinavian winter night. Each horse ran hard through the woods of fresh powder. Atop each horse, rode a daughter of Hosea draped in black. Each rider rode with such purpose that no words were needed. Each knew her destination. On the way, they encountered a time walker dressed in white by the name of Akina. Cil pulled on the reins of her steed and her sisters followed suit.

"Akina, all is as expected?" she asked.

Akina pulled back her fur lined hood to reply, "Yes, Auntie, all is as expected. But, you know that. Don't you?"

Cil said nothing but smiled before she kicked her heels into her horse and rode off into the darkness. One by one, each of her sisters proceeded past Akina. First was Deborah, who had, as Akina would later describe, a wide-eyed, overly-excited look on her face. It was almost a bloodlust. Next came Ruth Ann, with a thousand miles away stare on her face. Bringing up the rear was Sarah, with her ever-present sunglasses firmly in place. She rode past Akina flashing her trademark irrepressible smile. Sarah's opponents hated that smile and longed to wipe it off her face. The sisters followed Cil through the woods and towards the castle on the northern bay. They rode hard and fast through the woods as a winter's full moon illuminated their path.

As the sisters broke through the tree line, a castle and the wall that surrounded it were plainly in sight. They rode toward the guard tower along the outer wall. Nordic soldiers lined the top of the wall in a heightened state of readiness. As the sisters approached, a gate in the wall swung open and they passed through on their shiny black horses. Aunt Cil led them up the central corridor toward the castle beyond. Residents in the courtyard gasped as the four hooded riders proceeded, escorted by several guards on horseback. The ladies quickly dismounted in front of the castle and walked briskly towards the large wooden front doors. One of the guards barked out a command and once again a set of doors swung open before the women this time opening into a grand hall. The king and his court were sitting in their assigned places at the other end of the hall. It was clear that the Aunties were expected.

The members of the court were adorned in their finest coats and pelts. A feast for four was laid out on the great dining table, but the sisters paid it no mind. It was an offering of sorts, but Cil and her sisters had no time for such things. They stood before the court and removed their hoods. This action froze the crowd more than the weather outside ever could. The sight of the four black women standing shoulder to shoulder left their mouths agape.

Deborah leaned over to Ruth and whispered, "They're looking at our hair."

Ruth rolled her eyes.

Cil motioned for Deborah to step forward. Deborah did so and began to speak to the king and his court in their native tongue. Deborah had the gift of speaking in the tongue of many languages. She could even speak languages that she'd never heard before. So, she translated between the parties.

"King Helwig, Queen Helwig, and members of the royal court as our herald undoubtedly communicated to you, we are here to rid your realm of the terror currently approaching your gates."

King Helwig stood up, "We saw what your herald can do but what can you do that would warrant us putting our faith in you to resolve this matter?" He pointed at the Aunties as he made this last point.

Cil nodded to Sarah. She removed her shades which immediately revealed her glowing eyes. Then, she gazed upon a large urn of water and unleashed a red hot beam from those eyes that split the urn in half spilling the water it contained onto the stone floor.

Next, Ruth Ann stepped forward. She raised her hands, and in a single scooping motion projected a blue shell which scooped the remains of the broken and still smoldering urn into the air. The sphere hovered in the air spinning slightly before launching upwards bursting through the ceiling and into the night sky. The entire court could see the blue ball accelerate towards the great beyond and out of sight.

Then, when all eyes landed Deborah, she simply vanished. From the spot on the floor where she had stood, a spring sprung up spouting water thirty feet into the air. The geyser began to rage and quickly filled the hall with water. Suddenly, water began to flow into the hall from everywhere. Water flowed from every opening including the windows, the cracks in the walls, and the new hole in the ceiling. Members of the court scurried up the king's landing and to the throne to escape the rising waters. Just as her audience began to panic, the water disappeared and Deborah reappeared right where she had been when the phenomena began as though nothing happened.

Finally, Cil raised her staff but before she could demonstrate anything, the king motioned towards her vigorously shaking his head. There was little need for Deborah to translate.

Deborah glanced towards Cil and then said to the king, "About our fee…"

The king interrupted her, "Yes, your herald indicated that there would be one. What is it? Precious stones, gold coins or…," the king hesitated and then said "a sacrifice?"

Deborah shook her own head from side to side, "No, we don't want any of those things. We'd like you to take this box far across the sea to a location that we'll give you. Once there, you're to place the box on the ground and build a small barn around it exactly as depicted by the illustration carved into the box."

The king, not quite believing or understanding what he was hearing, repeated it back to the women, "You want me to take that box across the westward waters and place it on the ground? And, for that you will save my kingdom from the demons at our gates?"

Deborah nodded, "Yes."

The king released his doubts and directed his guards to take possession of the box. The sealed metal box was twelve inches by six inches and about three inches deep.

Cil turned towards her sister, "Okay, this is done. Let's go out and clean the yard." This was music to her sisters' ears. Often they had to restrain themselves due to the realities of their lives but in the isolation of the northern woods they need not worry about hurting innocents or showing mercy. Though the foe was powerful, the task was simple. In their lives, simple was a precious commodity.

Deborah leaned in towards her sister Ruth, "So, let's not go trying to catch snowflakes on our tongues until after the battle is done."

Ruth huffed back, "That happened one time. Must you bring that up every time there is the slightest bit of snow in the air?"

"Yes," laughed Deborah.

## THE TROUBLE WITH GRUBS 63

The sisters sang as they rode out to the tree line where the demonic beasts therein beamed a jaundiced eye. The whispering wind was filled with the lies of the serpent king, Jormungand. With his many tongues, lie overlaid lie.

One tongue asked of another, "Who are these before us?"

The other tongue replied, "I do not know who they are, but I know what they are. They are the children of the nameless One, who have claimed their birthright. Nonetheless, they will perish along with all the others who have come before us."

With her sisters spread out in a line behind her and a steady stream of new snow falling all around her, Cil rode back and forth proclaiming, "Hear me Jormungand, you shape-shifting son of Loki, and to your demon seed, this will be the last day that you foul the air of this blessed Earth. Today is the day of your reckoning."

She raised the cone-shaped End of Days Horn that hung around her neck towards her mouth. The horn could be heard both on earth and in the underworld. Cil's steed rose up on its hind legs when blew into the horn. The creatures of the dark cringed at its sound and at the sight of Cil's large, seemingly bottomless black eyes. When engaged, her eyes were reflection pools of one's own inequities. They somehow glowed a black light that was visible from deep within the woods before them.

With the wind rippling their black robes, Cil lifted her staff into the air and pointed it directly at Jormungand. He thought that he was hidden from human sight since he was currently in the form of a Minotaur. His whispering stopped for a moment when he realized that Cil could see him. It was a silence that reached across eternity.

Cil motioned towards Ruth and Sarah before galloping off in a direct line towards the serpent god with Deborah riding close behind. As Ruth and Sarah fired off force beams and searing beams of light into the demon horde, Cil and Deborah proceeded into the teeth of Jormungand's army of hell-born beasts. As she breached their line, Cil swung her staff so fast that it could not be seen by human or demon eye. Deborah who had made herself invisible along with her steed fired arrow after arrow from Athena's bow. The arrows from that bow formed at the archer's will and penetrated anything they encountered. Although she was invisible, Deborah continuously talked smack to her opponents as she was known to do.

"What you got to say now, huh? Y'all was howling and talking plenty of trash a minute ago. Oh, how I wish you'd say something now!"

At the frontline, Ruth and Sarah continued to push the demon forces farther into the woods. They could hear Deborah running her mouth even through all the wailing and gnashing of teeth. When Deborah began to use profane language, Ruth could be quiet no longer.

She yelled out, "Deborah!"

From somewhere in the darkness of the woods she replied, "Sorry."

Sarah chuckled and commented just loud enough for Ruth to hear, "You know your sister is crazy, right?"

Ruth just shook her head.

Meanwhile, Cil had managed to work her way to Jormungand. The demon, also known as the Serpent King, took on his true form as he rose on his broad tail.

He stood upright as he spoke to her, "Woman, daughter of men, you worked your way through my servants to your master, now here is your reward."

The beast blew from its mouth a killing frost, which instantly killed the trees and foliage between him and his target. Cil's body seemed to be immediately petrified like an old buried piece of wood. Jormungand arrogantly thought it would be simple to dispatch his foe. He tilted back his head and released a victory howl. Mid-howl, Cil leaped from a tree behind Jormungand and swung her staff hard and fast through the serpent demon's neck sending his head cascading to the forest floor. Deborah had cast an illusion of a frozen Cil which the son of Loki, the Norse god of deceit did not detect until his head was dislodged from his body.

Cil landed in the soft snow and then ran to her sister's side. Standing back to back with Cil, Deborah couldn't help but comment, "Huh. Close up, he looks more like a giant grub than a serpent."

Cil agreed, "Well, I guess 'Jormungand the Grub King' isn't going to scare anyone. Is it?"

The sisters then began to work their way back towards Ruth and Sarah dispatching spawns of hell left and right. Their path was clearly laid out by the blue and yellow glow beyond the immediate darkness. Many of the beasts who had the sense to run from that angelic onslaught were the very ones that Cil and Deborah encountered. As they approached the clearing again, the sisters were within sight of one another.

"Y'all better get it now because we're running out of fools over here," Deborah called out implying that she and Cil were doing the heavy lifting.

With the last of the demons vanquished from that level of existence, the four sisters stood near where they'd begun the battle staring back into forest. It was now completely ablaze. Their horses dug their noses into the snow searching for winter grass. The others watched as Ruth encased the burning wooded area in a large blue air-tight bubble to extinguish the fire. The women conversed in the gently falling snow as the king and his court approached through a line of soldiers set out about one hundred yards from the sisters.

"Sarah, look at her," Deborah nodded towards Ruth who was standing with her face turned skyward and her mouth open.

"What's wrong with her? I know I've got issues but I have a diagnosis and treatment plan. Here we are trying to make an impression on these locals and she's trying to catch snowflakes on her tongue again."

Sarah laughed, "Hey, you did say she could once we were done."

Cil gave her sisters a quick look which each of them knew meant to be quiet.

The king shouted something in his native tongue and Deborah gave a translation, "The king asks, 'What's wrong with that one on the end?'"

Ruth turned to Deborah and quickly stuck out her tongue.

Sarah asked Deborah, "Sis, please don't. We've got a long way to go to get home and I'm ready to get out of this place."

Deborah laughed, "You know I can't talk to you when you're all glorified." Sarah hated when she used that term. Deborah used the term in reference to how Sarah was when she was powered up and ready for battle. In that state, Sarah's eyes glowed. That was the reason she always wore shades. It was also harder to harm her in that state. Ruth always wore a thin invisible protective casing of energy around her body. Cil and Deborah were always powered up as well. Sarah could remain in that state 24 hours a day, but she chose not to. In her mind, being energized like that wasn't being human. Her sisters each had their own thoughts about her reasoning. They suspected that she didn't quite trust herself.

Sarah smiled and mounted her horse which was her way of restating her point that she was ready to go. Cil and Ruth also mounted their steeds.

Deborah gave Sarah a sideward glance before chiding her, "What's your hurry? Can't wait to get back to your boyfriend? Excuse me, I mean your boss."

# THE TROUBLE WITH GRUBS 67

The shade wearing Sarah didn't flinch. Her gaze was fixed on Deborah.

Cil called out, "Deborah!"

At last Deborah yielded the staring contest, for the moment anyway. She turned to the king and said to him that the threat to his kingdom had been eliminated. And she also let him know the fire would soon be extinguished. The flames were already fading. Deborah also reminded the king of his end of the bargain. She subtly suggested that they would not be happy if he did not follow through. She also reminded him of what happens when they're not happy but she did not communicate this last part to her sisters. When she was done, she mounted her horse and fell into line with her sisters.

After the flames subsided, Ruth lowered her shields and Deborah stretched out her hands towards the forest. Immediately tiny evergreen sprouts began to push up through the white snow. Deborah leaned down to whisper to the queen, "Your forest will be restored by spring."

Cil nodded to her siblings and the four of them began to gallop along the tree line away from the king and his court. As they rode, Cil began spinning her staff. She spun it faster, faster still, and it glowed brighter and brighter until a portal of light opened up before them. The king's court and many of the soldiers saw that the destination beyond radiated an alarming red. The portal revealed a place that each of them knew instinctively should be avoided.

One by one, each of the sisters atop their horses leapt into the void. The witnesses again stood with their mouths agape. They would have been more astonished if they had known the women's destination. Cil had opened a portal to The Pit. The Pit was a state of existence void of the veils of this life. Some called it Hell, others Purgatory. Still others simply said that it was here but devoid of the illusion of time and the flesh.

The Pit was a spiritual realm where our spirits take form side by side with the dark spiritual forces who seek to torment us. It was also a land where some from our own dimension had been cast as a form of punishment. It was filled with all sorts of beasts that crawled up from the depths of Hell. The realm was not constrained to the same rules of space and time as our own existence. Visitors could enter from one time and location and exit into another. Of course, running that gauntlet of horrors would be a non-starter for anyone but the Aunties. Most of the residents knew better than to mess with these ladies, but every time they passed through new residents tried them. They expected as much.

It would have been easier to arrange for Akina to transport them. Cil's sisters had asked her about doing so. Her reply was that Akina was unreliable and inconsistent. This became all the more true as Akina grew older but that wasn't the whole truth. Cil knew the threat that Akina would one day become to all the living and sought to involve her in their operations only when absolutely necessary. Time would eventually validate her concerns.

# 7
# TIPPING POINT

*September, 1963*

*The fruit we bear today is rooted in the blood sacrifice, of those who came before.*

Sometimes things are clear only in our most desperate moments. So it was for Hosea. As soon as he hung up the phone with Paul, Hosea knew what must be done. Turning, he called out to Ms. Elizabeth, "We're going to need to hide the girls."

Elizabeth replied, "I thought you said that Paul had worked out a deal for their protection?"

Hosea answered back, "A deal with a demon isn't worth the breath with which it is spoken. I don't trust any of it. Yet, I know as sure as the Sun does set that the Evil One will orchestrate something foul to lay in our path. It is who he is."

Elizabeth said in just above a whisper to Hosea, "What does he want with Elisa?"

Hosea shook his head, "I don't know but it can't be good. All I know is that in Matasis' mind he's getting the better of the deal."

Elizabeth nodded, "True. So, it seems that he sees that he is getting a sure thing in Elisa in exchange for possibility of whatever threat the girls might someday be to him or a dream box which might or might not actually exist."

"That's right," Hosea said.

Elizabeth asked, "So, what are you going to do?"

"I have a plan but it starts with their cousin Rob. He's always maintained that I could ask him anything. So, we're going to see exactly what that means."

After returning home and leaving the girls in Elizabeth's care, Hosea headed off to Rob's house. As he stepped onto Rob's street, a stiff wind nearly knocked his fedora from his head.

Cousin Rob's house was just around the corner from Hosea's in Atlanta's historic West End. Rob was a Special Forces operative. On paper, that's what he was. He really was something so far off the books that even some sitting presidents were unaware of his existence or of that of his team, Team Omega. They were a team of Marines all of whom had special talents. None of his teammate's gifts rivaled Rob's for he was able to summon the elements: fire, earth, water and wind. Each member of the team did possess a paranormal ability any of which would dislodge the world of the ordinary Joe or Josephine from its axis. Rob was their leader. Due to his country's call, Rob was seldom at home. His home was not like Hosea's which had a level of protection over it from the prayers of saints, but it did have protection of another sort. One of Rob's teammates, Louis, had established a psychic link to the property so that he always knew when someone came to the door and what they wanted. Louis could also tell you the history of an object simply by touching it. So, of course, he was into archeology.

All that Hosea had to do was to go to Rob's home and knock on the door which he did. Hosea didn't know when Rob would contact him but he knew that he would. Rob wasn't always around but he was always faithful to his family and his country. More importantly, Rob knew that Hosea would reach out to him only when necessary. And, truth be told, on more than one occasion Rob had reached out to Hosea for assistance as well. In the very small circle of those who knew about such things as exorcisms and things paranormal, Hosea was very well respected.

After inspecting the shrubs in Rob's yard, Hosea turned to make the short trek back to his own house. As he reached the sidewalk, a stiff breeze came rushing towards him. He walked up the street towards the corner, but once he turned the corner, he found himself back on Rob's street. He looked to the left and then to the right to see spaced out around him seven masked men dressed in long black robes. At the end of each street or alleyway, they stood like onyx statues. Hosea attempted to cross the street but again found himself back on Rob's side of the street.

Hosea realized that his predicament was the doing of Zi the Sorceress, who always rode upon the wind. He knew that if he trusted his own senses, he would be killed or he'd be lost forever. So, he closed his eyes and stilled himself so that he might hear the spirit within. Hosea paid no attention to sight, sound, smell, or touch He stood still for long moments with his eyes closed quietly waiting. Hosea let go of the world and the path became clear to him. He took his first step, then another, and then a third.

Hosea made his way past the black clad guardians and back to life as he knew it. Hosea was sure that this was done just to intimidate him. They wanted to make him go home, pack his bags, and leave. Hosea knew what they were doing and he didn't like it. Like any man, he had is pride. But, even his pride was nothing compared to his love of his children.

Back at the house, Miss Elizabeth and Deborah prepared Sunday dinner while the other girls napped. Cil had fallen into a deep sleep on the bed she shared with Deborah each night. When she awoke, she saw an angel standing at the foot of the bed. The angel was bronze and glowing. Its wings were so bright that Cil could hardly look at them.

The angel of the Lord called to her, "Cil, you have been chosen to bear this burden for your generation."

Cil, still in her church clothes, sat straight up, leaned slightly towards the angel, and whispered, "Me?"

The angel smiled at her and proclaimed, "So it is written, so it is. Look up, Lucille, and gaze upon that which few of the living have ever seen."

Cil looked up towards the ceiling but there was no ceiling, no plaster, no mortar and no roof. There was only heaven filled with the heavenly host. She stared in amazement at what she saw. It was nothing like she'd read or dreamed it would be. It was so much more. A smile washed over her face. Then, a stream of tears flowed from her eyes causing her brown cheeks to glisten. Just as suddenly as the tears had come she felt herself floating and free.

The angel of the Lord whispered into her ear, "No, not yet."

Cil awoke in the summer heat. She was still lying in her bed. She wiped the beaded sweat from her brow. When Deborah walked in, Cil was mumbling to herself, "It's all energy – our thoughts, our time and our tears – all of it."

Deborah stopped at the edge of the bed. She was truly concerned about her big sister. "What's wrong with you? You look like you're the one who just walked out of a hot kitchen."

Cil looked at her sister and then out of the open window as she wept, "You wouldn't believe me, if I told you."

Then, Cil heard her father returning home and leapt from her bed. She ran into the living room calling, "Daddy! Daddy!"

She was fourteen-years-old yet she leapt into her father's arms just as she did when she was three. Her white cotton blouse soaked up the summer sweat from his arms as she cried into his ear, "Daddy, I've seen everything. I've seen all that is to be for us. Oh, Daddy…," she cried. She gripped him tighter and spoke into his ear as the angel had spoken into hers, "I know what is to become of us all."

Sensing something of what his daughter may have seen, Hosea lowered Cil to the floor and said to her, "Darling, we're all going to die someday. Just as we are born to live so, too, are we born to die."

Cil looked at her father. She still had tears in her eyes. Her face expressed all that she could not, would not, say. She had seen the future often but, this time, it was different. After Cil's encounter with the angel, she knew, in an instant, all that would be for those whom she loved and for herself. She knew all there was to know about time. She knew more than man would know for a thousand generations. Time had been revealed as the illusion it truly was, For Cil, there was no turning back. She knew this would be the first and last time that she would ever willingly share that she could indeed see the future. She would not even tell her sisters.

Hosea took Cil's hand and led her through the house, out to the back porch, and away from her sisters and Miss Elizabeth. The two of them sat on the porch swing facing the small, wall-lined backyard. Hosea listened as Cil recounted her dream.

When she was done, he paused to gather his thoughts. Then, he said to her, "Darling, you've been called. You've been called to be a Gatekeeper. Do you know what that is?"

Cil nodded her head, "I think so."

Hosea spoke softly to her, "People are called to do many things. Some people are called to do particular things," Hosea paused in reference to himself before continuing, "and some particular people are called to a particular thing. In this case, that particular thing is being a Gatekeeper. And for you to understand what that means you must understand what the "gate" is that you're minding. Consider first that there is the world we see and the worlds that we do not see. And some of these worlds that we do not see are not so nice. Often the not so nice residents of these worlds want to come to our world. As Gatekeeper, it will be your job to make sure that they don't. But if they do make their way here, you are to send them back."

"How will I do that?" Cil asked.

Hosea replied, "Stop and think on it for a moment."

Cil did think. Moments later, her eyes opened widely. "At Big Mama's house there is an old staff buried in the backyard. It will be my key to the gate."

Big Mama was from the Atlanta branch of the Few family that grew out of the same plantation onto which Lola and Elisa were born. Big Mama's house was in northwest Atlanta.

Hosea took his daughter's hand and asked her, "You understand that accepting this role will come at a price?"

"Yes, Daddy, I understand," Cil replied.

Hosea also understood this call on Cil's life. "Okay, we'll go by there tomorrow. But, for now, let's have prayer together."

Cil nodded and bowed her head as her father prayed over her. When they were done, Hosea smiled and kissed Cil on her cheek before extolling her, "Come on, go wash your face then, let's make some beignets. We'll show Miss Elizabeth how we do it!"

Making beignets to celebrate family achievements was one thing that they brought from New Orleans to Atlanta.

Before reentering the house, Cil grabbed her father by the arm, "Daddy, why do you stay married to Mama? She's never here and you and Miss Elizabeth belong together."

Hosea stopped and took a deep breath before answering, "It's complicated, darling. Repeatedly, I have asked God that He might release me from your mother but each time He tells me that I cannot go just yet. Besides, my romantic life is not my top priority right now." Hosea gave his eldest daughter a knowing smile.

Cil took her daddy's hand and they both reentered the home. Cil's little sisters came running down the hall past her. Her youngest sister, Sarah, stopped Cil in the hallway and said, "Mommy Cil, I made this for you." Sarah pressed a handmade metal cross into Cil's palm. She'd made it using her gift to heat metal to the point that she could easily bend it. Then, she strung it on a shoelace long enough for Cil to wear it around her neck.

Cil knelt down to look Sarah in the eye. "Thank you, Sarah, but this is one of your shoelaces. How will you keep your shoes on without it?"

Sarah simply smiled.

Cil smiled back, "I'll treasure it always." She then placed Sarah's gift around her neck, stuffed the cross beneath her blouse, and squeezed it there before rising.

Cil looked around at her family soaking in the scene. Soon there would be powdered sugar everywhere and the night would end as they always did with Daddy's feet propped up, his reading glasses hanging from his nose, and a book resting in his lap. The next day they would retrieve the staff Cil needed from Big Mama's house. But, on that night, as Cil enjoyed her family she also realized what she must do and how those actions would cascade through the ages.

# SACRIFICES • *Alan D. Jones*

# THE BOOK OF DEBORAH

# 8
# SAD CONCEPTION

*June, 1981*

*Unmentionable things refuse to lie silent forever. If they are not spoken, they will find another way to the surface, even if they must ooze from every pore.*

Cil and her two youngest sisters lived together in their father's home along with Cil's husband of ten years, Joe.

Joe was a good man who left the place of his birth to follow Cil and her siblings back to Atlanta. In many ways, he helped Cil finish raising her siblings. While Rob may have been a surrogate father to them, Joe was more of a logistical daddy. He picked up the girls from school when they were younger, fixed their cars, and took out the trash.

Deborah was married to a man named William. Willy was his street name. Willy was the antithesis of Joe. Where Joe was dependable, Willy was not. Where Joe showed concern for others, Willy did not. Whatever Joe was, Willy always seemed to be the opposite. Willy was twenty-seven years old but acted like he was seventeen. Joe, who was pushing fifty at the time, possessed the wisdom of an older man. Willy was a short, light-skinned, pretty-boy, fake tough guy. Deborah always had a weakness for pretty boys. Joe was a dark brown-skinned man who stood six foot three and weighed about 230 pounds. Willy hated Joe. Joe paid Willy no mind.

One evening, Deborah and Willy stopped by the family home to make an announcement. A giddy Deborah barely allowed time for Cil to open the front door before she blurted out, "I'm pregnant!" Her sisters Ruth and Sarah rushed to the foyer to embrace their sister and share in her joy. Cil smiled at them and then back at Willy who was still on the front porch, "You can come in." Sheepishly, Willy stepped in.

"Is your old man in?" Willy asked.

Cil answered, "No, he's still at the shop."

"Cool," Willy replied.

Willy tried to hide it but he was a little afraid of Joe. Willy claimed he was from New York but he was actually born and raised mostly in Virginia. He did spend his seventh grade year in New York. That one year was enough for him to rewrite his life story.

After Willy entered the room, he stood off to the side. Ruth reached out to give him a quick hug. Sarah gave him a quick smile but refrained from hugging him. The two of them had argued on his last visit about his unwillingness to get a job. Deborah made decent money teaching English over at Spelman, but still it irked Sarah. Willy had been married to Deborah for almost two years and heaven help her if Sarah could recall him working more than a week or two anywhere in that time. Joe had offered him a job at his repair shop but Willy's pride would not allow him to get his hands dirty. Now, with a baby on the way, Sarah was hopeful that he would now step up. But, she wasn't holding her breath.

Willy could not stand Sarah. While he acknowledged to his friends that she was a very pretty woman, he felt like she was stuck up. It was his deepest desire to see her get her comeuppance.

Cil asked Willy, "How's the job hunt coming?"

Willy shrugged his shoulders, "You know, it's hard out here. Plus now, I gotta pay these student loans back. But, you know, I still get my hustle on."

Cil knew that meant that he spent most of his would be productive hours hanging out with his boys, but she didn't say anything.

"Would you like something to eat? There's some chicken and sides on the table."

Willy never turned down a meal. "Oh, good."

As he made his way to the table to load up, he asked, "Hey, if y'all don't mind, I'm gonna take this to the front porch and let you females talk about all this baby stuff."

Before he and Deborah were married, planning for the wedding had made Willy anxious. All this baby preparation talk was no better. In his mind, it was just more stress on him. His folks were established black professionals in the Atlanta area. There were certain expectations on him with which he was never comfortable. His family had put him in the best schools. They'd gotten him into Morehouse, a historically black college. And, they'd gotten him interviews at their friends' firms after he graduated. It was never enough.

Willy didn't like the white high schools. He resented being at Morehouse. He had applied at USC, Harvard and Notre Dame, but none of them would have him. Neither would Morehouse, until his daddy had made a call; his daddy was a legacy after all. Even marrying Deborah was pushed on him by his family. Although Deborah's family had no history in Atlanta, she and her sisters had excelled in their chosen professions. Despite the fact that Deborah was "a little dark" for his mother's taste, the fact that she was a professor at Spelman afforded the mother of an underachieving son something to brag about at girlfriend luncheons.

Deborah, like her mother-in-law, was color-struck in her younger days. Willy was a good-looking, college-educated man with wavy hair from an established Atlanta family. Despite his height and the lack of steady income, he'd met all of Deborah's qualifications for a husband. Most people who knew her thought that she could have done better than Willy.

Some women, beautiful women, fall in love with the challenge of love rather than the nature of love. This understanding only comes with the living of one's life. The understanding of what love should be, had puzzled young Deborah. It wasn't until after she was married that she finally understood.

After Willy made his way to the front porch the sisters pulled Deborah to the parlor to ask about the baby. "So, do you know the sex yet?" Ruth asked.

"No!" Deborah stated emphatically. "But, we do know there's more than one!" All the sisters squealed in delight.

After the screaming stopped and the tea was poured, the sisters were sat around the kitchen table. After her first sip of tea, Deborah asked her two younger sisters, "So, what about you two? Anything happening? Any prospects? Just asking."

Sarah who was an expert at hiding her cards said nothing. Ruth Ann, as was typically the case within the sisterhood, broke first. "Well, I finally heard from Jerome and…"

Impatiently, Deborah asked, "And what?"

Embarrassed, Ruth confessed, "He called me collect from the jail."

At this point, Sarah broke her silence, "What? And, you accepted the call?"

"Yes. What else was I supposed to do? He's in jail. I couldn't say no," Ruth replied strongly.

Cil who already knew each story the sisters would tell had an answer for Ruth, "The point is not to date guys who are in jail or are likely to go."

Where Deborah had a weakness for pretty boys, Ruth seemed to attract bad boys. In truth, her compassion and desire to rescue these men was the real culprit as was the fact that she was a bit naïve.

Deborah shook her head at Ruth and then turned her chair completely around to face Sarah even as Ruth continued to mutter.

"So…?"

Sarah interrupted Deborah's inquisition, "Ruth Ann, darling, please finish what you were saying."

Ruth took a breath and then released, "I know I haven't had the best success with men and they always seem to mistreat me. But, I really believe that they'd love me and treat me right, if they ever took the time to know me. They'd see how nice a person I am and they'd truly love me."

Sarah reached out her right hand to touch Ruth, "Darling you're full blown extraordinary. But, it's still your responsibility to make sure that these guys do indeed take the time to get to know just how wonderful you are, regardless of how long that might take. And, if they can't wait, then they weren't right for you."

Across the kitchen table, Deborah gave Ruth a forced smile that conveyed the lost cause she thought her to be. Then, she turned back towards Sarah and said again, "So?"

Sarah smiled. Deborah leaned in and Sarah just lifted one brow. Deborah sat back and stated, "I heard that you went to lunch with your branch manager again – your married branch manager – your white branch manager. What's up with that?"

Sarah set down her half-full cup of tea, "I can't go to lunch with my boss? Really? I didn't know that."

Deborah continued her questioning, "No, you can't. Not like y'all do. Anything more than once or twice a month is too much. See, now, if you were both married or even if you were both single, maybe you'd get a pass. But if the man is married and the woman is not, y'all can't be lunch buddies. Aren't there any other men around there who you can go to lunch with besides him?"

Sarah replied, "Gary is really just a very cool guy. I've never met a professional white man around here who is as open in public as he is. Besides, I go to lunch with the tellers just as much as or more than I do with Gary."

Deborah rebutted, "But the question is, who else does Gary go to lunch with besides you?"

Sarah acknowledged, "When he does take a lunch, it's pretty much just me. I really think that I'm the only one in the office that he feels he can have a conversation with."

"Yeah, right, a conversation. Is that what they call it today? I don't need to come down there, do I?" Deborah asked as she sat back in her chair. One of the most horrifying experiences of Sarah's professional life, was the sight of Deborah marching into her branch to confront her previous manager regarding the inequity of Sarah's pay. Through her own doings Sarah had arranged for a pay increase at the end of the year, but that wasn't soon enough for Deborah.

Sarah replied with a very smooth "No."

The two women sat in silence as Ruth Ann hid behind her cup of tea.

What Sarah didn't share was that on their last lunch date, Gary had said something that made her uneasy and dared her to dream all at the same time.

After lamenting the challenges of a new baby and a young wife, Gary said, "Seattle is more open than here. I really wish I could take you there. You'd love it."

"Now, just what the heck was that supposed to mean?" Sarah thought.

At the time he said it, she tried to ignore it. Was this man working his way up to ask for something more than a friendly cooperative relationship? The thought of such a complex relationship with a married man with a child – her boss no less – made Sarah uneasy. On the other hand, the thought of leaving the South, of running away from all it – including the family burden – was enticing. She'd started dreaming of easy lunches on the Pacific shore, with or without Gary.

Deborah asked, "So, what about the football player? What's his name?"

"James. He's nice but he's too young."

Deborah smirked, "He's of legal age, ain't he?"

"Yes, but I think he's just infatuated with me because I won't go out with him. As his personal banker, I can't. Besides, you know how professional athletes are? I don't think I could even date one while he's still playing."

Deborah leaned in again, "So playing Russian roulette with a married man is a better option?"

Cil wasn't a mind reader but she knew her little sister very well. She saw this flirtation with her boss as an emotional escape hatch from the burden they all bore.

Cil spoke softly to Sarah, "I know this life is not easy and that you want a normal life. I do too.

Cil felt for the cross hidden under her blouse. Sarah had given to her when they were children and it always hung around her neck.

"But, one day, you will have to pick up your own cross – be it here, in Seattle, or wherever."

While this conversation was going on inside, Willy ate his home-cooked meal, including the cornbread and sweet tea, out on the front porch. The little man sat out there salivating on his plot to get back at Sarah. If he had known that Sarah had prepared the food he was enjoying that day, would he have done what he did? No one will ever know. One thing is certain, once you set evil free, you have very little say about where it goes or how far.

When Sarah and her sisters returned to the front room, Willy stepped inside and mentioned the party a buddy of his was hosting nearby. He had already mentioned the party to Deborah on the pretext that he wanted Sarah and Ruth Ann to attend to meet some single men. He already knew that it was a school night and that Ruth could not attend. Sarah reluctantly agreed to attend. She would take a covered dish Deborah had agreed to contribute and, if she liked the party, she would stay. Sarah headed over just about dusk. By the time she reached the yellow and white house, she wished she had driven. She climbed the steps and found Willy sitting on a tall stool holding a glass of lemonade. Willy smiled as she reached the landing, "I saw you coming down the street so I poured you something cold and sweet."

Sarah peeked in through one of the front windows and noted half a dozen men sitting around the dining room with beers in their hands. She set the dish down, took the frosty glass, and commented to Willy, "Not a lot of folks here yet."

Willy smiled as Sarah took her first sip, "No, but you know how we do."

My mother nodded and said before taking a second sip, "No ladies here yet, either. You know I don't want to be the only woman at any party."

Willy replied as he stood up, "Oh, that's cool. Maybe you can come back later since it's just down the street. At least step in for a second to say hello to the fellas." He held the door for her.

In hindsight, Sarah said that she should have known something was up because he'd never held a door for her before. Standing on the hardwood floor of the dining room, she got a good look at the six men seated at the table each of whom lifted a bottle to her. She smiled that dazzling smile of hers then took a full gulp of the lemonade in her hand. The floor seemed to be shifting beneath her feet. She looked for a couch or something to lean on.

The next memory Sarah had was that of waking up in the backyard of the yellow and white house with a large black man kneeling over her telling her, "You're gonna be alright."

The man was one of the growing number of veterans from a war long since ended who found themselves living on the street. He recognized my mother as one of the sisters who lived in the community. He remembered how active she and her sisters had been in helping those in need. They fed the hungry and were always willing to share a smile and a word of encouragement. He tried to pull down what was left of her dress over her slip before he lifted her up into his arms. He knew the sisters' house so he carried Sarah home and rang the bell.

Ruth and Cil were sitting in the front dining room from which they could see the front porch. Ruth was asking Cil why her eyes were moist. Cil convinced her it was allergies. In truth, it was because she knew that last night was the night that her sister had been raped. She also knew that it was the night that a child was conceived. The terrible burden weighed heavy on Cil and the consequences cascaded through the ages and generations to come

Ruth and Cil sprang to their feet and rushed to the door. The Good Samaritan carried Sarah across the doorway and laid her down on the living room sofa.

"She was laying in the back yard of that yellow and white house on Lawson," he said before leaving.

Cil and Ruth kneeled down side by side to examine their sister. Cil directed Ruth to make some coffee.

Sarah was floating in out of consciousness. Later, she would only remember those early events in snapshots. She remembered a tearful Ruth holding the coffee cup to her lips while Cil held her. Her next memory was of a weeping Deborah holding her tightly and Cil covering her with a blanket. Eventually, just after three in the afternoon, Sarah awoke with some degree of clarity and, with that clarity, all innocence was lost. She realized what had happened to her. She pulled back the blanket to see her tattered, blood stained clothes. That, plus the pain between her legs, confirmed her violation. Sarah curled into a ball and wept.

Moments later, Sarah's face hardened and her eyes blazed with the red-hot fire of retribution.

She angrily shouted, "Where's Willy? Where is Willy?"

A weeping Deborah answered, "I've been calling him since I got here, but he's either not at home or isn't picking up."

Sarah suggested, "We need to call the police. They'll find him."

Cil nodded and Ruth agreed.

Deborah objected, "I want to talk to Willy to find out what happened before we call the police."

"What?" Sarah sat straight up. "What is there to know? I passed out after he gave me a drink. I woke up the next morning half-naked in some stranger's backyard after being sexually assaulted. What can he say to change that?"

Deborah argued, "He has a hard enough time finding a job now. The last thing he needs is to get caught up in something like this if he didn't have anything to do with it."

Ruth, who was still crying commented softly but loud enough for all to hear, "Your husband doesn't have a job because he doesn't want to work."

"Well, we should call the police, for sure," Cil added, "but if we call the police then we have to let the judicial system handle it. But if we don't…"

Cil gave her sisters a knowing look.

Through her tears, Ruth gave a firm, "Yes."

Sarah began nodding her head in agreement as vigorously as she dared, "Yeah, we can get him and all his boys."

"Hold up now! Y'all are talking about my husband! Not some demon from Hell. Y'all know the rules," Deborah protested loudly. "If you've forgotten the cost of personal vendettas, ask Aunt Elisa."

Elisa was cast into The Pit for avenging a personal wrong while she was being groomed to be an Elder. Since her return from The Pit over twenty years earlier she'd seldom spoken of it.

Sarah began to glow a fiery red and yelled, "I can't believe you're saying this! Look at me! Look at what they did!"

Deborah, never one to back down, shouted back as the room trembled, "I see you but you were unconscious. So you really don't know what really happened."

Sarah fired back, "I know what happened! I was raped by a bunch of cowardly men. What else do we need to know besides their addresses?"

Deborah paused for a moment and then reached for the phone to make one more call.

"Hello, may I speak to Willy? What? Look, I know he's there. Really? Look, heifer, you can either put him on the phone or I can come over there and drag his butt out of there."

Moments passed as the sisters watched Deborah in amazement, not quite believing what they were hearing. Even Cil, who knew the future, sat in real astonishment. Finally, Willy came to the phone.

"Willy, what happened last night at the party? Just tell me the truth." Deborah was silent as Willy spoke. She ended her conversation with a simple, "Okay."

She took a deep breath before sharing with her sisters. "He says that you got drunk and were hanging all over the guys but, when he left, you were fine."

Exasperated, Sarah asked, "And you believe that crap?"

Sarah's doubts were warranted since this would be just the first version of what happened to which Willy would swear. His second story was that he got drunk and passed out only to find out what happened later. His third story, after Uncle Joe encouraged him a bit, was that the special drink he gave Sarah was only supposed to loosen her up. He said that he fought to keep his boys off of her but they kicked him out of the house and he was too ashamed to go home afterwards. Since I don't have a connection with Willy, I really can't tell you which version, if any, is the truth. Liars lie.

Deborah said as calmly as she knew how, "Hey, that's my husband. And, if that's what he says, I have to go with that until I know differently."

In one movement, Sarah burst into flames and tears as she sprung from the sofa. The house shook as Deborah glared at her little sister. Between Deborah and Sarah there was a bright blue glow. At the center of that radiance stood Ruth. Using her force fields, she kept the two sisters separated from one another.

"Enough!" Cil declared, "We will call the police. There is too much at stake in the coming days for us to deal with this right now. We will stay out of it while the police do their investigation. But, if they do not press charges, as I suspect they won't, we will deal with this one way or another. I can't tell you what that looks like right now but, as hard as it sounds, we need to handle our business first and deal with this later. Too much is at stake. I'll call Miss Elizabeth and let her know what's going on."

Three minutes later Miss Elizabeth arrived and took over as was her way.

Just before five that evening, the police arrived to take Sarah's statement. By all accounts, she held up very well but she lost it when they brought out the rape kit. Seeing the kit and having Elizabeth and the female officer escort her to the restroom, opened the wound for her once more. Deborah tried to comfort her as well but Sarah pushed her away. Dejected and troubled, Deborah picked up her purse and exited alone into the darkness of night.

The next morning, Cil and Elizabeth headed out for work. They left Ruth Ann to care for Sarah. About eleven o'clock, Willy called.

"Ruth Ann, is my wife there? The folks at Spelman called and they said that she didn't come in to work this morning. She never misses a class. She loves those students more than she loves me. So, for her to just not show up without calling anyone, something must be wrong."

Ruth asked Willy, "So, she didn't come home last night either?"

"No, it doesn't look like it," Willy replied.

Ruth realized that Willy didn't go home last night either and paused for a moment. She knew she wasn't going to get anything useful out of him. "Okay," she replied before hanging up the phone.

Ruth's thoughts immediately went back to the times in her life when Deborah had gone missing. It was never a good thing. It had been several years since her last episode but each one was an all hands on deck event. Each time it happened, the sisters were reminded of the worst days of their collective lives.

The real concern wasn't Deborah's personal safety. On her medication or not, she was more than capable of defending herself from the locals. The biggest threat to Deborah was, and always had always been, Deborah. As a teen in the jungles of Central America, Deborah had tried to take her own life during one of her down times while Cil and her other sisters were away. A stranger found her and took her to the hospital. Deborah, in her delusionary state, always claimed that it was

Cil who had found her and rescued her. A secondary reason for Ruth's concern regarded the Council's constant recruitment efforts of Deborah. It seemed that over the years Matasis had seen something within Deborah that made him believe that he could turn her into a force of darkness.

Ruth called Elizabeth, Cil, and Joe to let them know that Deborah was AWOL. She tried not to wake Sarah but Sarah sensed something was wrong wandered into the living room as Ruth was finishing her calls. Sarah forced Ruth to tell her what was going on. Not wanting to wait on the others to arrive, Sarah threw on her house robe and sneakers and the two of them began to comb the neighborhood for Deborah.

Because of her gift, Sarah's vision was better than an eagle's. But she dared not take to the air anywhere near the house. She couldn't risk being seen. Sarah sent Ruth one way and she went the other. Sarah had little doubt that they'd find Deborah. Still she felt a sense of dread knowing that her sister's mood swings had no bottom.

Sarah sensed that her sister was reaching a point of no return. It was more than just a feeling; she could see the dark clouds gathering and felt a chill in the mid-morning June air. Deborah's emotions affected the weather. Somewhere, Deborah was teetering on the abyss. Perhaps, she could go airborne for just a bit? The years since they returned to Atlanta had been good years but, if she took to air, they'd have to move again. They'd done that before, when warranted, and this would certainly be such an occasion.

Before she took to the air, Sarah decided to check one more alley. As her teary eyes began to turn to fire, she caught a glimpse of two women in the alley seated on the landing of a side door. She rubbed the tears from her eyes to see clearly. Deborah sat quietly while the other woman spoke lovingly into her ear. The other woman was Aunt Elisa.

Sarah ran down the alleyway. Kneeling down to hug her sister, Sarah whispered into her ear, "Deborah..." After a long embrace she pulled back a bit to examine Deborah. "Are you okay?"

The disheveled Deborah answered back, "Yes, I'm fine. And, yes, I'm taking my meds."

"Oh, sister..." Sarah cried as she embraced Deborah again.

Sarah's gaze turned to Elisa who knew her question already, "Yes, I could hear her thoughts and I knew she was out here on that roof up there."

Then Elisa turned to Deborah before continuing, "Deb just needed some time to figure things out."

A tearful Deborah elaborated, "I'm leaving Willy. I just can't go on with him, not after this. I'm so sorry that I brought this curse of a man into the family." Deborah looked into her sister's eyes. "Please forgive me."

"Of course, but, there is nothing to forgive. He made his own choices."

Just then Ruth Ann turned the corner and came scurrying down the alleyway calling out, "Deborah!"

"I'm fine. But, I do need to check myself in for a few days."

Deborah laughed through her tears acknowledging that she needed help, "I'm going to need to make some changes." She smiled knowingly to Sarah.

Elisa stood up, "I need to get going before I'm missed. Cil and Elizabeth are pulling up to the house right now." Elisa was well aware that she was on borrowed time. As long as the Council of Nob needed her, she would be okay. Elisa had played nice over the years and even sought to convince them that she was on their side. But with Elisa's project coming to an end, she knew the knives would be out soon. Before she disappeared around the corner, Elisa turned and said to the three sisters, "The hardest thing to do in life is to let go of pain, but you get through it and you're better on the other side."

# 9
# SLIPPING AWAY

*September, 1963*

*Some are born to be shepherds of peace, while others couriers of chaos. And, yet, for all our protests, it is disorder that gives purpose to order. And, it is in the midst of the process that we are most like God.*

On a cool September morning, Hosea received the call that he needed to be in Paris by evening of the next day. A courier would bring him his plane tickets later that morning. The teenage son of an influential French politician had been confirmed as a victim of possession. The local priests had done their best and failed to terminate the possession. Hosea hated to leave his girls, but with Elisa in town and Rob arriving that evening, he knew that his daughters would be in good hands. Not to mention that mother hen Elizabeth would be there each evening. In truth, he knew that his girls were safer with those three than with just him. Still, he was apprehensive about leaving.

Hosea arrived at Charles De Gaulle airport at five p.m. local time. A driver waited for him at the gate, holding a sign that read "Mr. Hosea Johnson." Seeing the sign, he walked briskly to the black-suited driver. The driver took the larger of his two bags and greeted him, "Good evening, Monsieur Johnson."

Hosea followed the driver through the lightly falling rain to a black stretch limo located outside on the curb. Such audacious trappings always troubled Hosea's spirit given the nature of his work. He preferred the more humble locales and, yet, he always went where he was called. The limo stopped at a white brick building on Rue 16. Three of the local priests stood on the front steps like sentries, their long flowing black robes flickering as the street lights reflected off the beads of water on them. These events were always unique, but the energy that day felt more disturbing to Hosea than it ever had been since the first time he participated in an exorcism.

The senior priest extended his hand and greeted Hosea in a heavy French accent, "So, you are the one to whom God listens? I certainly hope so."

Hosea wanted to say how God had seemed so far away as of late, but looking at the weary priests, he didn't have the heart to burden them further. He had tried to sleep on the flight, but he couldn't. Here he was again before people who were full of expectations.

Hosea asked, "Where?"

The priest took him to a stone-lined room on the first floor. Immediately Hosea noticed the condensation on the outside wall of the room. The door to the room was soaked and beginning to rot. Hosea paused for a moment before the spirit within him told him to send the other priests away. He did although it was odd. Ordinarily, he would request that someone accompany him into the room.

After the priests left, Hosea knelt down and prayed, "Lord, it's me again. My God, oh, how you have blessed me time and time again. Even before the foundations of the Earth were set you were mindful of me. And words cannot express my gratitude unto thee. Lord, you know the troubles of my heart, you know my joy and my pain, you know my dreams and my fears, and you know my waking up and my lying down. Today, I accept your peace and I let go of all these earthly things. Lord, and yet you know that in the next breath that my girls are steady on my mind. Still, I release them freely into your loving hands and pray that I give this life fully unto thee."

# SLIPPING AWAY 97

With that, Hosea stood and pushed open the door. The room was dark and ice cold. The only light in the room was provided by the four candles that circled the bed. On that bed was a young man of about eighteen. His body lurched and heaved mightily against the constraints. Hosea called out, "Who are you?"

The straps holding the boy down grew taut as he pulled against them to raise his head, "Does it matter, Hosea, the fading star? My, how you've gotten old. You're not nearly the man you used to be. The end is near now."

"Your lips move, demon, but, as always, your words are void. You know well, this life is of no concern to me." Hosea said paying little attention to the beast as he opened his Bible.

In that moment the boy sprung from the bed snapping the bands that had held him. In an instant, he was across the room pressing his left hand into Hosea's neck and pushing him back against the nearly frozen wall. "The light has gone out of your eyes. Yes, we see it for ourselves now."

Hosea whispered "Submitto." The boy released him but began to growl. First, his eyes became jaundiced; then, his body began to transform. In the candlelight, the beast took on its true form. The demon, wings stretched wide and talons exposed, hovered over Hosea.

As it approached him again, Hosea whispered a second time, "Concesso" and the beast was suspended in mid-air. Then after adjusting his collar, as Hosea was prone to do even when not having been choked, Hosea pointed towards the limbs of the beast and said repeatedly "Ligare!"

Hosea pulled a bottle of water from his pocket and dampened his fingers from it. Then, he dabbed the pillow at the head of the bed. Hosea looked again at the struggling beast and steeled himself for the hard part.

"Separata! Separata! Separata!" Hosea called over and over again.

At long last in the flickering light, a shade of the boy began to appear alongside the demon.

Still Hosea called, "Separata! Separata! Separata!"

When the boy was fully separated from the beast, Hosea called out once, "Descendere."

At once, the boy's form descended to the bed. When his head touched the pillow below, his form condensed fully into human flesh. Hosea placed his hand upon the boy's forehead and said a quick prayer.

Then Hosea turned back towards the demon and commanded, "In the name of the Lord, God, potest albeit!"

The creature departed immediately into the wall and back to Hell.

Hosea picked up his Bible and pulled the door open to exit the room. He put his Bible into a small box and placed the box on a table just outside the door. Hosea attempted to have a seat next to it, but, instead, stumbled over the table and into the chair bringing the whole assembly crashing to the ground as he collapsed onto the cold floor.

∞

Back in Atlanta, Elisa and Lola were meeting with Miss Elizabeth to discuss care for the children in Hosea's absence. Lola sat stone-faced as Elisa and Elizabeth spoke.

"So, just what kind of deal did you make with Matasis?" Elizabeth asked.

Elisa responded, "According to Paul, as long as I agree to do their bidding, the Council agrees not to harm the girls. I'm supposed to meet them at their lodge on Auburn Avenue tonight for the details. I think the Council has something very specific in mind. And, I'm not supposed to have any contact with the girls while this agreement is in place. That's going to break my heart but I'd do anything for them."

Elizabeth reached out and took Elisa's hand as her eyes began to fill with tears. Elisa took a deep breath and let it out as she fought to compose herself.

Lola, who seemed oblivious to the gravity of the moment, smacked her gum and smiled, "The girls will be alright. They are always alright because I bore them and I'm always alright. Plus, you'll still be able to hang out with me right, since I'm not in the game?"

Elizabeth and Elisa gave each other a knowing look before moving on. Elizabeth laid her hand on top of Elisa's hand again before asking, "Do you want to say good bye to the girls before you leave? They're in their rooms reading and getting ready for bed."

Elisa smiled, "No, I don't want to say good bye. But, I would like to say good night." Elisa stopped by Ruth and Sarah's room first. Both girls were sleeping and Elisa gently kissed each of them on the cheek. Next she knocked and entered Cil and Deborah's room. She told each of them good night and gave each a hug.

Deborah sensing something was off asked, "Is everything okay, Auntie Elisa?"

Elisa smiled, "Yes, darling. Now go to sleep."

Outside the bedroom door a very nicely dressed Lola called, "Are you ready to go?"

Elisa replied softly, "Yes." Somberly, she rose and re-entered the hallway. "I'm ready. Let me grab my purse out of the kitchen."

Lola, being Lola, demanded, "Hey, I need for you to cheer up so that we can have some fun tonight."

As they headed for the front door, Elisa stopped for a second and asked Elizabeth, "So, what time is Rob due in?"

Elizabeth answered, "He's due to touch down around ten so I guess he'll be here before midnight. Do you want to hang out for a spell so that you can see him?"

Elisa just smiled and then turned to follow Lola out of the door. As she exited, she replied, "Thank you Elizabeth for all you do. Words cannot express my gratitude. I hope to see you again, soon."

As they walked down stairs to Elisa's car, Lola pointed out, "I love them kids, too, but I didn't get all dressed up to sit around talking to a bunch of other women. No offense."

"None taken," Elisa smiled. She knew that one of the main reasons Lola liked to hang out with her was because she had a car and money. Elisa could buy drinks when the men were either cheap or absent. Elisa had to admit, though, that when the two of them entered a bar or club, the men typically sat up and took notice. That was a rush for Lola whose self-esteem was often beaten down by the choices she made and by others' the responses to her choices. In nightlife, Lola found life like she dreamed it would be. Elisa had accepted that Lola was going to live and die as an addict. All she could do was to walk with her so that she might watch over her as she hoped for the day when she might turn a different way.

The destination of choice that night was a club off of Edgewood. It was near the building where Elisa would be attending her first Council meeting. Elisa pulled into an empty lot across the street from the club. As she got out, she sensed the presence besides herself and Lola. Deborah was completely invisible and hiding in the back seat. Somehow she'd eluded detection all the way to the club. Elisa knew that she was a bit distracted but that didn't fully account for her oversight. This girl certainly had advanced skills to remain hidden from her for so long.

Elisa called out, "Deborah, you can come out of the car now."

Deborah made herself visible and stepped out of the vehicle with her head hung low. Lola swore and then proceeded to ask, "So, what are we going to do now?"

Elisa gave Lola a look and asked rhetorically, "So, what do you think we should do?"

Lola replied with the question, "Take her home?"

Elisa nodded, "Hey, you go on into the club. Here's some money. I'll take Deborah home. It's not that far away and I'll be back in twenty minutes. Find a good table for us to hold court."

Lola took the money and smiled. She sang as she danced across the street, "I'm going to a Go-Go…"

You never want to give cash to an addict but Elisa had only given Lola enough to buy one drink. After watching Lola go into the club, Elisa turned her attention to Deborah. "So, what are you doing here?"

"I don't know. I saw you and Mama leaving and I wanted to go with you to see where you were going," Deborah said.

Elisa replied, "Well, you see where we are. No big shakes. I'm just going to hang out with your mama for a little bit. So, let's go back to the house."

"Auntie Elisa, may I ask you a question? You know what I can do, but what is it that you can do?" Deborah asked.

Elisa thought for a moment and then smiled and took Deborah's hand. She led her to a storefront window where the two of them could see their reflections.

"Well, I think you already know that I can read minds. I can do a number of things, but one of the things I can do is particularly special. For the longest time I couldn't do it, but it's come back to me of late."

Elisa stretched out her hand towards the glass and their images dissolved transforming the space into an opening.

"Come, this is a passageway to something very nice."

Deborah hesitated. The portal surface was murky and had a watery look to it. Elisa took Deborah's hand and said, "Trust me."

Deborah exhaled, releasing her fears. With a nervous smile, she followed Elisa into the portal. Instinctively, Deborah closed her eyes. Once on the other side Elisa said to her, "Open your eyes."

What Deborah saw next could only be described as paradise. She saw a land so lush in foliage that it seemed unreal. Winged creatures flew to and fro. Small four-legged animals scurried about. The air was so fresh, so clean that Deborah could hardly believe it.

"Oh, my goodness!" Deborah exclaimed.

"Yes," Elisa smiled, "it is breathtaking, isn't it. The sun here is a large red one, circled by a small white dwarf star and we are so close to them that it often looks like morning even in the middle of the night here. There's fruit everywhere, plenty of water, and, believe it or not, all the animals are vegetarian."

"Vege-what?"

"Vegetarian, meaning that animals here don't try to eat one another."

"Wow…" Deborah's mouth remained open in astonishment.

As the two of them walked hand in hand towards a clearing, Elisa continued to explain, sharing her world with little Deborah. In the clearing they found a large rock that they could both sit upon.

Deborah smiled and mused, "I wish I could live here all of the time. It's so pretty."

Elisa thought for a moment and confided to Deborah, "Well, it has been discussed. Would you like it if you and your sisters could live here all of the time?"

"Yes!" Deborah screamed.

"Well, let me see what I can do. I would love to have you here, but it's not just up to me." Elisa said honestly.

She had once proposed this when it was learned that the Council of Nob had begun operations in Atlanta, but the powers that be in the Circle, the ruling body over the Circle Knights and their Elders, rejected the idea. Although she'd once sworn an oath to obey as a Circle Knight herself, she was this close to going rogue... again.

Elisa looked up at one of the setting suns, as the smaller, brighter one took prominence, "It's time to go but let me show you one more thing. Look over there across the field."

Deborah stood up on the rock so that she could see and cried, "Ew-wee, is that what I think it is?" as she began jumping up and down.

Elisa nodded, "Yes, it is."

Back at the portal, Elisa took Deborah's hand and led her through it back to their world. As they exited the portal, they were greeted by seven cloaked men whose wide hats hid their faces. These were the Seven Warriors of Zi.

From behind them Zi called out, "Toshite moraemasu ka!" and the men parted revealing Zi the Sorceress, Isadora Queen of the Dead, Destry the Destroyer, and Matasis the Deformer. Zi gave a sly smile and commented, "Welcome back, old friend."

Deborah didn't know who they were, but she knew that she didn't like them. She whispered to Elisa, "I can get us out of here."

Through a forced smile, Elisa told her pointing at Zi, "No, darling, I know this one and the others are my new friends.

Although I'm not sure why they're here now when I'm supposed to meet them at their place at midnight?"

Matasis smiled a sly smile, "That was the plan. But, we ran into your sister Lola at the club and she told us that you were out here with your little friend. So, we came out to look for you."

"So, where's Lola?" asked Elisa trying her best to hide her anger at Lola.

"Oh, she met some guy and they went off together to who knows where, but you can imagine can't you?" Matasis teased, before going on, "Why don't you come on over now?"

"Well, I need to take the child home," Elisa answered.

Matasis smiled, "Oh, you can bring her. We won't bite, since we're all friends now. Besides the others are already in the meeting hall waiting on us. I was going to introduce you at the end of our meeting but, since you're here now, I'll bring you in at the beginning. Then, you can get this little girl home and get back to your evening out. Come on, you're one of us now."

Elisa realized that she had to go all in if this game was going to work, so she relented. She took Deborah's hand and spoke softly to her, "We're going to go and visit with my new friends for just a little bit and then it's off to bed for you."

Deborah told her sisters later that Isadora looked at her like she was a hot cheese burger on the grill, although each time she told the story she inserted a different delicacy: fried chicken, Seven-Up cake, pork chops, and the like. Elisa stepped in between Isadora and Deborah.

Isadora flashed a devilish smile as she tried to intimidate Elisa and Deborah, "I heard that you're not nearly the talent you were before. I heard that besides your gift with portals, you're not the woman of legends anymore. I heard…"

Elisa cut Isadora off mid-sentence, "Do you want to try me?"

Elisa's unblinking gaze remained locked into Isadora's eyes. After a tense moment Isadora smiled and turned away.

As they walked the short distance across the parking lot from Edgewood to Auburn Avenue, Matasis spoke quietly to Elisa. "Let me give you a tip. I know even though you're a Circle Knight castaway, it probably still turns your stomach to work with us. You wonder how you can ever trust these people. Well, let me tell you, now. You can't. I certainly don't. But, what I do trust is that every entity is true to itself. So, if you know what motivates someone, you'll know, within certain boundaries, what they will and will not do. So, I suggest you get to know them, disgusting as that might be to you, for your own safety. Since I need you on this project, I say this for my own benefit. My second tip is this – never, ever, try to play me. I know you're known by many as the Enchantress, but if I ever catch you trying to play with my mind, I will kill you and all you hold dear. Are we clear?"

Elisa nodded. She was well aware that Matasis took his vendettas as eternal matters.

Matasis took a step and then added, "Oh, and you need to lose your sister, Lola. She's a drug addict and her mind is weak. If I so much as hear her name in association with any Council business, I will kill her myself. Are we clear?"

Elisa answered, "Yes."

As they entered the Council of Nob's sanctuary, Elisa felt the magnitude of the bitter pill she'd agreed to swallow for the sake of the girls. The Sanctuary was filled with soulless dark water. Realizing there was no turning back she took a breath and plunged in. She'd never been the best swimmer, and to make things worse, the water in this room was so, so very cold. So, that day, to survive, she went cold as well, to survive the long night's swim.

Waiting in the Boardroom were Chase the Saint Killer and Poseidon the Space God along with several servants and guards. Elisa had expected to see all of them. Paul had informed her of the Council's current composition. But there was one more entity present that she hadn't expected to see that night. His name was Henri. He was a Frenchman and dear friend that Elisa had met many years ago in a lifetime far away before she'd ever tasted the bitter air of The Pit. Henri smiled at her. She exhaled softly and smiled back at him. Henri was a Nightwalker. In fact, he was an ambassador of the ruling Nightwalker clan. Elisa also knew Chase in the life before. She stared at him hoping for some response or acknowledgement, but his stark-white face remained like stone.

Zi entered the room. Seeing Henri, Chase, and Elisa, she commented "Oh, how the worm has turned."

It was a reference that only the four of them understood. They had come together under very different circumstances many years ago when they were the best of friends. Today, each stood alone.

Poseidon quipped, "What, another dreamer? Don't we have enough of those?"

Across the universe humans were often referred to as dreamers. The act of dreaming was an experience unique to Earthlings. But among the species on Earth that dreamed, humans were said to be able to see the future, past, and alternate realities through their dreams. Getting consistent results from any particular human in this matter was like chasing the wind. Many aliens, like Poseidon, had grown skeptical of these "dreamers" as if they were some sort of snake oil being pushed by fringe scientists and anthropologists.

Matasis smiled and formally introduced Elisa to the group at large. "Elisa here has some very unique skills which will allow us to reach our goal in a tenth of the time originally estimated. But rather than explaining what she does, let me show you what she can do." Matasis motioned to the servants to pull out a large full length mirror.

Before Matasis could continue, Chase asked, "So, who is the little munchkin tagging along with her?"

Matasis looked back at Deborah who was hiding as best she could behind Elisa's skirt. "Oh, she's Elisa's little niece, Deborah. She has some talents too, which perhaps we'll take a look at a little later."

Elisa cringed as she realized the depth to which Lola had sold them out.

Deborah, frightened by their hungry gazes, instinctively went invisible taking Elisa with her.

Chase quipped, "I guess she couldn't wait."

"And she took the big one with her," Destry commented.

Chase corrected him, "No, they're both still here." This was the first inkling that somehow Chase could still perceive Deborah when she was in her hidden mode even though he wasn't a mind reader like Elisa.

Elisa spoke to Deborah, "Darling, you can let them see us. It'll be okay. I promise." Slowly, they both came back into view. Still, Deborah clung to Elisa's skirt.

Zi plopped down into a chair and demanded, "Enough chatter, let's show everyone what Elisa can do."

"Okay, but first we'll need a volunteer. You will think of a location and Elisa will create a portal to that location." Matasis said as he looked around the room for a volunteer.

At last, Henri the Nightwalker, spoke up, "I'll do it. There's nothing to be afraid of. I've had the privilege of doing this before on a number of occasions."

Destry snickered, "Better you than me. I'm not gonna have some dame strolling around my head."

Elisa thought, "That would be a short trip." Besides, since Destry was completely human, his mind was easy pickings. Disgustingly enough, he thought about women constantly. Surprisingly, the woman most often on his mind was Zi who could not stand him or his kind. Maybe that's why he thought about her so much.

Elisa turned to her old friend, "Okay Henri, you know what to do. Just think of a place."

Henri closed his eyes and so did Elisa. A moment later, Elisa's eyes opened revealing two glowing orbs. She reached out towards the long mirror in the front of the room. Its surface became murky, as the storefront window had earlier. But unlike before, the lighting in the room allowed everyone to clearly see images from the other side.

Henri elaborated on what they were looking at. "What you're seeing there is one of our subterranean ports. And if you look closely, you can see our ships loading your first shipment." Everyone in the room was impressed. Even Zi, who also possessed limited teleportation ability, was reminded of how talented her old friend could be.

Matasis took the floor again, "Two things to note here. First, you see that Elisa is the rarest of beings which can combine telepathy and teleportation. Anywhere you want to go, on any plane of existence, she can create a portal to get you there. Secondly, unlike others who have created temporal or special distortions in the past, Elisa's creations are persistent. Meaning, that as long as that mirror remains intact and the exit on the other side is not blocked, you will have a working portal."

Poseidon sat up. "Can you do that with non-humans as well?"

Elisa answered, "Yes, I can."

She touched the space god and closed her eyes. A moment later she opened her blazing eyes and reached out with both arms towards the glass top conference table. Immediately, ripples appeared on the surface of the table and an ocean world beneath it. Items sitting on the table began to bob up and down, some of them sinking below. Poseidon reached into the table and pulled back his wet hand. Then inexplicably, he grabbed one of the servants and tossed him down into the portal. Deborah shrieked and Elisa tried to quiet her. Everyone else in the room was riveted peering into the portal as they watched the flailing servant struggle against the gravity of a new world. Holding his breath, he inched his way back towards the portal. But before he could reach it, Poseidon asked Elisa, "So, can you close these just as quickly?"

Puzzled, Elisa turned to him, "Yes?"

"Close it now then," Poseidon demanded. He was a sadistic creature when it came to humans but he also wanted to see blood on Elisa's hands.

Elisa looked to Matasis and he nodded for her to proceed. She didn't want to but Elisa knew that she had to stay in this game. She told herself that for the greater good she had to do this thing. Elisa held Deborah's face tight against her skirt with one hand as she reached out towards the table with the other. A moment later, there was glass where there had been an alien world. Poseidon nodded his approval.

"I think at last our intergalactic, inter-dimensional Omni Portal is a go as our waterlogged servant can now attest."

Isadora frowned and cackled, "I was going to sacrifice that one tonight."

Elisa interrupted, "Matasis are you done with us?"

Matasis gave an ominous, "For now. Be back here tomorrow evening right after sunset. We have work to do. And, you might want to pick up some winter wear while you're out tomorrow."

Henri the Nightwalker motioned to Matasis that he was going to escort Elisa and Deborah out. Among the four old friends, Henri had been the late night philosopher. His observations could be striking. Of the battle between French and English culture he would say well before Darwin ever set sail, "The evolution of a society is no less painful than the evolution of a species. Branches must die so that others might live and thrive." Henri expected that the French culture would come to dominate the world. I can tell you that in this distant future, that was not the case. Rather, it was the language of technology that decided the issue. Additionally, Henri would be sad to know that in this future age Nightwalkers are all but extinct. But Henri, unlike others of his tribe, never had delusions about that.

Henri called out to Elisa, "Madame, s'il vous plait attendre." He gently offered his arm for Elisa to take. "It is good to see you, old friend. I'm so happy that you escaped from The Pit."

"Escaped? I know what you mean. But, even when you escape Hell the stench remains, at least as long as you're on this side of the Jordan. But yes, I'm back. In fact, I've been back for a minute and, honestly, I'm a little surprised that I didn't hear from you sooner."

In truth, Elisa was a lot surprised, but she tried to hide her disappointment as her fingers dug into her arm beneath her long sleeve blouse.

"Yes, I'm sorry about that. Given the tense relationship between the Circle and Nightwalkers since we aligned with Matasis, I just couldn't risk it politically."

"Politically, really? I was locked away for nearly three hundred years, and made to endure unspeakable obscenities. So, now, you can't be seen with me?" Elisa shook her head.

Henri reached out to touch Elisa's shoulder, "Oh, my Elisa, if only you knew how I longed to see you again. But, since my father became king, my own heart, my own desires, are of no consequence."

Elisa pulled away a bit with the now sleepy Deborah clinging tightly to her leg. "Oh, I hear what you're saying, but at the end of the day you've abandoned your friends and gotten into bed with Matasis. That's a hell of a price to pay for blood loyalty."

"Elisa, I know it's horrible that we are reduced to doing business with the likes of these. But, the reality of it is that they have the upper hand right now. But, their season will pass just like all the others before. We just need to survive today, do the same tomorrow and all the days thereafter until their star sets."

"And then what?" Elisa asked.

"Then the knives come out. Assuming Matasis is eventually defeated and these things play out, those in my father's regime shall be blamed and cast out for our enemies to devour."

"And you're okay with that?"

"We do this for the survival of our people today, so that they might have breath tomorrow to curse us."

Elisa asked, "Gosh, what they're up to must be pretty awful? I wasn't in the room long enough to know everything they're doing, but I sensed enough to know that this thing they are building has a very a very dark purpose. Surely, you know this?"

"Oui, Madame," Henri answered, "they are building an inter-dimensional portal which they plan to use to permanently open the door between this world and a thousand others. They call it the Omni Portal. It will be indestructible once completed. It will allow easy passage to our world from Poseidon's world, Isadora's Oblivion, and …"

"And, the Pit." Elisa injected.

"Yes, the Pit where you were held all those years and a thousand other dark places you've never heard of before. If they are successful in building this, it will mean the end of creation. This is the gateway to destruction. Each being at that table has a particular thirst they seek to satisfy by doing this. And the problem is not just those miscreants in there, but it is who and what they represent. Poseidon not only represents his war mongering civilization, he also speaks for the old gods who were cast out of this realm and now seek to destroy it if they cannot have it. Isadora, Queen of the Dead, leads those spirits who worship death. She sees the creation of the Omni Portal as a means of increasing her empire of lost souls. Zi is the most dominant and influential sorceress in the world and she heads Espérons que des Abandonnés', an End of Days cult she became involved in around the time you left. Their sole goal is to bring about the end of this version of creation."

Elisa interrupted, "She still believes there's no hope for us?"

"Correct, she believes the sooner we can bring about the End of Days, the sooner the righteous can claim their place. But, unlike other apocalyptic minded people, Zi does not count herself among the righteous. You may not know about the Destry. They're new since you were cast down. The Destry leads a society of mercenaries dedicated to the art of war and suffering. So, the idea of starting the war of wars aligns with their theology perfectly. And, then, there is Matasis who relishes long painful deaths. Not only does he lead this group but he has the ability to corrupt others into doing his bidding."

Elisa lifted Deborah up into her arms as if to leave.

Then she turned to Henri and asked, "So, what's going on with Chase? There's coldness about him now, which I've never seen before. He wouldn't even talk to me, his closest friend!"

Elisa had reached out to Chase since her return from the Pit but her requests to meet with him had gone unacknowledged.

Henri paused and then sighed, "I've never seen anything more disturbing. Being a former Circle Knight himself and, given what happened, he seems to take the greatest pleasure in killing other Circle Knights. They call him the Saint Killer."

Elisa understood. Chase's quest for retribution inspired him. His life as an assassin had numbed him to death; the events of three hundred years ago had given him a target; and his thirst for vengeance made him relentless. Chase was also the most feared assassin in the League of Assassins but he cared little about such statuses. That wasn't why he killed. He sought out lives to take simply as a statement against those who proclaimed all life sacred. The bitterness resulting from events in the 1700's motivated him across the centuries.

Henri continued, "He's never said it to me, but I truly believe Chase is only involved in this because he believes that staging an End of Days event is the only sure way to bring the Elders to the battlefield. He's determined to make the Elders answer for what they've done."

Elisa gave Henri a knowing look and then shook her head for she, too, had reason to be angry with the Elders.

. "What about you? Why are you really here? Do you think that, in suggesting this arrangement, perhaps, Paul may have been compromised by Matasis? And of all those he could have offered, why did Paul pick you – an alpha-level Circle Knight?"

"I don't know about that alpha-level business anymore." Elisa was a shell of her former self and she struggled to do formerly simple things. "But regarding Paul," Elisa realized that she could only share a version of the truth with Henri. She hated that but too much was at risk to do otherwise, "I don't know where he is, but one thing is true. I trust Paul when it comes to securing the safety of these babies. And, if I'm the lamb to be sacrificed in the process, I'm fine with that. Plus, Paul was the only Elder who defended my case before the other Circle Knight Elders, despite the political cost of doing so. And I still respect him for who he was back when I last walked this earth."

Henri smiled, "Yes, those were the days – back in New Orleans."

Elisa, wanting to get Deborah home, motioned for Henri to follow her towards her car. "Yes, they were. But, in this new age, this new, serious Henri will take some getting used to."

"That Henri, for century upon century, was a child. But, these events have forced upon me a reality I cannot ignore."

"For you to become a part of the establishment, these must be perilous times, indeed, in the Nightwalker community."

Henri belonged to a flavor of the human experience commonly referred to as Vampires. They were a branch of humans that diverged from homo sapiens long before recorded history. There are many misconceptions about them; many of which are promoted by their community for their own protection. First, most of them are not immortal but, relative to humans, they do live for a very long time. Historically, their average life expectancy has been roughly eight hundred years. With modern medical advances that also benefit humans, the modern Nightwalker's average life expectancy is closer to two thousand years. Pure bloods, like Henri, claim to be truly immortal.

Second, Nightwalkers don't burst into flames when exposed to daylight. However, they are very light sensitive which brings up the third point. Originating from Europe, during the Ice Age, they lived in caves. Those who survived the harsh conditions and limited food supply did so by hibernating. After the ice receded and wave after wave of humans came up out of Africa, the Nightwalkers could not compete. Homo sapiens did not need to sleep through the winters because of their higher body temperatures. Armed with weapons, they decimated the Nightwalkers while they slept during the cold European winters. For their own protection, the Nightwalkers perpetuated myths and stories in the human community that taught humans to fear them. Actually, with the rise of human commerce, their extended life expectancies and ability to pass for human have allowed the Nightwalkers to amass great wealth and knowledge. Their libraries were the greatest on earth for, unlike so many humans, they loved and thirsted for knowledge. Humans use information to control one another; Nightwalkers use it to uplift each other.

However, some of the stories about Nightwalkers are based in truth. They are an arrogant lot. Most of them look down on humans and think them petty. Nightwalkers do tend to have large incisors. And, they do like to drink blood. That is a holdover from their Ice Age days. They prefer the blood of cattle and sheep to that of humans whom they think are nasty, disease-filled creatures. So, it does beg the question, if they are a part of the Earth's history, why haven't archeologists found any evidence of them yet? Well, they have, and lots of it actually. But archeologists refer to them by another name, Neanderthals.

Henri looked intently into Elisa eyes, "And, yet there is hope. We are hopeful that an age of enlightenment is upon mankind such that we can come out of the shadows and reveal ourselves to them within the next two hundred years. The rise of mass media will aid us in this.

But there is another thing. A handful of us, including the king, know about her. " Henri glanced at the sleeping Deborah in Elisa's arms. "I know that the circumstances of her birth were not optimal, but her birth may be our best opportunity to bring all three expressions of human existence together. Nightwalker royal blood flows through her veins which means that someday she could make a legitimate claim to the throne." Henri paused, "Particularly, if she had the guidance of her Auntie. I know I can't reach out to you, but if you reach out to us, it could work." Henri smiled slyly at Elisa, "Hey, think about it. I know that you would add a lot our community and to my own house."

"Your house?" Elisa smiled, turned and walked off towards her car. She looked back over her left shoulder and said loudly, "Bye, Henri…"

This was not the first time that Henri had made a not so sly play for Elisa's time and affection. This time he'd woven Deborah into his strategy. She too had a good sense of who Deborah's biological father was but Elisa saw no benefit in becoming entangled in Nightwalker political theater. Still, she was struck how the whole universe could be at stake and this man was still thinking about her skirt. This was not the time.

Elisa's thoughts raced as she started the car. All the old ways and old gods that tormented men throughout the ages were seeking to stage a comeback. They sought a return to days when demons from the underworld walked the earth and aliens propped themselves up as gods to be worshiped. She had been enlisted to return all humankind to an age of chaos and fear, at best. At worst, it would truly be an end to creation. It confounded her that after all she'd been through surviving in The Pit that she had been chosen to be one of the first to face this gathering storm. She glanced back at a sleeping Deborah and remembered what gave her the strength to leave The Pit. In her lowest moment, her beloved told her of these precious babies. So, even though she wondered just how she might have the strength to make it through all that was to come, looking at Deborah told her that she had no choice.

As Elisa's car began to pull away from the curb, Henri ran up to Elisa's open window with his hand extended. "Here, I think this belongs to you." He handed her the red sash she'd left at the café in New Orleans on that last sunny day, three hundred years prior, when she dined with Chase and Henri.

# 10
# OLD WOUNDS

*June, 1981*

*Sadness and Melancholy are not the same. The former is regret for what was, where the latter is a longing for what could be.*

Just before sunrise, Deborah, Cil, and Joe turned onto Auburn Avenue in the battered blue pickup truck. Sarah and Ruth Ann followed close behind in an older foreign sports car. Sarah was driving. Both vehicles stopped in a set of shadows between the streetlights.

Cil pointed out, "There it is."

The "it" Cil was referring to was the building that the Council of Nob had purchased nearly twenty years earlier. It was where they held their meetings during the time they were based in Atlanta and where Deborah had gone with Elisa when she was a little girl. The Council still owned the building.

Joe grunted, "Yes, I see it. Where do you want me to park?"

"This is good," Cil said.

Cil nudged Deborah, "Ruth Ann and I will go around to the back entrance and cause a commotion. That should draw some of the guards from the front. Then you and Sarah go in hand to hand, as best you can, through the front. Our intelligence tells us that all of the portals were moved to the conference room some time ago after repeated flooding in the basement. When you get to the conference room, destroy all of the mirrors on the walls and all of the free standing ones except for the one to Elisa's paradise."

"Got it," Deborah said as she exited the truck.

Deborah motioned for Sarah to follow her up the street to the Council's old lodge. Cil and Ruth headed down an alley towards the back of the buildings on that block. Although the sisters had planned this mission earlier, Deborah repeated Cil's instructions to Sarah as they walked along the sidewalk. They stopped at the bus stop right before the lodge's entrance. They could see armed men in black suits with ear pieces milling about the lobby. The Council no longer met regularly at this location but they still used it for storage.

A militia of Isadora's walking dead remained on site as protection. The dead were under the command of human lieutenants who typically set up in the lobby or the break room. The four lieutenants in the lobby looked like Secret Service agents.

Deborah and Sarah stood outside pretending to wait for a bus as they each slipped on a pair of gloves. The sisters slyly watched the lobby. Then they heard the sound of a disturbance coming from behind the building. Two of the men immediately exited the lobby. The remaining two moved to the windows and closed the blinds. That was Deborah and Sarah's cue.

Both women were dressed in short sun dresses with black leggings. They quickly turned and walked towards the front door. The sisters wanted to refrain from using their powers within the building because the building also served as an arms cache for the Council. Deborah reached the door first and, seeing that it was locked, nodded towards Sarah. She lifted her shades slightly and a burst of white hot heat shot out. The bolt and lock melted away and dripped to the ground. The sisters looked around quickly then Deborah pushed the door open. The stunned lieutenants reached for their guns, but Sarah disarmed them with her smile, as was her way, until she and Deborah were upon them.

Deborah cupped her hands and slammed them over the ears of the man on the left. Sarah karate-chopped the one on the right in the throat and hit him across his glass jaw with a wheel house kick. Deborah brought her foe down by slamming his face down into her knee. In moments, both of men lay unconscious on the floor. Deborah and Sarah quickly unzipped their sun dresses revealing their fitted black full-body tights underneath. Deborah strapped the golden bow of Athena, which she'd managed to hide under her dress, to her back. They laid their dresses on the front desk and moved towards an internal door. Deborah took the lead; Sarah followed. Deborah opened the door to the hallway that led to the conference room. There were four sentries in the hallway, two near the stairs and two at the end of the hall outside of the conference room. Each walking corpse stood about six foot four and weighed between 250 to 300 pounds. They all had a hunger for human flesh.

First, they had to disable the two undead guarding the stairwell. The sisters had no intention of going upstairs or into the basement but, by being in the hallway, these guys were in the way. Deborah went invisible before running and sliding between the legs of the first monstrosity and springing up in front of the second one. Using the base of her hand, she landed an uppercut beneath its chin as she revealed herself.

Sarah executed a perfect leg sweep on the first beast toppling it to the floor. She jumped on top of it pounding blows into its eyes. Though it couldn't feel pain from her blows, it still could not see without its eyes.

Just as Deborah and Sarah were incapacitating the first two guards, the two overgrown zombies guarding the conference room door rushed towards them. These two had been fitted with long, sharp steel fingernails and iron teeth. Deborah had no time or room to sling a golden arrow before the first creature was upon her. The beast swung at her. She ducked but not before one of his razor sharp talons scratched her chin.

She nodded her head and questioned the abomination, "So, it's like that, huh?"

Deborah unleashed a barrage of blows against her opponent. Still, he stood. She ran past him towards the Boardroom and he followed in close pursuit. But, rather than going through the door, Deborah ran towards the corner, bounded up the wall to the side wall, then moved back toward the monster. From there, she kicked him in the head so hard that several of his iron teeth flew from his mouth. The sentry hit the floor.

Sarah leapt on the back of her opponent's neck and placed her hands on either side of his head to scorch him into submission.

Sarah said to her sister, "You know you could have done that a lot easier by at least staying invisible?"

Deborah smiled, "Yes, but you know…."

All the sisters knew that Deborah liked to fight. She was an "I wish you would" chick, as some like to say. It also seemed that she was always trying to prove that she was just as tough as Cil.

As the sisters entered the Boardroom, Deborah exclaimed, "Whoa. It's been so many years."

The room was filled with mirrors. There were several large mirrors on the walls, but most were free standing full-length mirrors. All of the mirrors were draped with a heavy cloth. Blocking light into the mirrors shut down the portals. But this place held more than simply inter-dimensional gateways. It did and would always hold a certain sadness for each of the sisters. For Deborah, it was a bitter sadness.

Sarah seeking to move things along said, "Hey, I'm going to turn the lights up just a bit in here so that we can see what we're doing. Then we can pull these covers off of each of these mirrors and you can tell me which one is the portal to Aunt Elisa's paradise."

Deborah shook her head as if loosening cobwebs and replied softly, "Okay."

The two of them began pulling the cloths from each of the mirrors. After all the cloths were removed, they stood back to survey the room. It was amazing. Each mirror represented a portal to new and amazing worlds. There were some worlds where all they could see was mist. Others were glistening cities of light. Still others seemed to be pure darkness. But, there was one mirror, framed in cherry wood, that led to a world that appeared much like earth. It was a world where everything had two shadows. From where they stood, it looked like paradise.

Deborah called out, "That one. That's it."

Sarah instructed her sister, "Alright, pull that one into the hallway and I'll get started here."

She then removed her shades looked at each mirror. As she did, each mirror began to melt. She radiated something akin to a microwave at each one. She was almost finished when the doors to the conference room opened. Her three sisters stepped in. They were protected from the radiation by one of Ruth's blue shields. They watched as the images on the three wall mirrors on the left wall, one by one, distorted, drooped and ran to the floor in small reflective rivulets. When Sarah gave the all-clear sign to her siblings, Ruth lowered her shield.

They picked up the one mirror they'd spared and carried it down the hallway. Instinctively, they stopped at the stairwell. Each of them took a deep breath. All were thinking of the events that took place at the bottom of those stairs nearly twenty years earlier. In spite of themselves, tears began to flow.

Cil said through her tears, "It's alright. Let it go. It's okay."

Deborah asked, "Can we go down there?"

Cil responded, "No, not right now, we don't have time. But, when we're done, we'll come back. And we'll get all of these munitions and chemicals out of here as well."

They picked up the mirror again and marched off through the foyer. Once outside, Cil motioned for Joe to drive up to meet them.

Joe immediately jumped out of the truck took the mirror from the women and laid it in the bed of his truck. He took a heavy moving blanket and placed it over the mirror. After securing everything, he hopped back into the driver's seat.

"It was hard going back in there, huh?"

Cil only nodded.

Deborah looked back at the building and replied simply "Yes…"

# THE BOOK OF ELISA

# SACRIFICES • *Alan D. Jones*

# 11
# NEW DAY, OLD NIGHTMARES

*March, 1753 - Louisiana, Damascus Plantation, New France*

*The more challenged a love is, the stronger it becomes.*

Elisa awoke full of excitement. She had just turned fourteen and she would become one with her beloved today. Oh, how she had lived for that day! Her mother had always told her that at fourteen she could marry. Of course, her mother had no idea how soon that wedding day would come. All day long she sang and danced as she awaited her beloved's return from the sugar cane fields.

On more than one occasion that day her mother cautioned, "Elisa, don't you dare fool around and drop none of their crystal."

"Oui, Mama," Elisa said with a smile.

She was so happy that even her mother's constant fretting could not steal her joy. Twenty years earlier, an Englishman who was visiting New Orleans from Georgia lost Elisa's mother and ten other slaves in a card game. Elisa had heard English and French since birth and spoke both fluently, but her mother still struggled with the latter. Elisa's mother, Ola, understood French just fine, but butchered the language when she tried to speak it. Ola said she had a thick tongue. Their master seemed to enjoy the comic relief. Elisa and her mother both worked in the big house. Ola was a good looking brown-skinned woman. She was loved by everyone in the house, except for the master's wife who always looked to give her a hard way to go. Elisa, Ola's only child, was very fair-skinned with long dirty blonde hair that curled when she washed it. Elisa was so fair that she could pass for white which explained their mistress' distain for Ola.

Elisa's betrothed was a sixteen year old field hand. He already could out work any two men on the plantation. Elisa liked that he was so well respected for his hard work, but she loved him for his charm, kindness, and dashing smile. It was all that Elisa could do not to tell all who would listen that by sunset she would be married. Elisa's beloved had made arrangements with a traveling preacher to marry them. They were to meet underneath the bridge on the edge of the property. Once they were married and had consummated their bond, how could anyone object?

It was a Tuesday. On Tuesdays, Elisa had to prep the evening meal for her mother to cook. When her mother entered the cookhouse, Elisa was free for the rest of the evening. Although she'd often come back after dinner to help her mother wash the dishes, she would not that evening. She felt bad about that since she knew how hard her mother worked. But alas, this was her wedding day, surely her mother would understand.

Elisa worked feverishly, cutting, cleaning, and seasoning the freshly-killed chicken for the main house. Though her mother was never late, Elisa kept an eye on the sky. She hoped her mother would arrive before the sun set.

At long last, Ola entered the cookhouse. She tied an apron around her waist and nodded to Elisa which was the signal that she could depart and enjoy her evening off. Elisa literally skipped and sang her way out of the kitchen.

Elisa stepped into the small room she shared with her mother and dressed herself in the one flowered dress she owned. It was the same dress she wore whenever she was not working. When she was ready, Elisa bolted out the door. She held her dress up enough to allow her legs room to run and blazed down the dirt road towards the river. Once she got to the bridge, she scurried down the side to the river bank below.

The preacher man and her beloved waited for her below the bridge. Her husband-to-be held a handful of daises he'd picked on his way there from the cane fields in one hand and a broom in the other. He smiled at Elisa and her heart skipped with joy.

It was a quick ceremony. Only ten minutes later, they were married and had sent the preacher on his way. Before God, they laid out a blanket right there beneath the bridge and took knowledge of one another. There, in the darkness, they agreed to tell their parents of their wedded bliss. They didn't have a cabin of their own or even a single bed between the two of them. All they had was their undying love. That was enough.

When Elisa arrived back to the big house and found the servant door unlocked, she was surprised. In the past, her mother had threatened to lock the door should she returned home past dark. Ola had just finished their evening chores and was getting ready to soak her feet. Everyone marveled at how young Ola looked, but her feet appeared much older her thirty-six year old body. Elisa asked her mother to sit so she could pour the hot water over Ola's feet. Elisa knelled before her mother and started pouring the water.

Then, she said matter-of-factly, "Mama, I'm married."

Ola didn't have to ask to whom but she did ask, "So, where y'all gonna live? Whose bed y'all gonna sleep in?"

"We're gonna work all that out, Mama," Elisa replied.

"Mmmm," was all that Ola said.

Elisa wasn't used to her mother being silent about much of anything and had thoroughly expected to have a major argument about her marriage.

Elisa decided that she was far better off with a quiet Ola than a fussing one. So, she left her mother's side to wash up and retire for the night. Elisa was still awake when her mother joined her in the bed that they shared. Still, her mother said nothing. Elisa knew her mother well and this quiet began to make her uneasy.

After breakfast the next morning, Elisa was outside washing up the morning dishes when a flatbed wagon drawn by two horses pulled into the courtyard. Two white men sat up high driving the horses and one slave rode in the bed. Another white man rode the most beautiful horse Elisa had ever seen. He dismounted his horse and greeted master with some papers. Then, five field hands struggled to drag another bound and hooded slave from the stable. Elisa stood up. It looked like master was selling someone. Something about the hooded slave looked familiar to Elisa. She began to walk towards them. The bound man continued to struggle. When the hood was removed, she saw it was her beloved. Instantly, Elisa began to run, screaming "No!"

Before she reached them, one of the field hands grabbed Elisa, lifted her into the air, and carried her away. As she was being carried away, Elisa noticed that the man in the wagon bed was speaking to her beloved. Her beloved immediately calmed down. The man in the wagon bed instructed the others to unbind him. After he was released, he climbed into the wagon with the stranger. The stranger motioned for the man holding Elisa to bring her forward. At the foot of the wagon, the stranger took a hold of Elisa's chin and looked into her eyes. Where her beloved's skin was the color of chocolate, the stranger's skin was coal black, but his eyes were fiery.

The stranger said in English, "You can take her away."

He turned to the man who had been on the horse, "I thought I saw something but there's nothing there. Let's see if we can make New Orleans by nightfall."

"Bien, Paul," the rider said.

The field hand still held her fast as Elisa began to scream, "No, take me with you! Please, take me with you! Please! Please..."

The rider, wagon, and her beloved rode off towards the bridge where Elisa had been married the night before.

Suddenly, Elisa noticed that her mother, Ola, was at her side trying to comfort her. She had been speaking to her, but this was the first time Elisa had heard her since she began running towards the wagon. Elisa fell to her knees as the wagon moved further away.

When Elisa saw master looking at her, she ran to him and grabbed his leg screaming, "Pere, Pere, Pere..." which she never called him unless they were alone.

She had the sense that he wanted to explain but could not. Nor could he respond to her calling him father out there in the courtyard in front of everyone although the color of her skin would have made a denial absurd.

Ola grabbed her daughter by the shoulders to lift her up.

"Elisa, it's for the best, darling. With your looks and ability to speak French, you can have a better life than any slave we know. You can meet a rich man and travel world."

Elisa wailed, "But, he was my world, Mama, and he's gone. My world is gone!"

Master's daughter or not, slaves were expected to do their grieving on their own time whenever that might be. As Elisa grieved for the theft of her beloved, little did she know that plans were already in the works to send her away as well. But, destiny had its own plans.

Ola was the first to notice. On two consecutive mornings, Elisa had awoken only to run outside to vomit. On the third morning this occurred, she was certain of her daughter's condition. That morning when Elisa returned to their small shared room Ola informed Elisa that she was pregnant.

After the initial shock, Elisa smiled. She was positively beaming. Elisa thought her mother, Master and Master's wife were all out done by this change of events. She even dared to hope that this development might lead to her being reunited with her beloved. She knew that her people's families were broken up all the time. They learned to make the best of these events and to go on living as quickly as possible. But Elisa, at fourteen, wasn't quite ready to give up her dreams.

Although Elisa was married, Ola and Elisa's father treated her as though she had been knocked up by some traveling pelt salesman. They kept her indoors as much as they could. When she started to show, they dressed her in long flowing cotton. Everyone on the plantation knew that she was pregnant. But, when visitors came, particular attention was paid to keeping Elisa out of sight. Elisa cooperated. She had learned that her father still planned to send her to a fancy boarding school in New Orleans after the holidays. She didn't want any bad word getting out about her beforehand. When she reached New Orleans, she planned to find her beloved. The baby could room with her until she did. It was an overly optimistic plan, but she chose to focus on her possible happiness in the days to come.

One benefit of her pregnancy came during the last six weeks of her pregnancy when she was allowed to forego any heavy lifting. She still had her dinner and cleaning duties, but there'd be no firewood hauling or anything else that was better suited to men folks. During this time, she had more time to read. Reading was one of her favorite pastimes. No other slave on the plantation was allowed to read, except Elisa. Her father realized that she needed to be a proficient reader if she was going to pass for white high society. He didn't know she had shared her books with her beloved and had taught him to read.

Elisa's water broke the week before Christmas. Ola served as her midwife and her half-sister, Lauren, assisted. After hours of labor, Elisa bore a beautiful baby girl. After the baby was cleaned and wrapped in fresh, clean cotton towels, Master stopped by the cookhouse to get a glimpse at his new grandbaby. At first, he smiled when he saw the lily-white complexion and straight dark hair. But then he peaked under the soft cotton cap covering her head and saw her cinnamon colored ears. He frowned, turned on his heel, and walked away.

# SACRIFICES • *Alan D. Jones*

# 12
# THE TRUTH OF THINGS

*January, 1754 - New Orleans, New France*

*Fear binds, but true faith frees us to become who we were meant to be.*

A canary yellow sun hung outside of Elisa's window calling her to arise to a new day. The calls from the white cotton sheets to remain beneath the covers went unheeded. This was Elisa's first night ever in a bed of her own. It was also her first morning in Madame Beatrice's boarding school. She needed to get up. The halls were filled with the sounds of adolescents and young adults. Elisa dressed quickly and rushed downstairs to morning assembly.

Mornings were for inspections and the perfection of foreign language skills. Elisa learned quickly that although her understanding of the English language was nearly perfect, her pronunciation was lacking. The other kids teased her, but Elisa didn't care. She'd gone through so much just to get to New Orleans that the teasing of spoiled children seemed a mere trifle. All she had to do was to play along long enough to allow her time to find her beloved and return to her baby girl. Together, the three of them would run away and start a new life together. Back at the plantation, anyone who was asked said that Ola was the child's mother.

Elisa's time on the plantation served her well in Beatrice's home. She completed the chores assigned to her in less than half the time as any of the others. Her disciplined life back home had taught her to make the best use of her study time. That, too, she finished as quickly as any of the others. She quickly finished her work to take on the chores of others so that they might cover for her when she needed to slip away into the streets of New Orleans to search for her beloved. This afforded her plenty of time to ask about her beloved. Elisa quickly figured out that no one had heard of her husband but, every day, she met someone who had heard of Paul. No one person knew much about him but, from what they shared collectively, Elisa was able to piece together a perspective of who Paul was. He was the best known Negro man who wasn't in the arts. He made his money in the import-export business. Few knew exactly from which ship he did his business. Everyone simply assumed that he worked with some white captain who, because of the types of items Paul sold, didn't want to be publicly associated with him. Still, after nearly three months in New Orleans, Elisa had little idea of where Paul and her beloved might be. In April, Elisa got a break of sorts.

Elisa wandered the city one clear afternoon as she often did. She was still looking for information about her beloved. Suddenly, a young, dusty blonde-haired man touched her on her shoulder. At his touch, Elisa immediately felt an energy unlike anything she'd ever felt before.

She turned and he said, "Bonjour, este-vous Elisa?"

"Oui." Elisa replied.

"Can we speak in English?" Chase asked the strikingly beautiful Elisa. Chase explained, "I would prefer that not everyone be a part of our conversation. My name is Chase. I understand that you are looking for a Negro man named Paul?"

Chase was very handsome with the face of an angel and looked as though he were about eighteen or nineteen years of age.

"Yes, I am. Do you know him?" Elisa asked expectantly.

Chase smiled and answered, "Yes, I do. In fact, I know him quite well."

"Oui, oui, oui! Where can I find him? Is he with another negro man about your height?" Elisa shouted.

"My lady, there are plenty of those around here," Chase laughed.

"The man he's with has the most wonderful smile you've ever seen," Elisa said. She smiled to herself as she thought about her beloved's bright smile.

"Ah, yes, I've heard of this man. And, who is he to you?" Chase asked.

"He's my husband." Elisa said as she began to well up.

As awareness swept over Chase's face, he said again, "Ah..."

"Where is he? Tell me!" Elisa demanded.

Chase grabbed Elisa's hands pulling them down from his vest, "Relax. It's important that we not draw attention to ourselves. Are you alright?"

Elisa, feeling faint and sweating profusely, replied, "I'm fine, I'll be okay, but please tell me."

Chase helped Elisa to a bench, "Okay, okay, I'll tell you what I can."

Before Chase could say anything else, Elisa replied, "He's on a trip working as Paul's personal bodyguard?"

Stunned, Chase hardly knew what to say, "How did... what did you just do? Did you already know?"

An equally confused Elisa rubbed her eyes and responded, "Didn't you just say that? I heard you clear as day. What? You didn't? You think I'm a what?"

"A mind reader," Chase audibly confirmed, "and you're one of us."

"One of whom? Tell me because what you're thinking does not make sense," Elisa said in a quiet desperation.

Chase looked around and then leaned over to whisper into Elisa's ear, "What we are is a gifted blood line with special abilities that make us very different than most. Some say that we are descendants of the angels who mated with humans as mentioned in Genesis. That is what our leadership tells us anyway."

Elisa looked up at Chase and asked, "And, what do you think?"

Chase smiled and said even more softly than before, "I see the paradox of our existence as being no different than mortal men. For each of us, it still comes down to faith. At least with them there is a conclusion to the story. But, for us it is only mentioned that we were born. Maybe the Good Book is missing some pages for the likes of us? Regardless, those of us who walk in the light and are willing to serve are called the Circle Knights. There are twelve Knights called the Elders, to whom we report. And, they in turn report to a group of like-minded fully mortal saints called the Circle. These are mortal and religious leaders from around the world, some widely known, but others quite obscure. It is said that Saint Augustine founded the order, but that's just what some of the other knights say. Most of us have never met a member of the tthe Circle or an Elder beyond the one to whom we report. I report to Paul and, he never tells any of us anything about the other Elders. He simply shares with us their latest directive."

Elisa, her eyes still moist and yet hopeful, asked as she continued to look out towards the Mississippi, "And my beloved?"

"He is one of us now," Chase confirmed.

"But, he's not gifted like us. Is he?" Elisa asked.

Chase smiled, "Oh, yes, he is. And, very much so from what I hear. Did he never share these things with you?"

"No," Elisa said shaking her head. She sat silent for a moment. "And, in truth, what rips at my heart is that when Paul came for my beloved, he did not struggle more or respond when I called out to him. Is he not searching for me, also?"

"Ah, a lover's doubt, such a curse upon the young. Your beloved had little choice in the matter. Paul has the ability to control man and spirit alike. He only has to say a word into the right ear and fleets will sail and armies collide. Your beloved was no match for him. Some can resist him, but they are rare and far between." Chase, seeing the longing in Elisa's eyes, thought for a moment, "I'll tell you what I know, but it's not much. Through our own means, Paul came to hear of an extraordinary young man at your plantation. One of our scouts secretly investigated the reports and found that they were quite modest regarding his abilities. Paul decided right then that this young man could be his new bodyguard. I was his interim bodyguard, but the Circle Knight Elders apparently preferred that I revert to my previous role."

"And, what role do you play? Providing sugar cane for young girls on the river walk?" Elisa asked.

Chase sighed, "Oh, I wish that was the case. Let's just say that my ability to track targets and eliminate them with no collateral damage made me uniquely suited for my role in the Circle Knights."

Elisa was not afraid but felt compelled to ask, "Are you here to eliminate me?"

Chase tilted his head, "No. Actually, I planned to tell you that your beloved had traveled to the Northwest Territories. I planned to provide you a horse and a bag of coins and, then, to send you on your way to spend the rest of your days on a fool's errand. But, when I first touched your shoulder, I knew you were one of us. Often, our gifts do not reveal themselves until triggered by an encounter with another like ourselves. Sometimes it takes a second or third touch."

"And, what now?" Elisa asked.

Chase replied, "Well, what would typically happen, should you decide that you want to be one of us, is that someone would be assigned to you to assist you in mastering your gifts."

Elisa looked into Chase's eyes, "Gifts?"

Chase nodded, "Yes, gifts. Normally, you receive your primary gift first, but then some time later you receive your secondary gift which may or may not be greater than your primary gift. Most often, the primary gift helps you manage the secondary gift."

"And, my beloved?" Elisa asked again.

Chase frowned a bit, "I'm sorry to say that he left last fall with Paul. And I don't really know where they are, or if they are even on this level of existence."

Now that she could read his mind, Elisa knew that Chase was telling the truth. She also saw in his mind that Chase believed that Elisa's best chance of ever finding her beloved was to become a Circle Knight herself and hope that Paul would return with her beloved or that she might encounter someone familiar with his whereabouts.

Elisa blurted out, "Yes, I'll do it. Will you train me?"

Chase took her hand and said to Elisa, "They don't usually assign me to indoctrinate new members to our way, but I will ask if they will make an exception in this case since I was the one who triggered your gift. Ordinarily, you'd be groomed by someone more senior. Knowing a bit about how Paul thinks, I'm pretty sure that he will claim you for his own order, known to those who know, as The Willing. We are what many would call counter-intelligence. Other Elders may want you for their orders as well but, since we found you, you'll likely stay with us."

"This all is just so unbelievable. And, they treat people like me equally?" Elisa said referring to her own race.

Chase confirmed, "Yes, they do, at least at the highest level. I'm told that the Inner Circle is comprised of men and women of every race."

Elisa, reading Chase's mind, leapt ahead, "And, yet, they do not allow everyone a place at the table."

Chase sighed again in quiet acceptance, "No, not everyone."

The two of them sat in silence before the mighty river. Elisa reached for Chase's hand as discretely as she could.

She said, "You will always have a seat at my table."

"And, you at mine," Chase replied.

Elisa continued, "And, may we swear never to lift up arms against one another."

"It is so, my lady."

Again, they sat in silence staring out over the great river.

At last, Chase offered, "But there is one more thing I should mention. Another reason I think Paul will claim you for his own, is because…"

Reading his mind, Elisa's mouth flew open, "C'est mon…"

Chase answered for her in English, "Yes, he is your ancestor born many centuries ago, but still alive today. You, my darling, are a descendant of Paul."

# SACRIFICES • *Alan D. Jones*

# 13
# STAR FALL

*May, 1768 - New Orleans, New France*

*In your anger, sin not.*

As Elisa dressed for dinner, she glowed with thoughts of her beloved. She was meeting Chase and Henri, the Nightwalker, for an early dinner. She couldn't wait to tell them that her beloved, according to Paul's calculations, should be returning within the next few days. Through Elisa's field work with the Circle Knights she'd been able to reconnect with her beloved on many occasions but, since he'd been on assignments for over a decade, none of her friends had ever met him.

So much had transpired during those years. Her gifts had developed just as Chase suggested they might and well beyond. Her primary gifts were telepathy and telekinesis. Her secondary gift was the ability to turn any reflective surface into a portal across time and space. It was Elisa's ability to read minds that allowed her to reach into the minds of others to create the portals to places she'd never even seen. An assortment of other gifts had been bestowed upon her as well. Elisa looked into the free standing, full-length mirror in front of her. She stretched out here hand and thought of Paris and there before her the mirror turned into a window of a busy Paris street. All she had to do was to step into it to be there.

Elisa didn't really have an idea of where she and her beloved would go once he returned and got their child back from her mother. They would also have to make decisions about whether or not they could both continue to serve as Circle Knights once they were able to live as a family. They'd individually taken vows to serve but, certainly Paul and the Circle Knight Elders would understand that a family should be together. Once she became an Elder, she was sure to get her way.

Elisa also wondered how her beloved might adjust to this world he left so long ago. They were married as children. Now, he was a man. Master had emancipated her upon his death, but he continued under the legal status of slave.

Paul was the designated Circle Knight Elder in charge of counter-intelligence. He had taken her beloved with him into The Pit on a secret mission. The Pit was a place of horrors, but the creatures there feared Paul and obeyed his every command. Still, Paul needed her beloved to watch his back. Fourteen years and many adventures had passed for her. For her beloved, fewer than three years had passed by. Time does not flow in The Pit as it does in this realm. Her beloved would be eighteen years old and, worse still, his mind would be that of an eighteen year old. Their brief rendezvous in the Pit, facilitated by Paul, in no way reflected the realities of married life.

She was blessed to still be quite youthful in appearance as her body filled out into womanhood. More importantly, she had matured in other ways. And though he survived the Pit, had his time there had warped him in some unrecoverable way? The evils of that realm were soul changing to witness. And what of his return? Could an eighteen year old handle a family and someone like her who was now a grown woman? Henri tried to assure her that this would not be an issue for her beloved. "Trust me, it won't be a problem", a smiling Henri had said, inferring that any eighteen year old man would love to have a woman like her, and would do anything to keep her.

But, all of those questions could wait. Tonight was a night to enjoy the warm summer breeze and the conversation of good friends. Elisa arrived at the restaurant to find Chase sitting at an outside table. He rose to pull out a chair.

"Merci," Elisa said with a smile as she removed the red sash hanging across her shoulder and hung it on the back of the chair.

Chase then spoke to Elisa in English which they often did to avoid prying ears, "So, did you tell Henri that your husband is due in port soon? You know that Henri is totally in love with you, right?"

Elisa smiled again. Before she could answer, a calm and cool Henri came around the corner laughing.

"Oh course, she knows I love her, but I am an honorable man, most days, and as such, I'm willing to wait my turn. It wouldn't be the first time," Henri said this with a wink.

Chase poked Henri with his cane which hid a slender sword, "So, how are you so sure that he won't be like Elisa and never age a day past twenty-five?"

Henri acknowledged, "That may well be. But, gifted as he is, most of these Circle Knights are still bound by their three score and ten as are most mortals."

Elisa giggled a bit not quite believing what she was hearing, "Surely you jest, Henri?"

"Oh, no my lady and I will tell your beloved so when I meet him. But, I will also tell him that I will honor the sanctity of your marriage as I would expect another to honor mine were I married. Make no mistake. Thirty years or so from now I plan to take his place. No offense to him, but we're a special breed we three. To each of us time is a friend, not an enemy." Henri stated affirmatively.

Chase smirked and called out for the barkeep to send out their favorite wine, bread and cheese before leaning into Henri to comment in English, "Obviously, you began drinking before you came here to meet us."

Henri poured the last of the wine into everyone's glass and then offered a toast to Elisa, "To Elisa and new opportunities."

Clinking glasses and nodding, they drank to the fact that Elisa was all but certain to be designated as an Elder-in-waiting and would take the next available seat. That could be in months or in hundreds of years. Seldom was someone designated unless one of the current Elders was ill or had grown weary of the position.

Elisa reached over, touched Chase's hand, and whispered, "And, once I come into my own, I will handle that matter with your beloved. It is a condition of my accepting their offer. So, do not worry."

Chase smiled.

The three friends joked and kidded one another until their order arrived. They talked about the people they knew and told embellished stories about each of them including Elisa's young protégé, Zi. The breeze and the mood were light and the wine flowed freely. In those moments, Elisa could almost forget her racial identity and those she left behind, but reminders were all around her, some more telling than others. The servant woman who carried their drinks stopped about six feet from their table as a mild sense of recognition swept over her face. Then, she remembered her place as a runaway slave and bowed her head as she placed the wine bottle on the table.

Elisa reached out her hand and placed it softly on the woman's hand and tried to comfort her, saying in French, "Il est correct. Comment se fait-tout le monde?"

The woman didn't answer Elisa's query about life on the plantation. What she saw in the woman's thoughts made her blood run cold. Elisa sprang to her feet knocking the bottle of wine to the ground.

She took the woman by both arms and screamed first in French, "Quand est-ce arrive?" and then, "When did this happen to you?"

The frightened young woman said nothing, but in her mind revealed all that Elisa needed to know.

Elisa looked back at Chase and Henri communicating telepathically to them that they needed to leave the table immediately before turning to the glass window lining the store front of the restaurant. That was the only notice that she could offer them before she revealed herself. She walked towards the glass stretching out her hand before her. She walked into and through the window. The other customers sitting outside could not believe what they saw. Each swore it must have been a trick of the evening light or something in their drinks. None of them knew that Elisa had planted these possibilities in each of their minds.

Elisa stepped out on the other side into the dining room of master's house and levitated gently down to the grand dining table. The dinner table was surrounded by her father's family. With a single thought, she made each of them forget what they'd just witnessed as she lowered herself to the floor, exited the home, and entered the cookhouse. Elisa walked through the kitchen, not stopping to speak to her mother's girlfriend from the field who was cooking in her stead.

Instead, Elisa called out, "Mama," as she pushed opened the door to the small room she had shared with her mother all those years.

She saw Ola with Elisa's her fourteen year old daughter curled up in her arms. Elisa took a breath before sitting on the edge of the bed to reach out to her daughter, who had been raised with no idea that Elisa was her real mother. In fact, since she'd left the plantation, no one mentioned Elisa's relationship to anyone there. It was as if she had never existed, or as if everyone there was enchanted in this one regard. Elisa pulled Lola up into her arms and then turned her around as she pulled down the top of her dress to reveal her back. Her heart sank as she saw the fresh wounds over older ones from the overseer's whip. The marks formed a tree of agony on Lola's back.

Without taking her eyes off her child, Elisa asked her mother, "Where is he?"

By "he" she meant the new overseer who was brought on after master died. Master's eldest son now ran the plantation. He knew that Lola was his niece in blood, thus he allowed her to work in the big house. The overseer was not to touch Lola without his explicit consent. The overseer had gone too far and the new master demanded that the overseer leave their farm by sunset.

The overseer's name was Hugo and all the slaves knew that he wasn't right from the day he arrived. The field hands, like the servant girl working in New Orleans, knew that he was hell on earth. Ola tried her best to keep him away from the child, but she'd failed. Elisa pulled the answer to her inquiry from Ola without her saying a word.

Ola pleaded with her daughter, "Elisa, what are you going to do? Master found out what he's been doing to the children and told him to leave the county tonight. We all agreed that it would be best for our baby if we just made him leave and never spoke of this thing again."

Elisa shook her head and looked up at her mother, "What, more lies? Exactly, how have all of these lies protected us?"

Elisa stood from the bed and softly brushed the young girl's hair with her hand, "Don't worry. That bad man will never hurt you again, little Lola."

Elisa strode out the back of the cookhouse and through the courtyard past the stable. Some of the older field hands in the stable did a double take as she passed their way, but each wondered if the evening light was playing tricks with their eyes. The women whispered rumors of her being some sort of enchantress. Most could not clearly recall how they knew her.

Those who were mothers had no doubt where she was headed. Hugo, the overseer, lived alone in an old cabin between the slave quarters and the bridge leaving the property, the same bridge underneath which Elisa had been married to her beloved.

Outside his cabin, Elisa saw Hugo's tattered wagon tied to his equally tattered horse. Elisa could hear Hugo moving about and she could smell the alcohol before ever stepping foot into his cabin. Next to the wagon were several items that Hugo had not loaded yet including a very shiny piece of metal that must have doubled as a mirror and a table top. Elisa pushed it to the ground before walking up to the door. Hugo stopped what he was doing and looked up in a panic. He thought it was the plantation master coming to make sure that he was indeed gone by sundown. The frightened little man stuck his head through the doorway to look around. When he saw the beautiful Elisa, he grinned.

Elisa's eyes narrowed before she said a single word, "Hugo."

"Oui, Madame?" Hugo replied.

Then, suddenly, he was head over heels suspended in the air. Elisa used her telekinesis to hold him aloft by his ankles.

Hugo cried out, "Vous etes l'enchanteresse!"

"Oui, Hugo," Elisa replied.

Hugo had heard some of the slaves whisper about an enchantress, but he always laughed at their fears. Elisa stretched out her hand towards the shining metal oval now lying on the ground and it began to glow in shifting red hues. She moved Hugo right above the newly formed portal.

As lowered him into the portal, she called out to him, "Profitez de votre temps en enfer."

Thus, she lowered him into The Pit.

When he was gone, Elisa closed the portal and wearily, with tears streaming down her face, turned back to the road to the Damascus plantation. It was dark now and so quiet that she could hear the hoofs of horses approaching from nearly a mile away. There were two horses and two riders. It was Chase and Henri who had used the portal in her apartment which led to one hidden in the woods on the other side of the river. They'd taken a couple of horses there and were now riding hard towards her.

As Elisa looked back across the river, she noticed pillars of light of various colors forming all around her. Each pillar condensed into a being. The Elders of the Circle Knights had been summoned from all over. Paul was among the twelve. The chairwoman of the group, who was ethereal in her appearance, spoke for them all, "Elisa, you know, full well that we do not throw mortals into The Pit without written approval, especially not for the sake of vengeance. Even if you were a Gatekeeper, this would not have gone unnoticed."

Elisa could only read a few of the minds around her, but she knew that each of them was an alpha level Knight such as herself and all of them had far more experience than her. She would be no match for all of them should she decide to fight. She knew from the moment she left her mother's room that it would come to this, although she hadn't expected it this soon. Elisa said nothing.

The chairwoman spoke again, "As you know, in our order, we cannot have a Knight, much less an alpha level Knight, breeching one of our core principles as you have done. We are here to protect mortals, not to judge them. If we allow this, our whole purpose is challenged. Thus, we have voted, eleven to one, that you be condemned to The Pit for an indefinite period of time."

Elisa looked towards Paul, realizing that he was the lone vote in her favor. She could hear Chase and Henri riding across the bridge

They yelled, "Attendez!" over and over.

As a bright blue light began to glow around her, Elisa smiled and lifted a hand towards her friends before the chairwoman made her final pronouncement, "May God have mercy on your soul."

With that, Elisa was cast into The Pit. Chase and Henri rode up to the circle just as the Elders, including Paul, disappeared into the night. Both men screamed into the nothingness that remained.

SACRIFICES • *Alan D. Jones*

# 14
# VIPERS

*June, 1981 - Toronto, Canada*

*The assurance of heaven is not a palace in the sky, but a peace within.*

Elisa knew the day would come when they would betray her. Just as she had known the Circle Knight Elders would confront her after she tossed her daughter's abuser into The Pit, she knew that Council of Nob would turn on her one day. Matasis had spent nearly twenty years telling her that she would share in the spoils once the Omni Portal was fully functional. She'd never believed a word of it. Nonetheless, she played along. Elisa knew full well that once they had no further use for her, she was expendable. The only question in her mind was when they would do it?

Elisa knew that history would not be kind to her. Aiding in the construction of the Omni Portal, which could very well mean the end of all creation, even in exchange for the lives of her grandchildren, would be a very hard to justify. That wasn't the whole story, but history only notes the highlights. In this game of shadows, there were deceptions within deceptions many of which would never be known. Elisa was fine with that. The problem with this game was that Elisa was the bait.

Everything has a price. The evil are always hungry for blood and Elisa, knowing this, was amazed that she'd survived this long in a pit full of vipers. She liked to think that Chase had spoken on her behalf. His words would not have swayed the council one bit, but something within her hoped that, in honor of old kindnesses, he had at least spoken a word in her defense.

It had started simply. The worst days of our lives often do. Matasis called the group to convene at a cottage just outside of Toronto. It was June but the daybreak air was cool and calm. Elisa pulled into the gravel turnaround in front of the cottage and exited her rental car. A flock of geese graced the sky above her as they passed by on their journey north. Elisa smiled.

The cabin appeared to be empty. Elisa walked around to the back towards the lake bordering the property to see if the sea plane was in dock. Several of the Council members could not or would not fly commercial. As Elisa entered the back yard, she caught sight of the plane. A question began to form in her mind. Even as it did, a sharp pain erupted in her right shoulder. She fell back as her left hand rose to cover the bleeding wound. Elisa immediately created a telekinetic shield which protected her from the second burst of energy fired from the far side of the lake. In an instant, Poseidon appeared behind Elisa swinging down upon her. She'd caught a mental image of his intention as he was materializing, so she was able to partially protect herself. She quickly realized that Zi must have teleported him behind her since he did not have that ability on his own. Her telekinetic shield prevented him from making contact, but the force of the blow had produced a migraine.

The space god laughed with distain, "One blow and you wilt? As with all mortals who rise up against the gods, your desire exceeds your ability."

Poseidon reeled back and swung his oversized fist into Elisa's torso. Though her shield took on most of the force, his knuckles made enough of an impact to send Elisa flying, cracking two of her ribs. Poseidon removed one of the crystal prisms from his neck. He held it out in his hand before him towards Elisa, who was now on the ground and struggling to breathe. The jewel glowed bright blue and red in his hand and released the spirit in the form of a dark mist. The spirit being slinked across the ground as it took form. Its form was that of a black snake with shifting heads, each one reflecting a different monstrosity.

Elisa fought through her pain to take to the sky. She knew that Zi was nearby. Elisa was barely twenty feet off the ground when lightning from the clear blue sky sent her tumbling to the ground. Elisa staggered to her feet and managed to cross the tree line. The bloodied Elisa ran through the woods. Zi stepped out of the wind several feet behind her and unleashed lightning from her fingers into Elisa's back. Elisa's arms flew up before she fell to the ground again. Zi marched over and stood above Elisa daring her to rise again, but Elisa didn't move. She remained curled in a nearly fetal position atop the moist grass.

Isadora stepped past Zi, smiling, "See, Zi, you were wrong. I know her reputation too, but Elisa is not half the woman she once was. It's a shame that Poseidon didn't get a chance to experience her in her fullness."

Isadora glanced in the direction of Matasis as he and Destry emerged from the darkness of the woods.

Matasis called out, "I'm sorry, Elisa, our big day is this week and you were just a loose end that we needed to clean up beforehand. Your services were most helpful to our dark cause. Oh, and, in case you're wondering, we sent Chase on a little mission down in Atlanta. But not to worry, Isadora has a place for you in Oblivion. You'll make plenty of new friends there."

Matasis nodded for Isadora to proceed. As Queen of the Dead, Isadora was always looking to expand her collection. Her eyes went completely black as vapors from the underworld seeped up through the ground and grabbed Elisa. They pulled her down as she struggled in vain against darkness.

# THE BOOK OF ELIZABETH

# SACRIFICES • *Alan D. Jones*

# 15
# IN BLOOM

*June, 1956*

*It's never gonna be 50/50 in a relationship, so we must allow love to make up the difference.*

Elizabeth Patterson was born into chaos, but she never accepted that it had to be so. Born during the Great Depression, she grew up in an era when those around her lived and preached "survive at all costs." Elizabeth had her doubts about the family theology. She would often see her big brother perform petty crimes. He always gave the same set of explanations. If he took a loaf of bread from a window sill, he would rationalize "Well, someone would have taken it, so why not me?" Or, if a cashier happened to leave her register open and unattended, he would snatch the cash and say, "Who leaves a register open like that and walks away? She was practically asking me to take the money. I'm doing her a favor by teaching her a lesson."

As a little girl, Elizabeth would take much of what her brother gave her and share it with other kids in the neighborhood who were hungry. Since these acts of kindness angered her brother, she learned to be discreet. Elizabeth's father once owned a farm, but had it taken from him when he was arrested and accused of being draft-dodger. He'd never received the draft notice, but it was not uncommon back then for postal workers to withhold draft cards from black property owners for the purpose of disenfranchising them. After his arrest, not only did he lose his farm, but he was shipped to Europe anyway to defend the same system that had betrayed him. When he returned to the States, he also fought the bottle.

Elizabeth's mother was a simple woman who often just let things happen. Her husband was seldom around and she allowed her children to do as they pleased. Of the five of them, Elizabeth was the only one who took schooling seriously and completed high school. She also completed a year at Dillard College, before the money ran out. Years later, Elizabeth would realize that her mother was probably clinically depressed. But, back then, black folks didn't acknowledge mental illness. Nor could they afford to pay for treatment.

Elizabeth loved music, but her mother discouraged it. Instead, she steered young Elizabeth towards becoming a beautician. However, the choir director at their church encouraged Elizabeth to pursue music. He seemed to see something in Elizabeth that no one in her family did. Eventually, Elizabeth acquiesced to her mother's wishes and went to work as a beautician. Music remained her passion, that is, until the Civil Rights movement hit the Mississippi Delta.

Growing up in a family of petty thieves, Elizabeth had dated hoodlums and had even fell in love with a couple of them. In her heart she knew that such a life, or even affiliating with such a life, would only lead to sadness one day. But what else was there for her? The answer came on a cool December day in 1955 in the form a newspaper article about the arrest of Rosa Parks. The next day after church, Elizabeth attended the meeting after service. A meeting of leaders from the community churches was held in the back room of one of the local black-owned restaurants. When Elizabeth stepped into the room, all eyes fell upon her. She felt completely out of place.

Then, her choir director stood up and said in a loud voice, "This is Elizabeth Patterson, the best musician and singer in all of New Orleans you've never heard. I've been hiding her at my church to keep any of you thieves from stealing her away from me!"

One of Dr. King's lieutenants shouted from the front, "Have a seat and join us."

Elizabeth took a seat next to an Episcopal priest. At first, because of his collar, she thought that he was a Catholic priest, but then he introduced himself. "Hello, my name is Hosea Johnson. I'm the priest at the Episcopal Church around the corner. Welcome."

There, at twenty-five years of age, Elizabeth found her life's purpose. She got involved in the movement and, the very next Sunday, visited Hosea's church for the first time. While she didn't leave her home church right away, she was increasingly drawn to Hosea's church and their work in the community. She often marched alongside the goatee-wearing minister. The salt and pepper on his chin told her that he was at least ten years older than she was. But, she found herself attracted to the wisdom he displayed and his constant acts of kindness. Elizabeth actually looked forward to being bailed out of jail for civil disobedience by the handsome priest.

When Elizabeth met Hosea, he had two baby girls, Cil and Deborah. One day, as Elizabeth and Hosea were driving to a planning meeting for an upcoming march, they passed a very pregnant woman standing on the side of the road in the 9th ward. She looked wild and stood screaming and yelling at no one. Hosea immediately pulled over and got out of the car. Elizabeth did likewise and began to follow him down the street towards the woman.

Hosea glanced back at Elizabeth as they walked and said, "That woman is my wife, Lola."

The words and the context froze Elizabeth in her tracks for a moment.

She couldn't help but release an, "Oh, my...."

Hosea motioned for Elizabeth to stand back a bit and calmly walked up to Lola. He tried his best to catch her eye so that she would see and recognize him.

Hosea called out, "Darling? Lola? It's me, Hosea. Can you hear me?"

Lola cried angrily, "Of course, I can hear you. I hear everything!"

Her clothes were raggedy so Hosea offered her his jacket, but she pulled away screaming. Elizabeth had been around long enough to know that Lola was on a bad trip, but there seemed to be something else going on as well. Elizabeth edged up slowly towards the screaming woman. Lola was having a conversation at the top of her lungs with persons unseen.

"How dare you judge me!" Lola accused as she pointed her finger towards a vacant lot.

Her eyes were silvery blue and appeared to glow, but Elizabeth supposed that it must be the light reflecting in her eyes. It was then that Elizabeth noticed the huge wet stain on Lola's skirt.

When she looked at Hosea, he nodded and said, "I know. I know. We need to get her to a hospital."

Hosea reached for Lola's right arm and motioned for Elizabeth to do the same on her left side. The contractions were coming now. The pain made Lola yield enough for them to move her back towards the car. They managed to get her into the back seat. Elizabeth sat in the back with Lola as Hosea jumped into the driver's seat and sped off towards the hospital. Elizabeth peered under Lola's skirt. She gasped as she saw the crown of the baby's head.

She called out to Hosea, "She's not going to make it to the hospital. We're gonna have to do this here. Pull over!"

Elizabeth delivered Ruth Ann Johnson right there on a side street in New Orleans. She proceeded to present the baby to

Lola whose eyes were now brown. Elizabeth initially brushed off the inconsistency as being her own imagination. She looked into the front seat at a relieved Hosea and smiled. Not quite a year later, Elizabeth was also present at the birth of Sarah Jane Johnson although she didn't perform that delivery.

It was with the birth of Ruth Ann that the trouble escalated in the church for Hosea. Lola's erratic behavior and increasing drug use became more and more of an issue for Hosea in his role as rector. Lola and Hosea weren't together when Deborah was born, but most folks gave the couple the benefit of the doubt that Hosea had fathered the child before the break up, especially since the child was dark-skinned like Hosea. Still, people whispered. With the birth of Ruth Ann, few in the congregation could understand why Hosea took the child in and, worse, refused to divorce Lola. They began to lose respect for him. A movement to remove him as rector truly took root. Sarah's birth a year later only served to ease the consciences of those who rose against Hosea; they were sure that they'd made the right decision. Some even said that they were doing him a favor by offering him a chance to get his own house in order.

Elizabeth stood by Hosea through it all. She'd seen the reflection of God in all he did and she could not forget that the way so many others had. He'd fed the hungry, clothed the naked, healed the sick, and comforted the dying without ceasing. Hosea even bailed Elizabeth's criminally-minded brother out of jail and exercised his faith that God would provide him the money to pay his own bills by the end of the month.

Many people said that there was something going on between Hosea and Elizabeth. In a sense they were right. She'd never so much as kissed the man, but she was totally smitten with him. And, why not, she thought? Since meeting Hosea, she'd joined the Civil Rights struggle; stopped dating petty criminals; and, with his help, returned to Dillard to complete her degree. She had become his Girl Friday but she did want more.

Hosea seemed to be oblivious to her longings. How could he not see what everyone else saw so plainly? Finally, the day after Ruth Ann was born, Hosea finally asked her the question he'd had on him mind for some time.

They were sitting in the family waiting room of the hospital that Lola and the baby were in when he turned to Elizabeth and asked, "Why are you here? Can't you see all the mess in my life?"

Elizabeth sat back a bit and decided to reply honestly, "Hosea, how could I not be here after all you've done for me, my family, and our community? In fact, this waiting room would be full and overflowing, if only a tenth of those you've helped were here like they should be –supporting you."

Hosea smiled and leaned forward in his chair to look towards Elizabeth. He paused a moment before speaking and said, "You know, you really should be hanging out with folks your own age. You do realize that I'm forty…"

Elizabeth cut him off, "I know how old you are and what does it matter? Since meeting you, my whole life has changed and I will be forever grateful for that. If I can be that one person that reflects back to you even a fraction of the love you've given, how can that be wrong or unwise?" Seeing by Hosea's expression that he wasn't really buying her argument, Elizabeth added, "Why can't you let someone else take care of you for a change?"

"I'm concerned about you, Elizabeth," a weary Hosea said softly.

"I know," Elizabeth reached out and squeezed his wrist before reaching for her purse. "Hey, I'm gonna run and pick up Cil and Deborah. I'll take them to my apartment and make them some mac and cheese with ham. You know I don't eat pork, but they love that stuff. I can bring you a plate once my neighbor gets home to watch the kids."

Hosea thanked her, "Thank you, but I'll be fine."

Elizabeth tilted her head and smiled, "Hosea, you need to eat. I'll fix you a plate and be back around six or seven. Bye."

Later that evening, Elizabeth returned to the hospital. She parked Hosea's car, grabbed the still warm plate of food and walked towards the hospital's front entrance. As she walked up, she noticed a long, black limousine. She thought it looked a little out of place but in New Orleans you might see pretty much anything. What was odd was the sight of Hosea exiting the back seat. Seeing him now, reminded her about several months before when she had seen a black limo parked outside of his church when they arrived early one Saturday morning. She found that incident curious, but let it go. She caught up with Hosea just before he entered the foyer of the hospital.

She called out, "Hosea!"

He turned, "Hi, Beth, what's happening?" She loved when he called her Beth. He only did so sometimes when they were alone.

"You tell me. What was that all about with the limo?" she inquired. She'd known of clergy being involved with mobsters and politicians. She considered both lowlifes and her heart raced at the thought of Hosea being involved in anything criminal.

Hosea thought for a moment. He was trying to decide just how open he should be before he answered her.

"Those were some people that I do work for from time to time."

"Work? What kind of work?"

Hosea breathed in deeply, "The kind of work that requires me to leave tomorrow morning."

Elizabeth noticed that there was something in the inside breast pocket of his black suit jacket. So, she sat the plate of food down and snatched the envelope from his jacket.

"Beth!" Hosea yelled as Elizabeth scurried away turning her back to him so that she could see what was inside of the envelope.

Elizabeth froze when she saw what was inside. It was a plane ticket – a plane ticket to Sydney, Australia. Her mouth fell open as she handed the ticket back to Hosea.

"Wow."

She turned her face toward him looking completely puzzled at this man she thought she knew.

Hosea shifted into full disclosure mode, "Beth, have a seat."

They sat on the bench next to the plate of food. "How much do you know about exorcisms? Have you heard of the term?" Elizabeth shook her head and Hosea continued. "Sometimes this world of light and air is breached by portals into darkness. Sometimes the forces of darkness reach into our world through the souls of men. These breaches are commonly referred to as demonic possessions. Often these breaches are the result of some distant pain that has been allowed to fester in a person's soul until it becomes a stronghold for the enemy. But at other times we have no explanation at all. Regardless, when these breaches occur, someone must repair them. Sometimes that someone is me. Various religious organizations call on me when I'm needed."

"And they need you in Australia?" Elizabeth asked as she shook her head.

"Yes, Beth, that's correct and they want me on that flight tomorrow morning."

"To cast out demons?" Elizabeth said softly.

"Yes."

They sat there in silence for a moment before Elizabeth posed her next thought.

"So, who are the folks in the limo?"

Hosea answered, "I guess you'd say they are, for lack of a better term, my handlers. They report to an organization called the Circle. the Circle is a collection of like-minded people from around the world sworn to hold up the light against the darkness. When an incident such as the one in Australia is brought to their attention, they decide the proper course of action and they delegate the task to the proper people, such as the folks you saw in the car."

"And, your Cousin Rob?"

Hosea was stunned by the mention of Rob's name.

Elizabeth continued, "Oh, come on. I catch such a surreal vibe from that guy. He drips secret agent sauce. I thought he was FBI or something. So, is Rob a priest too?"

Hosea shared what he could with Elizabeth, "Rob is something else. At the very least, one would have to say that Rob is gifted."

"And, at the very most?" Elizabeth asked.

Hosea pondered for a moment, "At the very most, he is descended from the angels, as referenced in Genesis of the Bible where it states that angels laid with humans."

Mouth agape, Elizabeth paused for a second. She didn't know if she believed what she was hearing. She struggled to reconcile her disbelief with her faith in and love for the messenger before her.

"So, can he part waters or something?"

"No, but he can do some amazing things nonetheless."

"Descended from angels, huh?"

"Don't know for sure, but that's what some of the others like Rob say."

"So, there are others?"

"Yes."

"Lola?"

"Yes, but how did you know?"

"Out there in the street, when she was screaming, her eyes were silver and glowing. A few minutes later, they were brown."

Hosea stared at Elizabeth with a sense of longing for younger days free of his burden. "Beth, you're a young woman, too young to be caught up in these shadow games. You should be out enjoying life, doing what young girls do, not here in my situation."

The full-figured Elizabeth sat straight up, "Hey, I'm not quite 30 yet, but I'm a full grown woman."

"Yes, you are."

They sat in silence for a moment as they shared a smile that spoke volumes of what was between them.

"Look, Hosea. In every area of your life you fight for what is right. You are a true warrior for God, helping the needy, loving the unlovable, and a true living sacrifice in the midst of chaos, forgoing your own needs for the sake of others. Yet you are flesh and blood. You need someone to share with, someone to help you carry this burden, someone to walk with you through this chaos. You need someone on which you can lean, without asking you for anything."

Hosea shook his head.

Elizabeth continued, "Listen to me. Since I can remember, I have benefited from the pain of others. My brother stole and hurt others for my benefit and, with few exceptions, I turned a blind eye. From fifteen to twenty-five, I ran the streets with hoodlums who kept my belly and my glass full, and yet again, I turned a blind eye to the true costs. Each time I turned away, but I'm not turning away this time."

Hosea sat frozen by her words.

Elizabeth continued, "With a drug addict for a wife and three little girls, you could use some help. Some help you can trust, who won't turn away."

Hosea sat back and breathed out heavily, acknowledging Elizabeth's argument. "Okay, I have most certainly appreciated your help with the girls and I don't know what I would do without you."

Elizabeth smiled and Hosea continued, "But, let me know if it gets to be too much. No words can match the reality of these things."

Years later, Elizabeth would speculate on why the big loves of her life were either saints or sinners. Suffice it to say, for her love was struggle.

# 16
# SUMMER HARVEST

*Late June, 1981*

*Those who don't fear death are the most powerful among us. But those who don't fear love live on beyond the grave.*

Elizabeth had dreams too. No, not dreams of fame or fortune, but dreams that showed her a glimpse of what was to be. These dreams didn't happen often, but when they did she took heed. So, that Sunday afternoon when she saw Chase standing on her front porch, she was not surprised. She had been expecting him.

Elizabeth put down her book, The Autobiography of Malcolm X, and rose to open the door. Chase and she both knew that he could have walked through that door, but he showed her the courtesy of standing outside the screen door until she noticed him. Typically, on days like this, he doesn't knock. He doesn't wait to be acknowledged. He simply appears before his prey and strikes them down. Elizabeth opened the door.

"Chase," she said as he entered the living room.

She closed the door behind him, shut the one open window, and closed the curtains.

"Elizabeth," he answered as he stepped towards the armchair.

They both knew what he was there to do. Elizabeth asked her executioner, "Would you like a glass of iced tea?"

"Yes, that would be fine."

Elizabeth went to the kitchen and returned with a pitcher of tea and two tall glasses on a tray. She sat the tray on the table and poured each of them a glass of the sweet delight. Elizabeth took a sip and sat back on the couch again.

"So, Chase what took you so long?"

Chase took the glass in his hand, "I've been a bit busy of late."

They both knew that he was referring to the Omni Portal. "And, you, Elizabeth, after all those years on the run, why did you return to Atlanta?"

"Well, I couldn't go back to New Orleans. I left that life behind. My life is here now with the girls."

Chase continued, "But, I'm sure the Circle could have placed you in a safe location in return for all your years of service."

"I ran all those years for the sake of the girls. Otherwise, I've never been one to run from my troubles. Life is trouble, is it not? But, the beauty of life is in the struggle against the darkness that demanded of each of us, is it not? So, if I must be somewhere when the end comes, I'd rather be here, where I was happiest in this life."

Elizabeth took another sip of tea.

"So, where will you be when your life ends?"

Unlike his associates, Chase had no delusion that he would live forever. He traded in blood and fully expected to die in blood one day.

"Somewhere far away from my beloved New Orleans."

"So, you do still love something? And still you would destroy the world for the sake of vengeance?"

"Yes, when vengeance is all that I have."

"So, what will satisfy your vengeance? How many saints and Circle Knights must you kill to satisfy your vengeance?"

"I only kill the servants to draw out their master."

Chase lowered his glass back onto the coffee table and for the first time Elizabeth saw another meaning in his words. She'd known for some time that Chase sought to force the Circle Knight Elders to deal with him directly, so that he might have his revenge on those Elders who took his beloved from him all those years ago. But his words that day, in light of his work on the Omni Portal, conveyed so much more. He was striking out at God Almighty.

Elizabeth hid her realization for the moment and carried on, "So, does that include Paul?"

"No, Paul and Elisa were the only ones who stood up for me and my love. So, I will never raise a hand against either of them. But the rest have to perish until vengeance is served."

"Even the babies?" Here Elizabeth referred to Sarah and her sisters.

"Yes."

"They weren't even alive when all that happened."

"No they weren't, but they are agents of my accusers. Thus, my vengeance knows no limit besides those who defended me and my beloved in our hour of need. When you've done things for the cause that I have done, spilled the blood that I have to spare the innocent, taken on the weight of taking the lives of others, willingly sacrificed your own joy for the greater good and then to have that sacrificed rejected as unfit, then you can judge me.

"Chase, you know my story, living off the crumbs of murderers and thieves while I looked the other way. So, I certainly can't judge you."

Elizabeth took a last sip of tea savoring its coolness on her tongue before continuing, "It's just that I don't understand. Elisa, Zi, Henri, and you all seem so broken now. From what little I know of your lives before, oh, how you loved and sacrificed for one another and, now, it's like you're four strangers who've lost their way. It just doesn't make sense."

"No, I guess it wouldn't make sense in your eyes. Each of us has served our time in hell, as have you, and sometimes when you've been through hell, that hell becomes a part of you." Chase took another sip of tea. "Ah, I detect a hint of mint."

Elizabeth nodded, "Yes, that's my secret ingredient."

Chase lowered his glass for the last time as well and then froze for moment, "I smell something."

"Yes, that would be the gas. I've noticed over the years that you tend to shy away from Sarah and her gift of fire. So, I got this idea. I had to at least try to protect my babies."

A tear ran down Elizabeth's face just as tears had often run down her face in her dreams. But, never in the past eighteen years of her waking life had she cried until that moment. She smiled as she felt the wetness on her cheek. She realized that she had at last completed the circle.

Chase acknowledged, "Understood."

Elizabeth thought of Hosea and wondered if they would truly see one another on the other side. Her last thoughts were of how happy she was that she'd seen Cil, Deborah, Ruth Ann and Sarah grow into adulthood and how the girls loved each other. Elizabeth pressed the remote in her hand tightly and a spark ignited the gas turning the house into a one huge fireball.

A translucent Chase walked towards the sidewalk from the smoldering remains. The deaf and blind woman who had been sitting on the front porch across the street first felt the shock waves of the explosion and then the heat from the fire and rose to her feet with her hand slightly extended trying to feel something. Chase had been denied a kill, but he always respected those who were unafraid to die. Elizabeth always held Chase's respect and had done nothing that day to diminish that feeling.

# THE BOOK OF RUTH

# SACRIFICES • *Alan D. Jones*

# 17
# THE SUM OF THINGS

*September, 1963 - Atlanta, Georgia*

*Would not an all-powerful God who allows free will truly love a creation who seeks not their own way?*

For Ruth Ann, a gentle spirit, the world was a puzzle and each day a labyrinth of discord which each day was more and more out of tune. Many evenings, she would crawl into bed shaking from the trials of the day. When not consumed with hanging on for dear emotional life, she spent her free time in the library. She loved to read about a world she thought she'd never see. The places her father had been were of particular interest to her. She loved works of fiction, too, although she cried often upon reading them. When not reading, she spent her library days writing letters to Gabby. Sometimes she cried when writing those too. Gabby and Ruth Ann shared their hearts in their letters as well as their dreams of the life they imagined as adults.

Ruth often felt at odds with the world. Even among her sisters, she was the different one. Where they were witty and quick, she was weird and quirky. They all sang like angels, but her voice was always a work in progress. Her oddities were numerous and growing. She didn't listen to the right kind of music. She was obsessed with wearing something pink at all times even if it was just her nails. Her sisters all played piano. But, Ruth only wanted to play guitar, lead guitar at that. It was as if all her life she was playing a different chord.

In late September, 1963, Ruth sat on the back porch with her dolls at her side while her sisters sat around the radio listening to WAOK. Ruth felt a sense of melancholy. It was a longing for something more. Whereas Deborah's moods swung from one extreme to another, Ruth's life was a single note playing out night after night. She tried her best to forget the meanness shown to her day after day at school. So, many a night she sat out on that porch or sat next to a window trying to rediscover herself. Her daddy was good at cheering her up, but he was gone and that made her that much sadder.

Miss Elizabeth was cleaning up the dinner dishes while she kept an ear out for Ruth as she played outside. When she'd finished the last spoon, she stepped out onto the porch, and sat on the swing next to the eight year old Ruth Ann.

"Can I sit here with you for a while? My feet are so tired of standing."

"Sure you can, Miss Elizabeth." Ruth Ann said. She moved the doll on her right to her left to sit next to the one on her left as she pushed her eye glasses back onto the bridge of her nose.

"You telling your dolly all your problems?"

"Well, she has problems too. We try to help each other."

Miss Elizabeth stroked the top of Ruth's head down to the nape of her neck and said, "Oh, I see. Darling, I know you miss your daddy. So do I. But he'll be home real soon."

She didn't reveal that she'd received a call several days earlier that Hosea was actually in a French hospital recuperating from what was being called exhaustion. Still, she hoped that he'd return in the next day or so. Elizabeth hadn't mentioned any of this to the girls.

"Are the others girls at school messing with you again?" she asked Ruth.

Cil had moved on to the high school in the Fall. Deborah was still at the school, but she was too preoccupied with being a social butterfly to look after her little sister. Ruth Ann dropped her head and picked up one of her dolls in silence as slow, agonizing tears began to inch down her face. She tried to hold them back but gravity and emotion overwhelmed her.

Miss Elizabeth, knowing firsthand the sting of the cruel words of others, put her arm around Ruth Ann and pulled her into her ample bosom, "That's alright baby girl, let it go, let it all go. Those silly kids at school don't know a precious gem when they're sitting next to one every day."

Miss Elizabeth pushed to and from slowly in the home made swing rocking Ruth to sleep. As the child fell asleep, Miss Elizabeth noticed a bluish hue along the walls of the back porch. She didn't know what it meant, but she knew these children were different from any she'd ever seen. She picked up Ruth Ann and carried her off to bed. Later, each of Ruth's sisters stepped in to check on her and little Sarah climbed into the bed with her.

That should have been the end of the evening, with each of the kids in bed before 10:00 p.m., but it wasn't. Miss Elizabeth was back in the kitchen. She already had made the kid's school lunches for the next day. She'd just started organizing the food in the cabinets when the phone rang. She was hoping that it was Hosea.

The caller asked, "Hello, is Mr. Johnson available?"

"No, he's out of town right now."

Miss Elizabeth answered and, as she glanced up, saw Cil standing in the hallway watching her.

"Ma'am, do you know when he will be back?" the caller asked.

"No, I do not. What is this about?" she asked.

"Are you a family member of Mr. Hosea Johnson?" the stranger inquired.

"Well, yes," Miss Elizabeth answered.

The caller then said, "Ma'am, this is the Fulton County coroner's office and I'm sorry to have to tell you that we believe that we have the body of Mrs. Lola Johnson. We need someone from your family to come down to Grady hospital to make a positive identification."

Miss Elizabeth hung her head and thought for a moment, "There's no one here to watch the kids."

Cil touched Miss Elizabeth's shoulder and spoke softly to her, "It's okay. You can go. I'll stay up until you get back."

Although she hadn't shared it with anyone, Cil had known that this was the night that her mother's body would be found.

Miss Elizabeth grabbed the car keys and scurried out the front door. It was 10:55 p.m. Cil took her seat at the kitchen table and waited for everything to play out. For her, knowing what was to come was like trying to brace yourself before a tsunami you could see coming ashore. You know much around you will be lost, so your only goal is to hold on to those things you truly love.

The first person to wake up, just before midnight, was Sarah. She stumbled into the bathroom and went to the kitchen to see why the light was still on. There she saw Cil sitting at the table with just a glass of water. Cil offered the glass to Sarah.

"Have a seat," she said to Sarah.

One by one, Cil told her little sisters. Sarah cried softly and curled up into Cil's arms. Deborah who took every chance to vocalize how much she hated her mother wailed the loudest upon hearing of her death. But, when Cil told little Ruth Ann, she did not utter a word. While Cil chased Deborah around the house trying to hold her, Ruth stumbled out of the kitchen and unto the back porch. Stepping out into the small back yard, she fell to her hands and knees in the moist soft grass where she began to weep.

"Mama... Mama...," she called out into the dirt gripping hard the blades of grass.

# THE SUM OF THINGS

Around 1:30 a.m., Miss Elizabeth returned and she tried to comfort each of the girls. Still each of them longed to see their father. Around 4:00 a.m., their prayers were answered. Hosea, bags in hand, walked through the front door. Ruth and Sarah reached him first. Hosea wrapped one arm around each as he kneeled. Together, they told him that his wife, Lola had died.

He gripped them even tighter as he whispered to each of them, "I'm so sorry."

When he stood up, Cil hugged her father as she cried uncontrollably. Finally, she released him to the arms of Miss Elizabeth. They held each other for a long time. Neither of them was particularly surprised that Lola had died of a drug overdose, but it was still a tragedy. Lola never realized that Miss Elizabeth truly cared for her despite her feelings for her husband.

At last, Hosea asked, "Where is Deborah?"

Everyone looked around for a second before Ruth answered, "She went to the bathroom a while ago."

Sarah walked over to the closed bathroom door and proclaimed, "She's not in there." One of Sarah's gifts was the ability to see far outside of the wave length of visible light. So, not only could she see in infra-red and ultra-violet, but she could also see natural x-rays, which allowed her, when she focused, to see through doors.

Hosea rushed to the bathroom door and called out, "Deborah? Deborah. Deborah!" Hearing no reply, he forced the door open to find an empty room and an open window. Hosea walked briskly from the bathroom back into the living room. He asked Elizabeth for her keys. Then he picked up his fedora and his seldom used walking cane.

"Watch the girls," he said.

With that, he walked into the night in search of his daughter.

Miss Elizabeth sent the girls back to their rooms so that they might get a little sleep before the sun came up. Then, she went into the kitchen to put on another pot of coffee for herself so that she might endure another stint waiting by the phone. What she didn't know is that while she was in the kitchen, Cil had climbed out of her bedroom window.

Cil stood outside of Ruth and Sarah's bedroom window. Staring back at Cil, the two youngest sisters opened the window and Cil helped them down to the ground. Cil knew where Deborah was headed. She was headed to the Council of Nob office on Auburn Avenue. The three of them began their trek from their West End home. Alone, Cil could have made the journey in little time at all, but she knew the future and she knew that her two younger sisters were to be with her this night.

Hosea also knew where Deborah was headed. Deborah always longed to be wherever her Aunt Elisa was. With news of her mother's death, Hosea knew that Deborah would go looking for Elisa. Thus, Hosea realized that Deborah must be headed to the Council's stronghold. But he also realized that if Deborah had indeed found Elisa, Elisa would probably have contacted him telepathically or even by phone to let him know that his daughter was safe. Hosea pulled up to the curb two doorways down from The Council's front entrance. He exited his car and proceeded to the front door. At five in the morning, there was only one security guard working the front lobby. A mortal man, he stepped out to retrieve the morning paper and, as he did, Hosea stepped through the open door as quickly and quietly as a Shaolin monk. Letting go of the world, Hosea listened to the Divine within him, just as he had many times before. This time he was wearier than he could ever remember.

A couple of days in the French hospital had revived him somewhat but the heaviness was upon him again. Still, he pressed on. His spirit told him that he needed to go downstairs to find Deborah. From the partially-lit lobby, Hosea opened the heavy metal door leading to the stairwell that led to the Boardroom. Several centurions stood guard in the hallway. Their bodies were deformed as were their spirits. Hosea could literally feel the evil in his stomach. As Hosea stepped fully into the hallway, the first monstrosity raised his arm towards him.

Hosea called loudly and firmly, "Claudicatis!" which meant "halt" in Latin.

The beast froze instantly. Hosea proceeded to do the same to the others in the hallway, but each encounter drained him more than the one before.

Hosea reached the bottom of the stairwell and walked across the open floor. He came to another large metal door. This one was locked from the inside. Hosea wiped his nose and then pressed his fingertips against the door feeling the cold steel against his skin. He first noticed the blood on his fingers as it smeared across the door. The blood was from his nose. He did not stop. He stood back and knocked three times on the door in three different locations proceeding down the door. He reached for the door handle and turned it opening the door. The room was modestly lit by only the emergency lighting.

Hosea reached for the wall switch and called out, "Deborah!"

When Hosea flipped the wall switch, the dormant lights flickered as they revealed Chase standing on the far side of the room on a riser. In his left hand, Chase held his unsheathed sword while his right hand pressed across Deborah's torso holding her close against him so she, too, faced her father.

Chase replied to Hosea's call, "Welcome, Hosea. Deborah is right here. She came here looking for Elisa and found me instead. The others are out of town, but they left me here to watch the house. Imagine that."

He smiled a wicked grin before going on, "Deborah and I have been getting to know each other."

Hosea yelled out, "Take your hands off of her! We have a deal!" as he squinted. He struggled to adjust from the darkness to the now brightly lit room.

"Oh, I will and we do. As long as Elisa serves us, no one on the Council will take direct action to harm any of your girls, not that it really matters with this one, since she's not long for this world anyway; for there is a darkness building up within her already. But as for you..."

Chase released Deborah to the floor and swung his sword slowly.

"That arrangement does little for you. See, if one understands all of the variables, one does not need to see the future to know the future. I knew that Lola would overdose last night and I knew that Deborah would come here, and finally, I knew that you would come looking for her." Chase began to circle Hosea as he continued, "So, when the others decided to take a little field trip, I asked to stay behind. See, you were always the target. No, you're not a Circle Knight, but you are known and respected by all the relevant parties. Dispatching you will certainly be noticed by the Elders."

Hosea coughed and demanded, "Deborah, go outside!"

Deborah couldn't move. She lay on the floor sobbing.

Hosea called out again to her, "Deborah, get yourself up now! Go!"

Hearing her daddy yell got Deborah's attention. She lifted herself up and scurried out of the control room.

Chase teased Hosea, "Oh, you're a good daddy to want to spare your child from seeing me spill your blood. How thoughtful."

Hosea coughed again, "If it is my time, it is my time."

Chase swung his sword slashing its tip across Hosea's cheek, drawing blood.

"Well, aren't you going to ask me what happened? What made me go over to the other side? They all do."

"I won't. I, too, know something about how things work and how things fit together."

"Yes, you do, Hosea. We both know that you're capable of dragging this final act out, but we also know that this is indeed the final curtain. You know that your other three daughters will be here shortly, and that you would rather die quickly than run the risk of them confronting me in some ill-conceived effort to rescue you."

Hosea nodded slightly, "So, get on with it."

"Ah, no fear whatsoever. Oh, how I wish that you would do me the honor of putting up a fight. But since you are one of the few truly honorable men I've ever met, I will, as a gift to you and Elisa as well, end this now and take my leave. Good night, fair saint."

With those words, Chase ran his sword through Hosea's abdomen. Hosea grabbed his side and silently stumbled towards the wall. He struggled not to cry out in concern for his daughter outside. He collapsed against the wall, sitting upright and holding his side.

Chase wiped his sword and as he began to walk back to the lab where one of Elisa's portals stood, he glanced back at Hosea

He offered to him something that he seldom offered to any, "If all people of faith were like you Hosea, I would not be wedded to this pledge of blood and vengeance. Sleep well for you are one of the few who has earned it."

With those words, the assassin was gone.

Hosea sought to hang on long enough to see his girls one last time. Hosea's prayer was answered. Not thirty seconds after Chase's departure, he heard his girls coming down the stairwell and he smiled. He heard Ruth Ann asking Deborah why she was in the hall. Then, all four of his girls burst through the door.

They came in looking for a fight. Seeing their father on the floor and blood everywhere, they ran to his side, calling out, "Daddy!"

Hosea hugged them as best he could before chuckling just a bit, "I love you all so much, it hurts." Hosea coughed more blood.

Ruth cuddled right next to his wound, reaching her arms around her father as best she could. "Don't go. Don't go," she whispered over and over again.

Sarah was at his other side looking intensely into her father's face.

Cil, who knew this was coming, knelt at his feet weeping. Her tears fell upon her father's dusty black shoes.

Deborah stood off to the side crying.

Hosea called to her, "Deborah…"

She ran to him. Ruth moved a little to make room for her as Deborah fell to her knees grabbing her father around his neck and pressing her cheek to his. She continued to weep as she professed her love for him.

With his last breaths, Hosea continued to instruct them, "Go with Rob. Listen to Elizabeth. Take care of each other and always forgive one another, for to hate one another is to hate me and what I've taught you too."

This last part was something Hosea said often when he thought their bickering had gotten out of hand. Thus, Hosea passed from this world and to the next.

Ruth held on to her father gripping his jacket as tightly as she'd gripped the blades of grass the night before upon hearing of her mother's passing. She held on until Cil pulled her from his corpse. Throughout the years, Ruth only knew that she screamed and screamed because her sisters would later tell her that she did. Of her own accord, she remembered very little of those moments. Only in her dreams does she recall even a sense of those events in the basement, and even then it's more of an emotion than any detail.

She had been angry with her sister Deborah when they found her at the bottom of the stairwell, instead of in the Boardroom helping their father. As soon as she saw the pain and self-condemnation that blanketed Deborah, Ruth Ann quickly let go of those feelings. Where Deborah was about holding on, Ruth was about letting go.

∞

The funeral for Lola and Hosea was a closed event with few in attendance. What it lacked in number, it more than made up for in purpose. Cousin Rob and Miss Elizabeth were there. Uncle Paul was accompanied by a Circle Knight Elder. Paul's guest was a very fair-skinned woman with the bluest eyes Ruth had ever seen. The woman glowed; even her footprints glowed behind her whichever path she chose. Ruth overheard someone saying that Uncle Paul did, indeed, still have friends among the Circle Knight Elders. He had once been one himself, but he'd been forced to resign his post largely because of Chase's doings. Chase had been his protégé. When he went rogue, others argued that somehow Paul's acceptance of Chase and other non-conformists had emboldened them against the leadership.

Paul knew that his days as an Elder were numbered when he first volunteered to head up counter-intelligence. In that role, you can't help but get your hands dirty. Once your hands are dirty, your perspective can change. Some would say that it did with Paul. At least seven of the other eleven Elders said so.

Elisa was there as well. Ruth remembered well how Elisa hugged Lola's casket and wept bitterly over it. Uncle Paul tried to pull her off the casket, but she pushed him away. Finally, Cousin Rob came over and lifted her off the casket.

She turned to embrace him and cried into his ear, "Oh my baby, my baby. Our baby's gone."

Ruth heard the words but thought that perhaps she misheard or didn't understand the context.

The woman with the glowing footprints walked to Rob and Elisa and said to them, "From this hour forward, you must focus on the sisters, for when they are ready, neither the temples of Olympus nor the Gates of Hell shall stand before them. Equally, will they be dust beneath their feet."

From that day forward, Hosea and Lola's daughters were commonly referred to as "The Sisters".

Miss Elizabeth, for her part, when not attending the girls, sat in front of Hosea's casket in a brown folding chair speaking softly to him. Tears streamed slowly down her face. She told him how his girls were doing and how she was going to take care of them and that he shouldn't worry. While most of the crowd hovered around Lola's casket, Elizabeth remained alone with Hosea. She'd instructed the girls to take a seat on the pew after they viewed their parent's bodies, and they obeyed. Eventually, she motioned them over to her and the five of them said goodbye to Hosea one last time.

The girls realized that they were the only one's there to mourn their father, even though he was well known by other clergy. Everyone else there was there for Lola, or more accurately, for Elisa, Rob and Paul. This saddened Ruth but it made Deborah a bit angry and resentful towards Uncle Paul.

Rob and Uncle Paul came over to say goodbye to their brother in arms and then closed Hosea's casket. Everyone returned to their pews and a man Ruth had never seen before got up to speak. He didn't announce his name, but everyone seemed to know who he was. Ruth would hear later that he was an emissary from the Circle Council. He read through some scripture, said a few words, and then smiled at Ruth and her sisters. He was the first in a series of well-wishers, known and unknown, who took time to tell Ruth and her sisters what they already knew – that their father was a good and faithful man.

However, even Ruth, who always hoped her mother would change, was struck by the fact that Lola, who had been so rash and mean, was at the center of this event. Her father who sacrificed so much and loved so many seemed to be secondary at his own funeral. Ruth wanted to get up and shout "Oh, you simple people! Did you not know my mother? Why are you crying for her? Sure, we cry as her children for what will never be, but we cry for him for all that was and is now lost!"

Ruth knew that her sisters were thinking similar thoughts. Each of them managed to hold their tongues through the service, even Deborah, although her eyes were as cutting as razor blades during eulogies for their mother. Years later, Ruth would come to understand that Circle Knights and their associates still considered Lola to be one of them, albeit a wayward member of their clan. Although they all appreciated Hosea, most viewed him as a civilian. To their credit, throughout the years to come, anytime Rob would call on one of them to assist him in protecting the girls, they did not hesitate to respond. That, too, was their way.

After the funeral, Rob ushered Elizabeth and the girls to a waiting limousine. The bodies of their parents went directly to unmarked graves in a cemetery just west of town. But the girls went straight to the airport with their new guardians. Even though there was supposed to be a truce in place that said no one on the Council of Nob would attack the girls directly, neither he nor Hosea trusted Matasis or "those crazy folks that work for him." They were sure that they'd find some way around the agreement or pervert it in some way. Once at the airport, the girls met Rob's special operations team. Ruth would only remember a few of the details of those days, but she never forgot the feeling of Rob's buddy, Big Mike, picking Sarah and her up into his arms and carrying them to their gate.

The grownups let Ruth sit next to the window. Big Mike sat next to her on the aisle. Cil and Deborah were across the aisle and Miss Elizabeth sat with Sarah in the row in front of them. Ruth turned to Big Mike and asked, "Will there be horses where we're going?"

Big Mike answered her, "I'm sure we can round you up a few."

The little girl replied, "Good, we love horses." Ruth stared out the window and played with the pink ribbon in her hair as the plane soared into the heavens on its way to Mexico City. There, they would catch a small plane for an unfamiliar land in the Mexican peninsula, to begin a new life – a life of new blessings, haunted by old curses.

# 18
# WHAT SHOULD NEVER BE

*July, 1981 - Atlanta, Georgia*

*"If you tell it all, you'll have nothing left to say..."* Lucille Johnson

Cil arrived first. The fire crews were still hosing down Miss Elizabeth's house. Cil kneeled down in the wet glass, closed her eyes, and prayed. After kneeling there for about a minute, Cil said, "Hello, Akina."

Akina had materialized around the corner and walked up to Cil's side. "So, you really let this happen?" An incredulous Akina asked.

Cil knew well in advance that this day was coming. Yet, she did nothing to prevent it.

"Akina, you cannot change the future. You can only prepare for it."

The slender dark-skinned Akina turned her afro-crowned head away and stared up the street.

Cil stood up and said softly to Akina, "Don't you think if I could change these things, I would?"

Akina remained silent.

Cil spoke again, "How many times have you tried to change the future and how many times have you failed?"

"Many times or, so it seems. Perhaps I am not failing. Maybe I am changing the future, but the time paradox is preventing us from realizing it?" Akina proposed.

Cil smiled, "That sounds reasonable. But, as someone who can travel back and forth in time, wouldn't you know if you'd been successful? Simply go to the future, observe, return to the past make change, and return to the future and observe again. But you've done that, haven't you? In fact, you're in the past now trying to affect some change on your own future. But you're finding that your own efforts are simply a part of what was always to be. Now you're wondering if perhaps as a time traveler, you are somehow prevented from changing the future by some physical law, and now you want me to explain it all to you. You think that perhaps you are affecting change, but to some divergent timeline which you are prevented from seeing? And if time is indeed an illusion, perhaps this reality is as well, a common delusion between beings which exist between the synapses of a God we cannot see, even as I speak to you now?"

Akina lowered her chin, and answered, "Yes."

Cil lifted Akina's chin with her index finger, "Child, you can no more change the future than you can move a star off of its axis."

Cil said this as a physicist and a believer. In theory the future could be changed, but Cil questioned whether Akina, or most any mortal, had the power to do so. Time was the directional property upon which the heavens were laid.

Cil continued, "The others will be here soon, so unless you want to answer a bunch of questions, you might want to get going."

"They still don't know that you can see the future, do they?" Akina asked.

"No, they don't and I hate hiding so much from them."

Cil hugged Akina goodbye and thought to herself about how much she'd hidden from Akina as well. There was no mortal to which Cil could reveal everything. Too much was at stake.

As Akina walked away towards her own future, Cil's attention returned to Miss Elizabeth's smoldering home. The soft June evening breeze carried some of the ashes back to the earth from which they'd come, that the circle might remain unbroken. Cil who knew the future as well as any mortal, knew that the losing season, at long last, was upon her family again. The loss of Cousin Rob and Miss Elizabeth were merely be the first in a series of losses. A sadness descended upon Cil. She clutched at the cross beneath her blouse that Sarah had given her all those years ago. She released it before turning to see Deborah scampering down the street.

At the sight of Elizabeth's house, Deborah kicked off her heels and ran in a full sprint towards the burning home, screaming, "Miss Elizabeth, Miss Elizabeth!"

Cil caught her little sister and held on to her tightly.

Moments later, Sarah also approached the house, repeating "No, no, God no..."

Sarah walked past her sisters into the yard and towards the glowing embers. Since the heat and flames could not harm her, Cil made no attempt to stop Sarah. The firemen there had another thought on the matter. Two of them grabbed the star-laden woman to hold her back. In her grief and anger, Sarah began to power up.

Cil called out to her, "Sarah! Let it go. They don't know."

Sarah cried, waving her hands back and forth at first and covering her mouth, before turning to join her sisters in the grass on the edge of the lawn.

Ruth Ann was the only sister who not to own a car. She was supervising an after school program at her elementary school and could not leave immediately when she received the news that the fire trucks were at Miss Elizabeth's house. After the last parent retrieved their child, Ruth ran to the bus stop to catch a bus as she normally would before she realized that she needed to catch a cab. She had to chase one down. By the time Ruth arrived, the firemen were packing up. In the evening light, Ruth walked up the street to the blackened house from where her cab had dropped her. Though her three sisters stood in the yard, the whole scene was surreal to Ruth. Silently, she walked past her sisters, her eyes never leaving the sight of charred pine and oak before her. One word did escape her lips, "How…?"

Cil answered Ruth, "A gas explosion. The investigator says it was arson, but you know."

Ruth staggered a few steps forward and then swayed as if she might fall. She shook her head from side to side as tears traced a path down her angelic face before falling down to the earth below. Miss Elizabeth was the mother Ruth had always hoped for. In the cold reality of a hot summer day, Ruth realized that there was still so much that was never realized between Miss Elizabeth and her. Ruth had dreamed of her children sitting at Elizabeth's feet as she had done. This abrupt ending was so jarring that Ruth felt her own bones might shatter. She always thought they had more time.

Days later after Miss Elizabeth's funeral, Ruth and her sisters gathered at Big Mama's house. The old woman had been the matriarch of the Few clan since the girls were young. She was born in a time before Lola or Elisa, but not nearly as long ago as Uncle Paul. It was said that her birth father was Paul, or that perhaps her mother was Paul's oldest daughter. When asked how old she was, she would only reply, "Old enough." She'd been an old woman for several lifetimes when the girls first met her had become set in her ways. Regardless, she had opened her doors to Hosea and his girls. For years, they visited Big Mama and their distant cousins at least twice a year at Christmas and Easter. The house of Few had split centuries ago over a matter that was unknown to Deborah, Ruth, and Sarah. Cil knew but she wouldn't tell her sisters.

When they asked she always said, "We don't need to get caught up in carrying on crap started by a bunch of folks long dead and gone."

The tension was particularly strong between Uncle Paul and Big Mama. To her credit, Big Mama never let that affect how she treated Ruth and her sisters. When Lola was alive, Big Mama repeatedly tried to get her into the drug treatment program she founded and ran. Lola would never admit she had a problem, much less accept treatment. Despite all the history between the branches of the family tree, Big Mama was the one constant for both sides. She hoped one day to bring the sides together again. Ruth and her sisters adored her from the weekend they first met her when they moved to Atlanta from New Orleans.

Big Mama finally passed away in 1973, Ruth's sophomore year at Spelman College. Since Big Mama's passing, the house served as a Circle safe house and armory. Each safe house around the world had what was known as a Watcher assigned to it. The Watchers were beings who weren't powerful enough to be selected to be Circle Knights, but who served in other capacities. Within the confines of the safe house, their abilities were magnified. This amplification was the doing of the Circle Knight Elders. Just as the Elders had bound Elisa's gifts before casting her into The Pit, they also had the ability to enhance someone's gifts to a degree. Some of the Circle Knights looked down on these Watchers and considered them almost to be their squires. But, the level of commitment of the Watchers could not be questioned. Each Watcher was bound to their assigned safe house for the remainder of their days. They were bound to the community, the further away from the home they roamed, the weaker they became. If they ventured too far, they would die. The Watcher assigned to Big Mama's house was one of her numerous "grandkids," many generations removed. Her name was Grace Few and her striking green eyes and blonde hair stuck out in the West End community during that time. When Big Mama died and the Elders approached the family about making her home a safe house, Grace didn't hesitate to volunteer to be the Watcher.

The sisters, now grown, entered the home reminiscing of those days gone by. They hadn't been in the home in years. The last time they'd been there was when they retrieved Athena's bow which had been buried in the backyard. That was nearly ten years ago. After Big Mama died, Cil informed her sisters that this matriarch was not just a keeper of family history and heirlooms but of certain family armaments as well. Most were kept in a vault inside the house, but some were buried in the yard like Cil's staff and Athena's bow. After finding the bow, Deborah wanted to go on a treasure hunt in the back yard, but Cil demanded that they only search for an item when they had need.

On this day creating, rather than finding, was on the agenda. The sisters had agreed that, while Deborah was quite adept at mixing it up in hand to hand combat, she needed a top notch weapon for in close fighting. She needed a sword, but not an ordinary sword. Those were easy to find and just as easy to snap against the kinds of beings they battled. No,

Deborah needed a sword that would stand the test of time. She needed a sword that, from its birth, would be a legend in the making. What wasn't discussed was Deborah's seemingly insatiable need to prove that she was just as powerful as her sisters. The digging up of Athena's bow had been an effort to fill that need and so was this. The Circle Knight Elders had deemed Cil, Ruth, and Sarah as "A1" knights; their powers were top-rated in effectiveness and scope. They graded Deborah as "B1." B1 was higher than anyone on Big Mama's side of the family tree had ever been graded which, in itself, was cause for some friction in the family. This perceived slight left Deborah with a large chip on her shoulder and led to regular discussions among the sisters about Deborah taking chances in battle just to prove the Elders wrong. What was never discussed, however, was the underlying emotional need for Deborah to somehow fix what happened the night her daddy, Hosea, was killed by Chase after he found her at the Council of Nob. Deborah battled the need to prove to herself that she was good enough. The problem of having such a goal is knowing when you've reached it.

The ladies moved with a sense of order and purpose even though chaos swirled all around them. Sarah had been raped just one month earlier. She'd not had a night free of nightmares since. Deborah was nearly three months pregnant with twins, but estranged from her own husband who had lured her sister Sarah into a den of wolves and abandoned her there. Sarah and Deborah's relationship was more strained than ever. Sarah alternated from feeling of rage to intense empathy for Deborah every time she opened her mouth.

The Day of Reckoning, when the forces of darkness intended to open the Omni Portal was less than a week away. They'd not heard from Auntie Elisa for some time. That was not completely unusual, but she had a habit over the years of making contact with them before the big events of their lives. With the biggest of days looming, they'd not heard a word. Miss Elizabeth had burned to death just days before. Ruth was never afraid of dying, but she was terrified that she would let her sisters down. She was so anxious about not messing up that she could hardly keep any food down the last two days. These panic attacks were nearly disabling for her. For Cil, all that can be said is heavy is the head that wears the crown.

The metalworking was a respite for each of them. It took them back to their childhood days of working in the stable shoeing the horses. The metallurgy they were now performing was far beyond anything they even dared to dream of in their youth, but the sense of separation from the world was much the same. They started with a blend of metals – some were common, others uncommon. Sarah melted down a portion of each as Cil directed it into the stone mold. When the mold was halfway full, Cil stopped the process and took a dagger from her waist. She made a small slash across the palm of her hand and allowed the blood from the wound to drip into the mold. Her sisters each did likewise. With each drop, the molten metal glowed brighter still, illuminating the darkened room even more.

When they were done and the sword cooled, Cil took the silvery black sword and stood before Deborah, with Ruth and Sarah taking their places on either side of her. Deborah was puzzled for a moment before realizing what her sisters were doing. Cil spoke, "In recognition of your dedication to the cause and in support of that cause, we present this Ebony Sword, to you this fifteenth day of July, Nineteen Eighty-One. In your hands may it protect the weak, vindicate the innocent, and lay waste to the bloodthirsty."

Deborah's eyes moistened. "Thank you," she said over and over to her sisters as they each hugged her.

The Watcher of the home knocked on the door and asked to come in.

"Sure," Cil replied.

Grace stepped in and handed a large envelope to Cil. The envelope contained four plane tickets, six signed documents and a single handwritten note. The note was from the Circle Knight Elders.

It read simply, "All arrangements have been made."

# THE BOOK OF GABRIELLA

## SACRIFICES • *Alan D. Jones*

# 19
# SISTERHOOD

*July, 1981 - North Hudson Bay, Canada*

*Love is patient, love is kind. It does not envy, it does not boast, it is not proud. It always protects, always trusts, always hopes, always perseveres.*

Gabriella, a loving soul, always hoped for more. Gabby, as she was often called, had been born to a preacher and a nurse. Looking after others was in her blood. As a little girl, she often tended to calves and foals. But, she was truly joyful when her mother allowed her to accompany her on visits to the sick.

Gabriella's mother, Alejanda, was a strikingly beautiful woman. She had passed on her good looks to her one, and only, daughter. Alejanda was a loving and forgiving woman and had little tolerance for meanness. She was unafraid to call out a bully when she saw one, be it a child or a government official. Gabby's father, Jorge, was a big man of six foot two. He was a gentle giant who was always willing to help others, even those who didn't seem to deserve his help. Although he stood in a pulpit on Sundays, most days he could be found under a car or truck working as the village mechanic. At night, after everyone else was asleep, Gabriella enjoyed sitting in her father's shop while he made late night repairs. It wasn't until she was older that she realized that most men could not pick up an engine block with their bare hands. Though there were few frills in Gabriella's house, she had all that she needed and she loved her parents dearly. Still, there was one thing she always hoped for: a little sister. She often asked her parents for one. Then, one week her parents took her with them to a church conference in a large city and her hope was granted. That was when she met Ruth Ann.

Gabriella's and Ruth's fathers had known each other for years and had worked together often. They didn't typically bring their families to these conferences unless it was driving distance, but this time they did. Meeting Ruth and her sisters had been planned although the girls didn't know it at the time. At the large circular table in the basement of an old country church, Gabriella had been seated next to Ruth. The two of them hit it off instantly. They talked incessantly that very first meeting, so much so that neither of them finished their dinners. That week, the little girls spent every day together. Gabriella's English was not so good although it was better than her French. Ruth's French was better than her Spanish although she mastered neither. Still, the two of them managed to communicate. After a full day of playing together, Gabriella began to see that Ruth was extremely shy around others. This made Gabriella love Ruth all the more.

Ruth viewed Gabriella as everything she wish she could be – beautiful, strong, and confident. Ruth was small and slight of build for her age. Many people mistook her for the youngest of the sisters. People constantly commented about how strikingly beautiful Cil, Deborah and Sarah were. They called Ruth cute. Ruth's siblings always operated in a sphere of complete confidence, but she seldom did. Ruth saw in Gabriella all the things she did not see in herself.

Gabriella saw Ruth for the beautiful person that she was. Behind those glasses, she saw a sister in spirit. Gabriella saw her goodness, her kindness, and her willingness to forgive. She also saw a quiet resolve that was so much like her own. She quickly came to realize that with sisters who were larger than life, like Ruth's, it would be easy for one's light to be hidden.

In addition to her primary gift of inhuman skill and strength like her daddy, Gabriella also possessed the gift of encouragement. It was a gift that she shared freely with Ruth. Early on, this put her in direct conflict with Deborah. Deborah was often critical of Ruth Ann. Deborah thought her criticisms helped to toughen Ruthie; she used harsh words to make her stronger. Gabriella saw a sapling that needed nurturing and room to grow among the redwoods.

As Gabriella grew into womanhood she saw less of her American sisters. When she did see the sisters, it was typically assignment related. When she was nineteen, Gabby started going out with Rob's Special Forces buddy Big Mike. By that time, at thirty years old, he was divorced with two kids. They didn't publicize it, but everyone knew about their relationship except Jorge. When Big Mike showed up at Gabby's college graduation with flowers, Jorge finally figured it out. Mike wasn't a Circle Knight, but he had a little something extra in his DNA. That made him a real beast in the field.

The inter-racial nature of Mike and Gabby's relationship proved vexing for the more intolerant they encountered when not in Latin America. Their relationship withstood that challenge, but the distance was more challenging. The final hurdle, which severed their relationship the year before, was children. Gabriella wanted to get married and have children. Mike already had two kids who he seldom got to see. He couldn't see how the two of them could actually raise children unless they quit the very thing they were called to do in this life. They hadn't seen each other in the year since they split until she arrived shipside aboard the central command vessel of the force gathering to stop the Omni Portal. Mike met her in the galley once he found out she was aboard. He hugged her for a long time telling her how sorry he was to hear about her mother, father, and other family members who had been slaughtered in the raid. She was grateful that he understood her need to compartmentalize all of that until this battle was over. There would be time for grieving over many things, but this was not the time. The two of them left much unsaid, but the look on his face told her that he regretted walking away from the best thing he ever had in his life. For the girl who had always hoped for more, his realization was not unexpected.

The next morning aboard a northbound freighter in the Hudson Bay, as Gabby offered her morning devotion to the sounds of shells exploding in the distance, she thought of her father and mother and how they died. The pain threatened to take her breath away. She focused, instead, on how they had lived and was inspired to push on. Her thoughts then turned to Ruth. She thought not of the earliest days when they first met, nor the later days when they battled side by side against the darkness. She recalled the day her sister came to live with her. Rob and his crew brought Ruth Ann and her sisters to Gabby's town. She remembered the girl with the pink ribbon in her hair stepping off her plane clutching a Raggedy Ann doll. Ruth screamed when she saw Gabriella. For security purposes, Rob had not told the girls exactly where they were going when they left Atlanta. Gabriella offered to share her room with little Ruth Ann and, finally, her prayers were answered. She had a sister.

Gabriella heard a helicopter landing on the flight deck above her. She had a pretty good idea of who might be coming aboard. Gabriella scampered up the stairs outside her cabin to the flight deck. She saw the copter. The door was open and, after a couple of military types exited it, Gabriella saw them: Cil, Deborah, Sarah and, lastly, Ruth. The sisters were all dressed in form fitting white body suits and wearing matching white ski jackets. Gabriella could see Ruth with her single pink lock, looking around, searching, so she raised her own hands and waved at the sisters. When Ruth saw her, she smiled and returned Gabriella's wave from across the deck. Ruth pointed out Gabriella to her sisters and they all began to head over. Her sisters were intercepted by Navy brass, but Ruth pushed through them towards Gabriella. As they drew close, tears flooded each of their eyes.

Ruth reached out to hug Gabriella, "You're alive! You're alive!"

Ruth and her sisters knew that Gabriella was not among the dead in the village from the attack, but they'd not heard anything about her whereabouts. The sisters had heard through Circle back channels that Gabriella was unharmed. Even though Circle Knight protocol dictates going to silent when an attempt is made on your life, they had been concerned.

Ruth took a breath, "Gabby, I'm so sorry about your parents, so very sorry. We came as soon as we got the call, but we were too late."

Still embracing, Gabriella answered her back, "Oh, I know. I was on a mission when it happened."

As the other sisters arrived and hugged her, Gabriella broke down in tears. Somehow being with them and the common bond they shared, allowed her to feel comfortable enough to let go. When they told Gabriella about Miss Elizabeth, the only mother the Ruth and her sisters had ever known, the five women began to cry again.

Just as quickly as they released their emotions, the ladies pulled themselves together and followed their escort to a briefing room. They listened as the Special Forces operative explained the battle plan. Everyone in the room knew that the leaders of the world, the people to whom these officers reported, had hoped that the Circle Knight Elders themselves would join the battle, but they had declined. Instead, they communicated a list of Circle Knight resources who would be made available.

An armada of warships from around the world that had been decommissioned had been assembled. These off the book ships had been retrofitted with the latest weapons. Only the command ship carried meta-humans like the guys in Rob's unit and Circle Knights like the sisters. Most of the crews on the other ships had little idea of the nature of the enemy they were bombarding. Everything remained compartmentalized. Everyone involved knew only as much as needed to perform their jobs. Even those who knew, didn't fully understand or, in some cases, believe what they'd been told about these special resources. Only select leaders around the world have been aware of these demigods since the dawn of recorded history.

The battle plan, in short, was to blend all available meta-human resources in with the infantry assault forces, with the exception of the four sisters. These forces would engage the enemy from the west and push towards the Omni Portal while heavy ship artillery rained down on the forces of darkness from the south. When the enemy's attention was drawn to the west and south, the sisters would establish a beachhead on the eastern shore and drive towards the Omni Portal located on the southeast shore. None of the women were happy about Gabriella being assigned to the western front, but those were the orders from the Circle Knight Elders. The thought was that Gabriella's talents could easily blend in with the other ground forces, which would maximize her effectiveness. Whereas whenever the sisters entered the fray, there'd be no hiding their presence.

When the briefing was over, Deborah reached out to grab Gabriella's hand.

Deborah pulled her close and whispered in her ear, "Come with us." And as they began to walk Deborah said, "By the way, you were right about Willy. I knew he was a bum, but I wanted him so much."

Gabriella winced, "Oh, I'm sorry."

"Oh, don't be. As usual, I had to learn the hard way. I should have known that when even Ruth Ann spoke against him, I should have run. So, being rid of him, in no way hurts my heart in the way that my foolishness has hurt my family."

Sarah heard her sister's words as they walked through the corridor and reached over to comfort her.

Deborah continued, "Yeah, there are a few things we need to update you on."

The women retreated to Cil's cabin. The five of them chatted as they recalled their lives with Gabriella's parents, Rob, Miss Elizabeth and Elisa. They also realized that their season of loss still might not be over. In fact, each of them knew that this battle would indeed be the middle passage of their generation.

Finally, came the knock on the door that each of them expected. The seaman said that it was time for Gabriella to join her western flank team for departure.

Deborah told him, "Just a minute, please?"

The women joined hands and formed a circle for a quick prayer.

When they finished, Ruth hugged Gabriella for a long moment and pleaded into her ear, "Gabby, please be careful."

Gabriella whispered back to her, "Have faith. God has made you for such a day as this."

Ruth smiled as her sisters stepped in to hug Gabriella as well.

Gabriella stepped into the corridor to join her escort.

When the door closed, Ruth burst into tears. Ruth had never exhibited even a hint of a sixth sense like Cil and Deborah. Yet, her heart grieved for Gabriella.

# SACRIFICES • *Alan D. Jones*

# THE BOOK OF ZI

# 20
# THE NOR'EASTER

*May, 1764 - China's East Coast*

*The moment when we lose ourselves is only revealed to us in retrospect as we are falling into the abyss, when we dare not even hope for salvation.*

Zi was born of the wind and the waves during the worst storm of the century in 1746. Her father fished her out of the ocean when she was a newborn. He found her wrapped in a blanket and floating in a basket. He took her back to his small fishing village along the east coast of China.

Zi loved her parents dearly. Zi also loved the water and the occasional typhoons that roiled the ocean. During the worst of storms, Zi would stand outside to soak it all in. The wind danced around her.

Ten years later everything changed. One dark fall night, Zi was awakened by chaos. She entered her parent's room and saw her mother on the ground. She didn't fully understanding what the men around her were doing. It was her mother's cries that had awakened her. A body clothed in her father's robe lay near the doorway. Its head was missing.

Suddenly, a large man came from behind her and scooped Zi up in one hand and walked toward the front door. He held something she could not see in his hand. Outside in the moonlight, she watched the man toss her father's head onto a pile. Zi screamed and screamed. To silence her, the man struck her in the head with the butt of his sword knocking the little girl unconscious.

Zi awoke the next day shackled in the hull of a slave ship headed to Japan. There were other children chained beside her. Some of them she knew, but most of them she didn't. Her village had not been raiders' only stop. Slavery had been banned in Japan some years earlier, but the practice continued among the elites in the more rural areas. The hugely profitable human trafficking market tempted anyone with a vessel worthy of the high seas. Zi and the other captives on this ship would be warehoused until they could be sold.

The ship had encountered a persistent head wind which made progress slow. They sailed for days as the vessel tacked back and forth. The closer they got to their destination, the fiercer the winds became. The crew became frightened as supplies dwindled. After a while, they decided that a sacrifice was needed to appease the seas.

Zi watched as one of the crew members dragged a girl up to the deck. The frightened girl had been one of Zi's playmates. From below, Zi could hear the girl's cries. Each one was more gut wrenching than the one before. Soon, Zi's friend went silent and blood dripped down the stairs. The crewmen tossed the girl overboard and waited for the seas to calm. Down in the hold, Zi wept. Outside, it rained.

The next night the head winds were stronger than ever. The crew decided to try another sacrifice. Two of the men came for Zi. They tried to pull her away from the wall. Each time they pulled her, she resisted. The whole ship lurched. The men regained their footing and tried again. Each time, Zi fought them and the waves rose up. The ship was cast towards its side. At last, the men gave up. Later, they returned with several other sailors to demonstrate to them how each time they struggled with the frightened young girl, the ocean would rise up against them.

The men began shouting, "Majo!"

The men unchained her and dragged her up to the deck despite the rolling of the seas beneath them. The more afraid she became the more the waves battered the ship. The ship rocked back and forth as the men tried to throw her overboard.

The captain saw the commotion and intervened. He saw with his own eyes how the waves roared beneath a clear sky. He heard the fear in his men's voices. To calm the situation, the captain proposed setting the girl adrift in one of the raiding party boats. The crew feared retribution from the evil spirit they thought Zi was serving. So, they let the captain place the young girl in a boat and set her adrift.

Zi floated upon the sea alone. She was lost and the boat had no sail. The oars were too heavy for her to heave. She wanted to go home, but there was no home to which she could return. Her condition seemed hopeless.

When she was thirsty, rain fell. Zi opened her mouth to drink. Still, she drifted. On the second day at sea, hunger set in. By the end of the third day, delirium overtook her. In her altered state, Zi had a vision. A voice from heaven told her to reach her hand into the sea. She did and grabbed a large fish. It was so large that she had trouble pulling it into the boat. That night, after she'd eaten she slept deeply. Zi dreamed that she was going to Japan. In the morning, a fresh breeze arose out of the west creating a current that pushed her boat towards the western shore of Japan. Two days later, she reached her destination.

Zi made her way to town. She found herself relying on the kindness of others. Most people, when they saw that she was Chinese, looked the other way. Eventually, she made her way to a fishing village. Zi could be persuasive when given the chance. She used that skill to convince one of the fishermen to allow her to assist him in exchange for food and a place to lay her head. Since Zi had helped her fisherman father since she was four or five years old, she knew what to do. She quickly gained her employer's trust. To help keep her safe, he dressed her like a boy. Only the fisherman, his wife, and their young son knew the truth.

Zi was horrified by the sight of others from her country working as slaves, but she kept her pain hidden. This arrangement lasted for three years, until one rainy day the fisherman's son, who had grown jealous of the favor Zi had earned in his father's eyes, told Zi's secret to one of the local Shogun's soldiers, including how she'd escaped the Shogun before at sea. The soldier went straightaway to tell his superiors.

The fisherman's son confessed to his father what he had done. Upon hearing the news, the father gathered Zi and took her to the docks. He found a ship bound for the New World. He paid the ship's captain half his family savings to take Zi with him to the New World. He explained to the captain that he was not paying him to transport Zi but, rather, to protect her. The captain agreed and decided to make Zi his cabin boy.

The hours until the ship set sail were anxious ones. From the captain's quarters, Zi could see her protector in the harbor casting his net. At long last the rain ended, the clouds parted and the ship set sail at last. As the ship moved into the harbor, Zi saw them. The Shogun and his men in their boats entered the harbor, searching from boat to boat for the fisherman. One of the other men on the water, pointed him out. The soldiers boarded the fisherman's boat and dragged him off of it. As her ship moved slowly out of the harbor, Zi watched as the men interrogated the fisherman. They struck him in the face. He pointed towards the hills. They clearly did not believe him because they struck him again. Zi cried out in anger. When she did, a huge wave formed in the ocean and moved towards the troops and their boats. The wave picked up all of soldiers in their boats and dashed them into the docks. Zi screamed and jumped up and down in panicked horror. Her wave also carried the fisherman into the unforgiving coastline.

The captain rushed in and fell to his knees wrapping his arms around the quivering Zi. He attempted to comfort and still her. After a time, Zi stopped shivering, but she remained at the window silently staring back into the harbor. Hour after hour she stood there, well into the evening, until the lights along the coast line were no longer visible.

The captain rose from his writing desk and kneeled down beside the young girl. He spoke to Zi perfectly in her native tongue.

"You are among friends, now," he said.

As Zi calmed down, so did the winds and the sea.

The Captain continued, "No harm will come to you. You are special, but you are not alone. I am taking you to a safe place called New Orleans. It will take a long time to get there by sea. There, you will have friends and will have no need to worry."

"Is this a slave ship?" Zi asked.

"No."

Zi couldn't decide whether to believe the captain or not, but something inside her said it was okay to trust him. In the coming months, Zi learned a decent amount of French as she got to know the ship's crew and her captain, Henri.

Months later, the ship made a brief stop in Haiti. There, Zi saw poverty and oppression like she'd never seen before. She also had her first encounter with the 'Espérons que des Abandonnés', a Haitian End of Days cult. A few short days after that, Zi finally found herself in New Orleans. Everything she knew lay in dust ten thousand miles away. In New Orleans, she found a new family – a family of people who, like her, had secrets. Zi tried to put her past behind her. Elisa took her in, and after some time and lots of questions, Elisa shared her faith with Zi. The concepts were foreign to her, but she listened. She wanted to please Elisa.

At fourteen, Zi met a runaway slave named Sam. He was sixteen, but he looked and claimed that he was eighteen. Sam was an attractive boy of mixed blood. His mother was from China. His father was from Haiti. Two years earlier, he'd managed to stowaway aboard a ship bound for New Orleans. He found work at the same fish house as Zi. The work was hard, but didn't last all day. He left work with the sun still high enough for him to work on his paintings. The hours were also perfect for Zi who wanted to continue her studies at the feet of Elisa, who'd taken her in. Sam carried the day's catch from the wagon to the cleaning stations which were staffed mostly by women, one of whom was Zi. Sam spoke French quite well, but Zi was taken aback his Chinese. His dialect was very similar to Zi's own. His mother could not have been born too far away from where Zi had been raised.

She felt comfortable with Sam. She told him many things about her past. Zi shared what happened to her in her village and how she watched helplessly as her adoptive Japanese family was slaughtered before her eyes. She cried as she told him about the guilt she felt because her parents died trying to protect her. But, she could not share how she caused the tidal wave that killed the fisherman in Japan who took her in once she arrived there. She'd often cried at the realization that if either family had turned away from her, they'd still be alive. Their mercy was repaid with their blood.

Sam trusted Zi, too. He shared the horrors he'd seen with his own eyes and those his parents told him of as well. They both swore that they'd rather die than return to a life of oppression. They longed for a world free from hatred. The commonality of their experience gave them a feeling that they were destined to be together. They quickly professed their love for one another.

Despite this, Zi did not share anything about her gifts or her friends who watched over her in New Orleans.

One day, Zi arrived at work to find that her bin was empty and that Sam was nowhere to be found. Her co-workers had no answers. Zi ran into the street desperately seeking some clue to Sam's whereabouts. She asked some of the shop owners and street vendors near the docks if they'd seen anything. Everyone she asked claimed to have seen nothing. Then, she asked an older gentleman selling delicate flowers from a bucket. Though his disheveled appearance gave Zi pause, his words were clear and rang true to her. The man told her that bounty hunters the night before had captured an Asian-looking black boy with curly hair and dragged him onto a slaver's ship headed back to Haiti. The ship left port before sunrise.

When she heard this, Zi hiked up her dress to her knees and ran to the pier. She held the crumpled ends of her skirt in each hand as she ran down the pier. Zi found a free dingy, untied it, and called upon her gift. A wind rose behind her and a current beneath her vessel that carried her down the Mississippi towards the gulf. Just over an hour later, she caught up to the slave ship in the bay of New Orleans. The sailors on deck were astonished and frightened by her approach. She had no sail or oars and yet her dingy moved as though an unseen hand pulled it along. Without warning, a fierce updraft over the starboard side of the ship lifted petite, teenaged Zi up and onto the deck. She demanded that they bring up to the deck the mulatto runaway slave they'd just picked up in New Orleans. All of the sailors pointed to the bay. They said that the boy had jumped overboard as they entered the bay and had drowned trying to swim to shore. Zi sensed that they were telling the truth. She called a second mighty wind that carried her back to her dingy. As her boat proceeded towards the marshlands, Zi glanced at the slave ship and, with a mere gesture, called forth a fifty-foot wave that capsized the ship. Zi did not look back after that. Zi was hopeful that she would find Sam. The fact that the sailors did not see Sam surface, did not surprise Zi. He had faked his own death in Haiti. As part of his plan to escape his enslavement, Sam fell off of a fishing boat. He had the ability to hold his breath for long periods of time. He swam underneath the boat to freedom on the far shore. Zi held out hope and searched along the marsh frantically until, at last, she found him. Sam's lifeless body was tangled up in the reeds. He'd almost made it. Zi jumped from her dingy and dragged him back aboard. She rocked him back and forth as she recounted how three times she had given her heart to love and three times her hope had been crushed by the cruelty of men. Zi cried bitterly.

Through her tears and sobbing, she heard her name being called, "Zi."

She turned to see Elisa.

Elisa asked, "Qu'avez-vous fait?"

Elisa already knew what Zi had done, but she needed to hear Zi acknowledge it.

Even though Zi had taken no vow of allegiance to the Circle Knights, her actions would not go unnoticed or unpunished by the Elders. She would not stand before the twelve for immediate judgment. They'd assign someone to deal with Zi.

Elisa said, "You must go. You will not be safe in the open."

Zi knew about the Elders and their harsh ways towards those like themselves. Elisa would attempt to convince the Elders that this was a one-time event driven by the passion of a young girl. Besides, she was not of age to be accountable anyway. Then, Elisa chastised Zi.

"We do not have the luxury of responding to the passions of our hearts against mortals, no matter the crime," Elisa said. "Go, now. I will do what I can to help with the Elders."

Elisa hugged Zi. She reminded her protégé of her training. She nodded and the young girl closed her eyes and stilled herself. A moment later, her body became ash and began to dissipate into the gentle breeze bound for whichever corner of the earth that sorrowful wind should take her. Even the Circle Elders know not from where the wind comes or where it goes.

Zi did indeed take to the wind as Elisa suggested, allowing it to take her wherever it might blow. In the subsequent years without her mentor present, Zi's life was also like the wind, shifting and hard to grasp. She would avenge the fisherman who saved her, by slaying the Shogun and all of his mail sons. She fell into witchcraft and somewhere along the way became consumed with the end times, believing that they were imminent. Word of Zi's deeds reached Elisa even in the Pit, taking her soul to an even deeper level therein.

Thus, sending Zi away was one regret that haunted Elisa daily.

# SACRIFICES • *Alan D. Jones*

# THE BOOK OF CHASE

# SACRIFICES • *Alan D. Jones*

# 21
# CHASING GHOSTS

*July, 1981 - North Hudson Bay, Canada*

*If you cast your brother into the wilderness don't be surprised if he adapts.*

"At last," Chase looked out over the icy battlefield and said, "the curtain rises on the last scene in the theater of life."

A confused Destry asked, "What are you talking about, Scarecrow? This is the last day for our opponents, you mean."

Through the softly falling snow Chase smiled and thought "How do you explain the End of Days to a fool? And who is the bigger fool in such a conversation?" If this man did not understand that, by making a deal with the demon Matasis, he had essentially made a deal with the devil there was nothing that Chase could do for him now.

The nearly completed Omni Portal had reappeared on Earth nearly three days ago at which time mankind began their futile assault on it. Chase and the other Council of Nob members had expected this. After all, Earth possessed its own oracles. Despite their efforts, all that remained to be done were the final calibrations. Destry's mercenaries worked feverishly to complete final tests and last-minute adjustments. Destry grinned at the thought of turning the portal on at last.

Chase knew that Destry and his lot had envisioned a world of constant war with the portal's opening. Actually, there was very little that would be constant about it. In a short time, the earth would perish and the forces of darkness would proceed to the next world.

Chase viewed the war monger, Poseidon, as a fool, too. He was a fool for believing that his armada could stand against the forces on the other side of the portal. Poseidon imagined Earth would prove the perfect training ground for his forces to engage all manner of being – flesh, spirit, and everything in between. They had weapons that were effective against both. Poseidon was so confident in his forces that he didn't see what was on the other side of the portal as a threat; he saw them rather as worlds to conquer that had been previously unavailable to him. Chase, however, understood probabilities. He knew that the chances of Poseidon and his civilization being the final winners in this cosmic melee were infinitesimally small.

Isadora's designs, on the other hand, actually had a chance to succeed. A small chance but a chance nonetheless. The Queen of the Dead knew that her realm, Oblivion, was one of the most feared of the portal destinations. She knew that her kingdom wouldn't be high on anyone's list to invade. This bloody chaos would allow her to claim countless lost souls and time to prepare for any potential attacks on her dark realm. Chase refrained from mentioning to her that chaos is, in fact, chaotic. Thus, the odds of things playing out exactly as Isadora wished weren't great. Chase did believe that she would have a bit of time to enjoy a heightened status as the bodies piled up. But, ultimately, everything and everyone, including her and her land of the dead, would be destroyed.

Chase knew that Zi saw these events as the closing act on creation, at least this rendition of it. Zi saw this as the necessary destruction of the current flawed age in order to bring about a new and better age.

Chase saw finality. Unlike others, Chase expected to die that day regardless of who won or lost. His singular goal was to engage the Elders and have them answer for the fate of his beloved. In fact, his life for the past three hundred years had been completely about holding the Circle Knight Elders accountable. Chase had dreamed of this day for centuries. Yet, he could hardly fathom that he'd reached the precipice of his goal. All he had to do now was to fall. It was so simple. "Surely, the twelve would be in attendance today of all days," Chase thought. When the Elders arrived he would engage them. Chase knew that he stood no chance against them, but he would speak his piece and the name of his beloved before he died. Their acts would be revealed before Heaven, Earth and Hell.

The Elders were not here. Chase reasoned that they'd found some means of cloaking themselves. Still, how could they allow Matasis and Isadora to proceed so far without intervening? The portal would be active momentarily but not a single alpha-level Circle Knight was in play.

Silver-haired Matasis stepped out of the command tent. As he surveyed the battle below he asked, "Chase, you were once one of them. So, tell me. What are they up to?"

From their camp located in the high ground of the north, Matasis and the other council members could see the entire field of combat.

Chase surveyed the field before answering, "I think they're holding their alphas back until we enter the field. Right now, it's just a fireworks show. They've mixed in most of their paranormal personnel with the regular troops in a full out assault from the west. Our combined forces from The Pit and Isadora's Oblivion are holding ground easily. From the south, their ships and planes fire munitions at the portal at the price of some of our workers. But, of course the Omni Portal remains unharmed, for it is indestructible."

Matasis grinned, "So, basically you're telling me that you don't know either."

Chase hesitated for a second as he tried to add context to something Zi had mentioned in passing. It was something she'd heard on the wind. Then, finally disregarding it, he simply nodded.

Matasis continued, "Oh, this is a rare day that Chase the Saint Killer, does not know something. But, then again, you're not particularly concerned with the outcome of the battle are you?"

Chase gave a half-nod conceding the point. He wanted to know why the Elders cast his beloved into The Pit. The stated reason was for the practice of witchcraft since Circle Knights are prohibited from the practice, but Chase never accepted this. Others had done as much but had not been punished so. He knew that the Elders were too intelligent to openly deem their relationship as unnatural. There had been others before Chase and his beloved, and yet he wondered... was there something they'd done differently? Were they too open with their love? If they had simply lived in the shadows, would his love still be here? The unanswered questions still burned within him all those years later.

"And, no sign of the Dream Box?" Matasis asked.

He had spared the girls in their youth mostly in exchange for Elisa's services. But, he also held out hope of finding this dream box. With the Dream Box in hand, he could destroy God's creation and use it to recreate the universe in his own image.

"Dream Box? You don't actually believe that it exists do you?" an incredulous Destry asked.

"There's a story that has spread from one dark lord to another that the Creator gave the other side something called a dream box. I've never seen it. If they've not used it by this point, I guess it stands to reason that it doesn't exist," Matasis said.

"So, no Elders, no Dream Box and not a single alpha level knight. Are you disappointed?" Chase asked.

Matasis laughed, "Certainly, I would have rather personally shed the blood of the Elders in battle, but I guess the lot of them are off somewhere serving each other last rites."

Down below, Destry's comrades signaled that they were done. Destry turned back to Matasis, "Showtime, boss-man."

Matasis called into the tent for the others to come out so that they could witness the beginning of the end. Chase was quietly stunned by the arrogance that Matasis showed. The demon did not entertain the thought that the Circle Knights might outsmart him in some way. At least he was concerned. The Elders weren't just going to let this be. Still, down below, the Omni Portal roared to life. Its roar was so mighty that the earth shook. The Omni Portal was shaped like a ring. It was sixty stories tall and the same in width. Its surface, when inactive, was stone-like in appearance. Once activated, it turned to bright and shining gold with streaks of silver. It was the same in thousands of locations. All of the portals were activated simultaneously. During its construction, the portal had traveled to each of these locations and then disappeared shortly after its technicians had captured their coordinates.

Almost immediately, figures formed inside the Omni Portal. The first beast through the portal was a Tambrin Tiger. The demon seed walked upright and had a head that looked much like a tiger's head. When it opened its mouth, a dark, dreadful mist spewed forth. The Tambrin Tiger consumed all who came into contact with the mist. Their flesh dissolved as the beast digested them externally. Several of Destry's mercenaries made the mistake of being too close to the portal when the beast appeared. They were no more.

From the eastern sky came a glowing golden arrow that struck the Tambrin Tiger in the head. The creature fell backwards and its killing mist withdrew within it.

"Ah, the Sisters are here. I figured they'd send them. Let us stain the fresh snow with their blood," Matasis crowed as he strutted through the ever increasing snowfall towards the battle field.

"It's harvest time", Isadora said. She flashed an evil grin and took flight.

Zi looked to Chase, "Care to place a wager, old friend?"

Chase smirked, "That's a fool's bet. If we're still here tomorrow, you win. If creation dies today, I win but you never have to pay off."

"I never said it was a good bet."

With that, Zi laughed and took to the wind. It should be noted that among their foes that day, Cil had the most respect for Zi. This was largely because Cil viewed Zi as the most humble of a vain lot. Like Chase, she recognized her own mortality despite the fact that she was not aging. However, unlike Chase, Zi realized that the future is an uncertain thing and that one should plan accordingly. Chase's predictive ability infected him with a level of arrogance – to a lesser degree than the demons, but more than Zi. His gift allowed him to see all the logical possibilities of a situation and to rank them in order of probability. As an event drew nearer, his predictive abilities became essentially flawless. Chase had figured out early on that Cil could see the future. He had the uncanny ability to analyze a thousand data points instantly and determine a course of action in nanoseconds. In all his years, Chase could not recall a time when his abilities had truly failed him. This accounted for his arrogance in battle. Zi, on the other hand, always assumed that something unexpected might happen and planned accordingly. This was the shred of humility that elevated her in Cil's eyes.

Poseidon's armada was stationed in a low Earth orbit awaiting his call to engage. He had weapons at this disposal that Destry and the others had never even dreamt of before. The spirits imprisoned in the crystals that hung around his neck were evidence of the effectiveness of their technological success. Still, Poseidon was a fan of the old ways. He wanted to satisfy his own personal bloodlust before he called in the big guns. For hundreds of thousands of years, he had lived the warrior's way. Even though he was an admiral, he still liked to get his hands dirty. He lusted for the kill. Like Chase, he'd hoped to encounter one of these Elders in hopes of repaying them for past transgressions. Poseidon sought retribution for being driven from the Earth along with the other gods and goddesses of his age. Adding insult to injury, one of these cursed half-breeds had taken up the golden bow of Athena. His wrath had been building since the day he left this cursed land, but he needed to wait just a little longer. He needed the Elders to show themselves before he sprang his trap from the heavens. Once the Elders were imprisoned, he would turn his attention to his Council of Nob associates. He deemed them fools. The armada in orbit was just one of many. His race had conquered countless star systems in many galaxies. They eagerly awaited the opportunity to use the Omni Portal to easily access other civilizations.

Chase's plan was not so grand. He would kill Cil. She was the Gatekeeper and a favorite of the Elders. If this did not provoke either the Elders or God to show themselves, at least he would have made his own pain known to all. But, how do you trap a woman who was as fast as lightning and could see the future? Chase had a plan.

# THE BOOK OF SARAH

# 22
# THE COST

*July, 1981 - North Hudson Bay, Canada*

*As the years stream by, I find that life is less about finding the right answers, than it is about asking the right questions. Energy spent chasing after answers to the wrong questions, can never be recaptured.*

Sarah and her sisters rode from the aircraft carrier towards the eastern shore of the island in the cargo bay of a large helicopter. Snow fell softly to the ground. Through the port window, they could see about one-third of the battlefield. In the distance towards the west, they could see flashes of light as shells fell upon the enemy's position. They cringed when they witnessed flashes of light cascading across the land and into the bay. They wanted to rush to the defense of the sailors and soldiers, but there was a plan.

Henri was also on the chopper. He spoke quietly to the sisters, "I know you ladies have got this, but I have my Red Guard and two legions offshore beneath the sea. I know we've played along with Matasis, but we have no intention of going quietly into the night if things go awry."

Cil smiled and glanced at Deborah. Cil knew that they were also there because of their interest in Deborah's well-being.

Henri conceded, "Well, yes, but that's a secondary matter. Now, isn't it?"

"Yes, it is. And, for that reason, I'm going to need to ask that you trust me when I ask you to stand down regardless of what you see."

Henri shook his head, "Okay, but I don't get it.

All four sisters were dressed in snow white thermal with their hair pulled back tight. This afforded a rare instance where one could see their common features, such as their cheekbones. Their beauty testified that they were indeed their mother's daughters.

Sarah went over strategy with Big Mike, Cil and Ruth Ann. Deborah paced back and forth. She talked a lot of trash and punched members of Rob's squad in the shoulders to get everyone hyped for battle.

The chopper hovered offshore in near-total darkness. Even the instrument panels were barely visible. From a high altitude, they watched for the signal. Then, the portal came to life.

Big Mike called to the pilot, "Okay, that's it. Take us down."

The back of the copter opened up and the men started pushing munitions payloads out into the night. Their chutes opened to guide them towards the eastern beach.

Sarah grabbed Deborah's arm , "Hey, remember. Leave Chase to me or Cil, okay?"

Deborah just smiled as she tied a metal staff to her back.

Ruth called out, "Look! They're already coming through the portal. It's one of those Tambrin Tigers."

"Hey, that's our cue!" Deborah shouted above the din.

She drew Athena's bow and released a golden energy arrow towards the Tambrin Tiger as she jumped out of the back of the helicopter.

A stunned Ruth looked at Cil and cried, "She can't fly!"

Cil responded, "So, I guess you better go get her!"

Ruth grabbed another of the metal staffs and jumped. Sarah glanced out of the side port just long enough to see that Deborah had hit her mark. The golden arrow lodged itself into the giant demon's head.

"How does she do that?" Sarah exclaimed.

Then she asked in a low voice, "Cil, what of Elisa? She's not here?"

"Is that a question? Set your sails and fret not about the wind, for that is wasted breath." Cil smiled and rose touching the cross beneath her garment, "Have faith, little sister."

Cil grabbed her staff in one hand and a thin metal one in the other before jumping into the chaos. Sarah gave Big Mike and the rest of Rob's crew a wide smile before illuminating and flying, staff in hand, out of the back of the craft.

Ruth had, indeed, caught Deborah as she went free-falling toward the eastern shore. They landed in a blue glow followed in quick succession by first Sarah and then Cil. Cil twirled her rod rapidly to create a cone of air and snow to cushion her landing. Upon landing each of the sisters tied a red flag to each of the staffs they carried and drove them into the icy snow. The blood red flags flapped in the western wind

Cil stepped between her sisters and pulled out her horn. She looked out across the beach towards the battlefield before placing the horn to her lips. Then, she blew louder than her sisters had ever heard her blow the sacred horn before. Three times it sounded. Each time, more wicked ones turned towards the East. Many of the demons within hearing range knew the sound of this horn all too well. Although Cil wanted to aid the forces in the west by drawing the attention of the demon hordes with the sound of her horn, announcing their presence with the horn was primarily for the benefit of the Council of Nob. Matasis and his compatriots would become enraged. Cil could use that anger to her benefit.

Ruth set a blue wall of energy across the beach to protect the special forces that would be landing after them. Then, the four sisters formed a battle square on the bluff overlooking the beach and girded themselves for the onslaught. Cil held her staff with two hands. Deborah removed her glistening Ebony Sword from its sheath. Ruth generated a glowing blue sword with rotating teeth like a chain saw. Sarah tossed her shades aside to reveal her eyes. They glowed brightly orange and red. In her hand, Sarah held a flaming sword of her own making that could burn through both flesh and spirit.

This was the close in combat they had trained for with Cousin Rob for all those years. Their goal was to clear the area of enemy combatants. A lot of these lesser demons ran about in this melee. Any one of these opportunistic creatures would jump at the chance to stab one of the sisters in the back. In blowing her horn, Cil drew the demons into the open.

As the first wave arrived, Cil called out a rotation, "Red."

Red signified a certain movement pattern much like commands called out within a Roman battle square more than a thousand years before. A large demon stood before Cil, with its mouth agape as it roared foulness into the air. As quickly as it had begun to roar, it fell silent. Its head landed in the snow.

Deborah made herself and her sword invisible. Then, she proceeded to make mincemeat of demons approaching from the rear. The enemy could not see Deborah, but her sisters knew exactly where she was. Her animated smack talk, as well as their years of training , let her sisters know exactly where she was at all times. The sisters crisscrossed the landscape in a well-rehearsed pattern.

Ruth shouted to Deborah, "You know they don't understand you, right?"

Sarah, laughing as her light dissipated the dark shadows that had gathered around her, replied, "And, you remember your sister is crazy, right?" She said this loudly enough for Deborah to hear as well.

Deborah cracked back, "You're just jealous because I'm more entertaining than you'll ever be."

After the initial wave, the sisters began to shift their square back and forth along the bluff. Their synchronized movements were a thing of beauty. It was as if they were all playing a song that only they knew. Just as when they played music together late into the night, they kept time with one another on the battlefield as well. They continued their dance until they'd cleared the area enough for Ruth to expand her protective shield. It now protected the beach and the bluff enough to set up a staging area. The barrier would keep out the majority of monsters, but it would give the troops a place to retreat to, if needed.

As Big Mike and the other Special Forces team descended from the sky, Cil turned to Sarah and said, "It's time."

Sarah took to the air alone. She ascended rapidly like a rocket shining ever brighter as she gained altitude.

Ruth asked, "She will be okay, right?"

Deborah replied quickly, "Sure she will be. Isn't she always?" Still Deborah added her own quiet prayer, "Godspeed, little sister."

Cil fought back the tears. Then, gathering herself, she called to Deborah and Ruth, "Alright. Their 'A' team will be here in just under sixty seconds. Remember, remember let's rope-a-dope these clowns."

Big Mike and his team climbed the bluff. They moved quickly inland to the predetermined high ground to provide sniper cover across the battlefield. The five positions were spread out over a couple of miles. Mike marched off to the western side of their location so that he might better assist Gabby and the other forces in the west whenever the opportunity arose. It was thought that the remnants of Rob's team were gifted enough to protect themselves even though each of them would be isolated in their own foxholes.

After Mike's team left, the entire Council of Nob gathered before the Sisters. There stood Matasis, Isadora, Chase, Zi, Destry and Poseidon.

Matasis mocked, "Oh, you bastard children of fallen angels, why do you struggle so hard?"

Matasis looked at Cil and nodded his head. In the next moment, Destry and Zi began a full on assault against Cil. First, Destry launched several mini-missiles from his armor towards Cil's feet and followed up with a disintegration beam. Both actions caused Cil to jump back just a bit. But, an opening was all that Zi needed. She reached towards the ground and, immediately, a giant wall of ever-growing ice rose around Cil. The ice enveloped her as it grew. Cil spun and swung against it only to have more ice take its place. The block of ice grew in height, width and depth until it became a small glacier sliding north along the bluff away from her sisters.

At the same time Cil was attacked, Isadora and Poseidon set their sights on Deborah.

The space god shouted, "Quickly, before she disappears again."

But, Isadora was already in action breathing black smoke from her mouth. The smoke behaved very much like iron filings around a magnet. Poseidon then lifted his trident towards the smoke-covered Deborah and hot bursts of energy streamed from its tips into the target obliterating her.

Isadora complained, "Oh, I so wanted to take that one home with me. She was spunky."

Poseidon, never missing an opportunity to speak ill of a "mortal" added his two cents, "Yes, a good court jester is hard to find."

Matasis and Chase turned their attention to Ruth. For this encounter, Matasis reverted to his original form. Long black wings sprung from his back and his face elongated horribly. His clawed feet burst through his boots and his hands became talons. Chase silently drew his sword and marched through the snow towards Ruth.

Matasis crowed, "What a shame that you will die, never truly knowing who or what you are. I'll do you this favor. Your Uncle Paul is not a descendant of an angel as you were led to believe. No, he's actually an angel... a cast out one. See, he was a part of the rebellion, just as I was and still am."

Matasis smiled wickedly and continued, "Now, though he is damned, he fights for your team. But, me? Well, I'm still working to tear all of this down, and if I can possess the Dream Box, I can start anew, building creation in my own image. So, where is it, darling?"

Ruth shook her head. She'd heard the prophecy, but she didn't know much about that. She left those matters to Cil as did her other sisters.

Matasis nodded in Ruth's direction signaling Chase to proceed. Chase became intangible and continued towards Ruth. He swung his sword as he marched through her protective veils. Stumbling, Ruth fell down into the snow. Suddenly, Ruth realized that Matasis saw her as the weak link. He had split the sisters up so that he could corner her for the information he wanted. This realization angered Ruth so much that she stood up and scowled at her opponents.

Ruth, who didn't curse, shouted, "Look, A-hole, I don't know who you think I am, or who you think I'm not, but I ain't telling you a darn thing."

With those words Ruth threw up her hands towards Chase, firing a series of bubbles at him. At first, Chase laughed. But, his laughter didn't last long. Chase soon discovered that these bubbles were not like the ones Ruth typically used. They were elastic and sticky. Even though he was in his intangible form, these bubbles had the effect of surrounding him in blue bubble gum.

Ruth launched herself through the air like a missile headed directly for Matasis. She hit him right in his midsection wrapping her arms around him and taking him down like a linebacker. Matasis dislodged Ruth just long enough to regain his balance. He gripped her in his talons trying to infect her with his spirit of deformity and disorder, but her personal shield held firm. Ruth formed a wedge of blue energy to free herself from Matasis. The demon then unleashed a beam of ethereal energy which Ruth fought to deflect. As she did, the snow and air around her blackened. Ruth didn't know what Matasis was doing, but she knew that it would not be good for her. So, she took to the air.

Ruth issued a series of three bubbles towards Matasis with the apparent intent of capturing him inside one of them. Matasis responded by opening his mouth and spawning three demonic minions, one for each bubble. This was what Ruth really wanted. Years earlier, Ruth and her sisters had noticed that when Matasis spawned a demon, he closed his eyes. As the demons were flying out of his mouth, Ruth was diving through the air towards Matasis. She collided with him midair delivering a blow so powerful that it drove him back to the ground.

Before Ruth could press her advantage, she felt a coldness that she'd never known before. It was Isadora swiping her hand down Ruth's back. The demon queen stared into Ruth's eyes, trying to absorb her essence. A soul snatch would have killed most Circle Knights. Ruth dropped to her knees. Poseidon followed up Isadora's move with a tremendous energy burst from his trident. The strike drove Ruth back and down into the permafrost.

Slightly up the coast, Zi, who had more respect for the sister's abilities than did her comrades, continued to pile ice onto Cil. She wasn't sure how much ice it would take to keep Cil imprisoned. So, she kept adding to her glacier. Suddenly, her second sense told her to duck. As she spun, she saw locks of her black hair fall onto the white snow. Zi immediately became mist riding the wind up and away from the attack.

Destry exclaimed, "What the heck?" as he rode his battle wagon skyward as well. He realized that Deborah was on the ground and he released a series of concussion bombs. The individual bombs were incredibly small, but the blasts they created were comparable to conventional bombs. While making his bombing run, Destry drifted a little too close to the glacier. When he did, Cil sprang from the ice and onto his chariot. Even though the chariot had its own force shield, Cil balanced herself atop the shield long enough to rattle off a series of blows before Destry was able to shake her off. His shield was state of the art alien technology, but still it flickered beneath Cil's blows. Destry saw that Cil could levitate by spinning her staff at supersonic speed. Destry sped off to the south to rejoin the other Council of Nob members.

Zi had been casting bolts of lightning down through the smoke at Deborah. Deborah returned golden arrows upward towards her. Neither could see the other, but they could sense one another. Zi shook her head as her teammate retreated without her.

She couldn't help call out, "That punk!"

Cil landed in a whirlwind down below pushing the smoke away just enough for all three women to see one another.

When Cil observed, Destry fleeing, she asked Zi, "So, that's who you aligned yourself with?"

"Pitiful isn't it?" Zi confessed.

Deborah said, "Elisa told us about how hard you had it growing up and how things got even worse once she was cast into The Pit. She also told us how the Elders hunted you. So, we get that you think the world is crap, but are you so into the whole destructive creation thing that you're willing to do this?"

Zi called down, "Look at the world. We're not heading to Hell. We're already there. The sooner we bring about Armageddon, the sooner we'll end all of this suffering. There is a certain kind of peace in such a death."

Deborah twisted her head and asked, "So, that's what you got from Bible Study three hundred years ago?"

"No, that's what I got from my life the last three hundred years." With those words Zi became mist again and left them.

Cil and Deborah shared a sad glance. Cil felt that if Zi had not been head of the cult she led that she might have walked away from all of this. It was almost as if she was doing this to save face with her followers. Or perhaps she wanted to support Chase in return for his kindness to her all those years ago.

Farther south along the beach, the other four Council of Nob members were taking turns trying to keep Ruth down. She kept getting up.

Chase complained, "You guys have had your turn. Let me put my blade in her and she'll stay down.

Isadora commented, "Hey, just wait a minute. You've killed your share."

Chase replied, "And?"

Poseidon chirped, "And, wait. This is the most interesting thing today. Honestly, I thought they'd put up a better fight. But, this one with the bubbles might be worth keeping alive to study."

Ruth stumbled to her feet as though she was drunk. Poseidon motioned to Isadora and Matasis to fire upon Ruth in unison with him. Ruth put up her hands but was blasted back onto the beach and into the frigid water. Their collective blast created a crater on the beach which the sea quickly filled. The four of them waited long moments as a couple of empty waves crashed the shore. On the third wave, Ruth washed ashore. The villains watched anxiously for a moment. They let out a collective gasp as Ruth rose to her hands and knees. Poseidon shook his head. He was truly impressed with a human for the first time in several thousand years. Poseidon was so impressed that he looked skyward to call down a capture team from his armada.

Before Poseidon could utter a word in his native tongue, Chase called out, "Wait..." At that moment, Chase realized the meaning of the phrase Zi had heard on the wind: rope-a-dope.

Destry rode toward them frantically shouting, "Cil and Deborah are free and headed this way."

Suddenly, a brightly-glowing missile came out of the western sky and hit the beach next to Ruth. Sarah had returned.

Without a word, Chase ran to the staging area that Ruth had shielded with one of her bubbles. First, he and his sword became intangible. He swung his blade against the barrier. The metal hit the blue field and stopped mid-air. The sword vibrated vigorously in his hand. He tried to stick his own hand through the blue wall. No matter how hard he tried, Chase could not breach the barrier. Chase knew that every Circle Knight was trained to keep one skill or one move secret from the world. At long last, he knew what Ruth's secret was. Her ability was adaptive. She had the ability to adapt her barriers to withstand any force or weapon she encountered. This little exercise of allowing the Council members to isolate her from her sisters was part of their plan. The show she'd just put on, as well as all the little skirmishes over the years, were making her invulnerable against their attacks.

"Rope-a-dope," Chase said to himself.

Chase realized that sticking with the rest of the Council would jeopardize his own agenda. So, he separated himself from the group. Chase knew that, if he played his cards right, his own secret ability would win the day for him.

Poseidon ripped two of the crystals from his neck and tossed them into the sea behind the two sisters. Within moments one sprung up as a leviathan and the other as a kraken. The size of the creatures was breathtaking. Mortals within sight of the bay lost heart at the sight of them. The kraken reached ashore wrapping both Ruth and Sarah in its tentacles and dragging them down below the surface. The leviathan breached the surface before it dived in after them. Cil and Deborah arrived on the scene as their younger sisters were being dragged down.

Isadora turned to Poseidon and asked, "I thought you killed her?"

"Deborah the Deceiver is a fitting name, then. We shall make sure that it is on her tombstone."

Poseidon tilted his trident towards Deborah and Cil and a flood of water flowed from it like a mighty river. Deborah stretched out her hands, palms up, as her eyes rolled back in her head. The ground beneath the snow rose up to create an earthen wall that steered the rushing waters to the sea. Deborah then replicated herself. Multiple images of her formed all around the beach.

Isadora called up Ammit, a monster from the underworld. The immortal beast had the head of a crocodile and the body of a lion. He was the size of an elephant. Ammit was a well-known consumer of bodies and souls. Around his neck was a mane of vipers.

Cil moved away to draw the beast toward herself. When Ammit opened his mouth, a rush of air, snow, demons, walking dead, and mortals were sucked into his jowls. Cil spun her staff faster and faster until a portal to The Pit opened up.

The abomination cackled. It had originated from one of the lower levels of The Pit and had no fear of it. If Cil sent him back there, he would return with two more like himself. Cil turned to her left and created a second portal into The Pit before the first one could dissipate. She spun her staff back and forth between the two ever faster.

Then, she said the words just as her father had taught her, "In the name of the Almighty, potest albeit!" The beast was pulled apart between the two gates Cil had opened.

Cil turned to Isadora and asked her, "Do you have any more servants you'd like sent back to Hell? We're running a two for one special today."

As the day was fading, lights flickered beneath the turbulent sea. A bright light, the color of the sun rose from the water into the sky like a beacon and a horrific boom echoed across the island. In the next moment, Sarah and Ruth erupted from the boiling water into the air.

Poseidon's mouth dropped open. Pieces of his monsters floated on the water's surface. He looked skyward and attempted to call down air strikes from his armada. He called to them three times. Nothing. Then, a shadow passed over the eastern beach and a deafening sound like the horns of a thousand tankers pulling into port at once rolled over the entire island. Poseidon knew that sound was the imminent impact siren. Still, he did not believe what he feared. He looked to the west and saw his smoldering fleet, ship after ship, descending from the sky like rain. The first one landed with a crash that shook the entire island. The ground trembled with the impact of each subsequent ship.

Deborah commented to Isadora, "I think you made my little sister upset. That was not a good move. In fact, I think you've made them both a bit mad."

A flash of blinding light erupted from Sarah's eyes. The beam was so bright that it blinded any who gazed upon it. The target was Destry's sky chariot. The chariot, despite its force shield, was sliced it in half. Destry barely managed to escape and jetted behind his comrades where he tried to hide from Sarah.

All eight remaining images of Deborah, who had been quite busy playing a deadly game of cat and mouse with Matasis and the space god, jumped up and down and shouted, "Them my sisters!"

Shaken, Poseidon made a beeline through the air to the sea. He reverted to the first tactic he'd learned as a child nearly a million years ago. He created a tidal wave. By the time it reached shore, it was at least twenty stories tall. Ruth lifted up her right hand and created a blue wall that held the building wave back. As she did, the sky grew dark in the west. It was Zi. In her short absence, she had conjured not one, but two, category four tornados. Each was headed towards the beach. Several of the soldiers were in their path. Cil raced off to carry them to safety.

Ruth didn't say a word. She stretched out her left hand and created a second barrier to the west that reached from the ground to the clouds. It would have been easier to divert the tornadoes to the south, but the allied fleet was in that direction. Instead, Ruth steered the twisters to the north. She focused completely on the task at hand. There was no room for error. Sarah and Deborah kept Matasis, Isadora, and the undead minions away from Ruth. A single bead of sweat rolled down Ruth's forehead to the tip of her nose and froze there. At last, the storms passed to the north. The tidal wave waters crested and flowed back into the sea.

Destry couldn't help but utter, "My God...," before fleeing inland.

Cil returned to the beach and they readied for the next round with their opponents. The sisters knew that Zi could spin up tornados with a lot less effort than it took Ruth to divert them. One of them would need to shut Zi down quickly. Plus, Chase the Saint Killer, who by name and record was the deadliest of their opponents, was AWOL.

Suddenly, over the cresting wave, the sisters saw a brown and gold winged beast soaring across the sky. A lone figure rode the beast. They swept to the south before turning north and descending to the beach. The sisters knew before the dragon landed that its rider was a friend rather than a foe.

"Hello, Ladies. Am I late?" the rider said before dismounting.

Collectively, the sisters said, "Elisa!"

Elisa was dressed in black with black gloves and a black cape with a reflective lining. She had escaped the trap laid for her by Matasis and crew, in part, by causing them to see what she wanted them to see. Also, she had never revealed that she didn't need a reflective surface when only teleporting herself. Keeping up the pretense across the centuries was a burden at times, but it did, as she imagined it would one day, save her life. She smiled at the girls before getting down to business.

"First off, since all our cards are on the table, let's dispense with the charades. Just call me 'Grandma'. Secondly, see that arrogant, soul-stealing heifer over there with her mouth hanging open?" Elisa said as she pointed at Isadora, "See, that's the face you make when you realize that you underestimated your opponent. You don't ever want to have that face. Thirdly, I'll take care of Zi. I owe her that."

Elisa spoke softly into her dragon's ear as she pointed to the demons, monsters and zombies before smacking her on the side and saying loudly, "Go girl!"

The dragon took to the air again and incinerating the creatures as they ran amok.

Elisa turned to her granddaughters and said, "Meet me at the Omni Portal when you're done. I've got some cleaning up to do."

With those words Elisa marched off towards the west and disappeared into the falling snow.

Ruth motioned towards the sea before asking Sarah, "So where is he?"

"Right there, on the sea floor," Sarah said. She pointed.

Ruth looked back at Cil and Deborah, "You can wait here behind the barrier until we get back, if you like. It won't take long."

Deborah laughed at the inference in Ruth's words.

Ruth turned towards the water and, after closing her eyes briefly, stretched out her hands. Moving her arms in a parting motion, the waters parted down to the bay floor revealing an awestruck Poseidon standing on the sea floor about one mile from shore. His red and blue skin made the giant easy to spot in the valley between the two walls of water. Sarah glided in and landed about twenty yards in front of the space god. Sarah smiled, but it was not friendly. She removed a piece of paper sealed in a thin blue film from her waist. Sarah unrolled the document and read, "To the space alien known as Poseidon, it has been declared by the Circle Knight Elders…"

"What is this?" an incredulous Poseidon asked.

As Sarah lifted her right hand towards the heavens she replied, "You really don't know what this is?"

She twisted her extended hand and every falling snowflake across the island became a burning coal that ignited any wicked spirit they fell upon.

Poseidon exclaimed, "Am I to be executed like some common criminal?"

"Oh, no," Sarah said as she walked towards Poseidon, "you're worse than a common criminal. But, know this, while I could have struck you down from a hundred miles away, I chose not to. Because before your death I wanted to offer you an opportunity to understand something of how the countless beings you have slaughtered felt when you took their lives and, in many cases, their entire world as well. No, you do not deserve a quick death from afar. And even today is not the justice you deserve, but that Day of Judgment awaits you as well."

Sarah's flaming sword then appeared in her hands again as it had when she landed on this island. Poseidon shot at her with every spectrum of energy weapon he possessed, but none of them were as powerful as the energy pent up within Sarah. Then, she was upon the giant. He swung with his right hand above her head. She countered with her flaming red hot sword across his abdomen. A bright red and blue light began to beam out of the gash, followed by a glowing jelly like substance. Poseidon stumbled back a step, but before he could take a second step back, Sarah sprang into the air spinning counter-clockwise. As she did, a flaming silver dagger appeared in her right hand. She drove it through the execution decree and into the forehead of the space god. Poseidon fell backwards landing on the sea floor with a thud.

Sarah glanced up at Ruth before blasting into the sky and back to shore. Ruth released the waters so they washed over Poseidon. When Sarah landed, the two sisters turned to see fire falling like snow across the island and the resulting chaos. The mortals took a moment to realize that the fire would not burn their flesh although it was a hazard to their clothing.

Sarah turned to Ruth and said, "Your turn."

Destry and his ilk had a record of trying to take their opponent down with them when they realized that their cause was lost. Destry had no problem with taking out half the island in any death cry that might be awaiting him. For the moment, although he realized that the tide had turned, he hadn't fully given up on the battle. He needed to get away from the beach so he could consider his options. Destry could call in reinforcements from the war camp deep in the Amazon jungle. Using alien technology, he would have a hundred well-armed, chaos-hungry soldiers there in twenty minutes. He had supplied some of the technicians from the camp to support starting up the Omni Portal, but had held back contributing any regular troops. He didn't send more troops because Poseidon's armada had been floating in space above the island. His men would have been sitting ducks. Poseidon had promised that the Destry could work as mercenaries in his global conquests once the Portal was done, but Destry never trusted Poseidon.

The good news was that the fire fall Sarah had created incinerated many of the roaming flesh-hungry abominations that had begun to assault him when he left the beach. On the downside, he wasn't sure how much longer his battle armor would hold up against the firestorm. It didn't burn his skin and seemed to be mostly for demons, but it was causing his armor to peel. Dark magic had been a used in its creation.

Destry's other option was to leave. With a tailwind, his battle suit could get him nearly two hundred miles south. He could blend in for a while until the other Destry caught up with him and returned him to their camp to stand before the tribunal. According to Destry law, retreat was the only offense punishable by death. Still, that was a better option to him than to be killed by a bunch of women. For Destry, that was worse than any possible outcome.

Ruth caught up with Destry near the middle of the island. He was walking west and mumbling to himself as the occasional bullet from one of the Special Forces snipers pinged against his fading armor. Ruth landed right in front of Destry stopping him dead in his tracks. Nervously, Ruth removed the Elders decree from her waist and began to read it to Destry.

Destry shook his head, "You can't be serious? You mean to tell me the ghosts in the mist sent shrinking violet out here to execute me? Why can't those yellow-bellied cowards step out from behind the veil and do it themselves? I can't have this. My entire legacy will be stricken from our books if I let this go down like this."

Ruth tried to interject, "Actually, this decree is for the Destry, plural…"

"What? Look, sweet britches, I actually think I could take you, but I'd rather not risk it the way things have been going here the last few minutes. So, I'm pressing this here button and taking out me, you, the trigger happy fellas on the hill over there and half this island with me. Enjoy the ride, Senorita!"

Destry had initiated the countdown on an alien explosive device that had the destructive effect of a nuclear weapon without the residual radiation. Ruth knew that she had about five seconds before the device detonated. She stretched out her hands towards Destry, releasing bubble after bubble, each of which enveloped him. Right before the blast, Destry's expression turned from jovial to disappointment. The energy from the explosion shone like a new blue star through Ruth's bubbles. Ruth continued to push against the blast force as pressure continued to increase against her, but she refused to give up. Finally, it stabilized and Ruth sent the small new star up into sky where it belonged.

Further south on the island, Elisa caught up with her protégé.

She called out to her, "Zi!"

Zi squatted in the snow as she had as the little girl Elisa took in so long ago. But, this was a far different place, both physically and spiritually. Perhaps, it was not so different for Zi emotionally. As the fire flakes continued to fall around Zi, electricity arced from her into the ground or into any hostile beings with designs on her. Zi looked at her former mentor through her tears. Black mascara streaked her face.

Zi laughed a bit, "So you are here. I knew you weren't dead, but I didn't say anything."

"I know."

"But if you're here, I know you have a plan to shut that damn thing down. You always have a plan."

"No, not always."

"Like when you killed that overseer?"

"Yes, those five minutes of anger took me away from you when you needed me most. Please forgive me."

Zi asked, "Forgive you? How could you not avenge your daughter?"

"You may have heard but you still don't understand. When I marched out to his shack, I knew that I was going to kill him. He was packed and ready to leave. And, yet, I proceeded, even though I'd sworn as a Knight not to take personal vengeance. I knew the law and that the Elders would judge me and banish me to The Pit. I knew all these things, but I didn't care. I put my anger before you, Chase, and being a part of my own daughter's life. In giving in to my anger, I failed you all."

"I'm tired, Elisa."

"I know."

With tears rolling down her face, Elisa walked over to Zi and pulled her up from the ground to embrace her inside of her cape. She held Zi for long moments. Then, Elisa began to glow brightly and Zi appeared to vanish within her.

Elisa looked over her shoulder to see four giants step through the portal.

She sighed, "Oh, no."

These four giants were the Four Pillars. They were some of the earliest predators in the universe. Believed to be indestructible, they were known for drinking the life out of every planet they visited. When Elisa saw them, she sent a telepathic message to all military personnel to abandon the island. Then, she flew towards the portal.

Meanwhile, Ruth and Sarah confronted Matasis and Isadora in an icy plain. Many of the demons that were not outright destroyed by Sarah's fire fall were driven back into the Omni Portal. Even those that persisted, like Matasis and Isadora, grew tired of their flesh burning and sought refuge. There was one small patch of ice beneath small decaying building where the flaming snow did not fall. Matasis and Isadora hid there with other trapped demons.

Matasis cried, "There is no need to continue this battle. The deed is done. So, why do you persist?"

Engulfed in flames, Sarah smiled back, "Is it?"

"Be gone, mortal. Your riddles bore me. Shortly, your world will be no more and I'll be here to witness it," Isadora ranted from the only patch of land on the island free from Sarah's fire fall.

Sarah simply smiled. She placed her hands on her hips and nodded at Ruth Ann. Ruth removed two rolled-up decrees from her waistband.

Ruth read, "To the spirit currently known as Matasis, it has been declared by the Circle Knight Elders that you shall be imprisoned until the Day of Judgment."

Matasis smirked, "What? None of you has the power to bind me."

"So you say, but our daddy did." Ruth replied.

"And, does," Sarah continued, "Buried beneath your feet is a box containing my our father's Bible along with several other items he carried with him whenever he performed an exorcism. Though he may be gone in body, his spirit still remains in those cherished items he in battle and in prayer and in us his children. We are bound to our father by a love that is foreign to you and beyond your comprehension. The love that he had for us his children, made even more perfect because it was a love he chose, a love of sacrifice, which fills us with his spirit so that we might speak and act on his behalf even more so than when he was alive. Thus…"

Then Ruth and Sarah spoke collectively as Ruth raised their father's prayer box into the air, "In the name of the Holy One, we bind you Matasis to this case hidden from long ago, that you may be contained there in."

Matasis could feel the effects of their decree almost immediately.

He cursed the sisters openly, "Damn you!"

Matasis' form became as vapor and he transitioned to the box sitting on the blue pillar Ruth had created. Matasis's face now adorned the lid and sides of the box and his ghoulish screams could be heard across the frozen land.

Ruth and Sarah turned to Isadora.

Before they could utter a word, the Queen of the Dead exclaimed, "Hey, I'm out of here. I can sit on my throne and just wait for the dead to roll in when the dust settles."

Isadora vanished in a puff of smoke as she returned to Oblivion.

"No, that heifer didn't," Ruth said.

Sarah answered, "Yes, she did. So, we're gonna need to go get her when we're done here. That's going to be a mess."

Feeling the ground tremble, the two sisters turned towards its source just moments before each heard Elisa's voice in their consciousness. It was the Pillars and with each step they took the Earth shook.

Evacuation helicopters rushed to the island from every direction, even as the giants marched into position. They were unstoppable. One faced the north, another south, another east and the other the west. The sisters scurried about trying to clear the area so that they could use their own gifts more fully.

As they tried to impede the progress of the primeval forces visited upon the Earth, Matasis laughed, "Foolish, foolish mortals, it's over. Save your breath and ready yourselves for death. Where are your Elders? Where is your God?"

Hearing his words from some distance away, Cil said into the wind for those with an ear to hear, "For those who love life and others more than themselves, God is within."

Chase could not hear Cil. He continued to wonder. He had done all of this to draw out the Elders or The Almighty One to answer for what had so arbitrarily been taken away from him. Chase had no problem with the world ending for his world had ended over two hundred years ago. But, he couldn't have it happen before he had his day. In the midst of the chaos, Chase saw an opportunity. It wasn't what he hoped for, but it was likely his best chance. As three of the sisters and Elisa struggled against the Pillars, Chase approached Deborah as she rushed to join the others.

Deborah drew her sword eager for a chance at redemption.

Chase taunted, "So, what are you going to do with that against me? Send me one of your sisters." He said this to provoke her

Deborah could have created a thousand different images of herself and escaped to assist her sisters against the Pillars. But, an old shame burned within her. She couldn't just walk away even though each of her sisters had asked her not to take Chase on. She told herself that by engaging Chase, she was helping her sisters' focus on the Four Pillars.

She took an on guard position and spoke sternly to the Saint Killer, "Come on, Chase. Let's do this."

Chase removed his sword, "Well, if you insist."

Deborah and her ebony sword became invisible. Chase and she attempted a first strike against one another. There was difficulty in this battle for both sides. Chase was intangible most of the time solidifying only when impact was imminent for his blade or when his blade was inside of an opponent. Deborah was invisible and possessed an uncanny sixth sense. However, Chase had the advantage of his predictive abilities which was common knowledge among the knights. He had an ability of perception that was well beyond that of any of his opponents. He also held a secret that only he and some of his victims came to know of in their dying moments.

Chase and Deborah parried back and forth in a close contest. Deborah made blind strikes and moves that even impressed Chase. Chase played the role of would be assassin although he had no intention of actually killing Deborah. But, he did draw blood on three separate thrusts. Chase raised the ante by knocking Deborah to the ground and grabbing her ponytail.

He confessed, "Child, I could always see you on a plane you know nothing of."

A bruised and tattered Deborah became visible. Just as Chase pulled back his sword to cut her head off, a blur passed before of him pulling Deborah away. He was left with a handful of dark hair. It was Cil, the one who the Elders, God, and all the heavens loved so much. Chase could not have asked for more in his dark quest. This is how you defeat a superfast woman who can see the future. You limit her choices. With a bloodied Deborah laying behind her on the edge of a high bluff and the Four Pillars positioning themselves at the Geo-Magnetic North Pole to end the world, Cil had few choices. She needed to dispatch of Chase quickly but she also needed to protect her injured sister. The first condition placed a time constraint on her, the latter, a positional limitation. Chase believed those limitations plus his intangibility and predictive powers put him on even footing with Cil. His last trick would surely give him the undisputed advantage against Cil. Thus, he would kill a beloved of Heaven or he would force the Elders or the One they serve to intervene. Chase was assured a win.

Chase proclaimed, "Cil, behold your death."

Chase played his final card which living being had ever seen. The assassin became invisible and silent, reflecting neither light nor sound. This ability was, in part, how he had been such a successful assassin. He could come for his victims like a thief in the night. The intangible assassin could not walk the stars or from one age to the next like Akina, but what he could do was to unhinge himself ever so slightly from this dimension so that he might disappear from your left only to reappear to your right an instant later.

Cil countered by closing her eyes. She closed them so that her eyes would not deceive her from a future she knew to be. Cil seemed to be performing some sort of shadow boxing for the martial arts against her invisible foe.

As she countered his every blow Cil said, "The flesh that you see is not me, but rather I am the sum of the light that I have reflected back to the universe. Thus, no stroke of the sword can diminish who I am. But, what about you? Brother, consider as you fall to the snow below returning to us with your last breath."

Chase laughed, "The fanatic 'till the end, eh Lucille?"

The two of them had battled to a point where Cil was standing almost directly in front of the injured Deborah. Deborah stood and pulled back her bow, waiting for the moment when her intuition would tell her to fire her arrow so it would pierce Chase when he became tangible, but her fear for her sister's life froze her in doubt. Deborah stood on the edge of the bluff like a statue as Cil battled in front of her. Cil trusted the vision she'd been given all those years before.

Each parry and counter move was directed not by sight, but by what she knew to be true. Their blows were furious as each rushed to what would be. Sarah could see the battle from her position out of the corner of her eye. She knew that Chase was the toughest of opponents, but she'd never seen Cil lose a battle. No one had. Therefore, the next few moments were utterly surreal. In lightening quickness, Cil leaned to her right in front of Deborah and then an instant later, redness appeared on Cil's white top.

An angry and teary Chase made himself visible again and tangible enough to put his raised foot against Cil to push her off of his blade and over the bluff, as he called out, "May the heavens take note of this day."

Deborah fell to her knees and screamed, "No!" She stretched out her hand to where Cil had been standing.

In an instant, light flashed behind Chase and Cil reappeared, unharmed, and with the Ebony blade in her hand. She drove the blade into Chase's back.

Chase gasped and looked back in confusion as he fell over the bluff into the snow drift below. Chase cried out to heaven as he fell.

Matasis, who had been watching these events at a distance from his prison, was struck with a realization.

He exclaimed "She is the Dream Box!"

Indeed, she was.

Cil reached down to Deborah and pulled her to her feet.

"Lord, in Heaven!" Sarah cried.

For two full breaths, Elisa floated frozen high above the scene. In the third breath, she called to her grandchildren in a halting voice, "Here, girls, we need to deal with this now."

Elisa looked at each of her babies. Her eyes glistened and she forced a smile as she fought to keep her composure.

"Okay, ladies, do we turn Sarah loose on these four giant guys and see what happens?"

Ruth shook her head, "I don't know that I can contain that that kind of energy. If even a tenth of that energy gets past me, all life on earth will be destroyed."

Sarah nodded in agreement, "We have got to have a better option than that."

Elisa replied back, "There may be another way. I don't know if you ladies truly understand who you are and what your role is in this life—one to lead, one to create, one to destroy and one to protect. There is nothing that you cannot do together if each of you will give yourselves fully over to your purpose. But you must be willing to sacrifice to become who you were meant to be."

Each of the four giants opened their own unique orifice to consume the energies of the Earth. Light emanated from them. The four sisters joined hands on the snowy ground in the middle of the four giants. They let go of all earthly concerns, even for their own lives, and allowed the power that had been given to them to flow freely. They trusted the spirit within. The sisters began to glow and a pillar of light rose from their circle to the heavens above. For the briefest of moments, these four orphaned girls took on their true inheritance. They glowed brightly and time seemed to stop as the beam of light arced from them into the sky above. It was as though the world began to revolve around that beam of light, faster and faster. First, the snow and dust around the sisters began to twirl. Then, the whirlwind expanded. It grew wider and wider until it began to engulf the four stone pillars. As the light and wind reached the four ancient creatures, their stony flesh crumbled to dust and swirled in the whirlwind as well. For billions of years they'd roamed the universe consuming heavenly bodies. On this day they returned to dust.

The sisters gave each other a hug then quickly turned their attention to the Omni Portal. Ruth had tried to block it. Since it was an inter-dimensional portal, her barrier against the face of the portal was not very effective. Sarah's firestorm was largely effective against the demons, but was ineffective against the portal itself.

Deborah, still in a good deal of pain asked, "Can we do what we just did to get rid of this thing, too?"

Elisa smiled and said to them as she levitated once more, "No, that only works against living things."

"So, how do we destroy the portal?" Ruth asked.

"We don't. That was never the plan," Elisa replied, "If we do that, in a hundred years some other demon will rebuild it. See, this portal and its various entry points all lead to the same place. So will any new such portals. It is the unholy grail of universal and inter-dimensional travel. All Omni Portals, past present and future, are forever linked across time and space. In that dilemma, is an opportunity."

Elisa approached the top of the Omni Portal.

Sarah became distraught, "Grandma Elisa, what are you doing?"

Elisa motioned to Sarah and the others, "No, stay there. This is something only I can do."

Elisa said to her granddaughters, "It's alright. Really, it is. If I remain, they'll hunt for me without ceasing until the true End of Days. Besides, this way I take my last secret with me."

Atop the portal, the wind rippled Elisa's black cape. Her arms, now bare, revealed the self-inflicted scars collected since she first entered The Pit. The marks revealed how she had hurt herself over the years so that she might channel her anger and remember her humanity and not hurt others.

Elisa looked to heaven and made her final petition, "Lord, I know I've let you down before, many, many times. But if you will but restore to me, here today, the power of my youth, which you gave to me, I will follow after you Lord, with all that I am."

Elisa stretched out her hand towards the sea behind the portal. The water began to swirl slowly. Soon, it became a whirlpool. As the waters swirled faster and faster, the waters rose up from the sea bed and arched towards the Omni Portal like a cyclone spawned from the ocean. As the sea rose up to meet the giant portal, several beams of sunlight cut through the cloudy sky to shine on Elisa one last time. Those last rays of light brought a peace to Elisa's face that she'd not known in three hundred years.

As the spinning sea drew near the portal and Elisa, the sisters could see that she was not only raising the sea, but that she was also holding back the effects of her destination from our world. Everything that was pulled into Elisa's watery portal disappeared from sight once it crossed the event horizon of the portal. She had created a window to a black hole, but held back its full fury balancing it on the edge of the point of no return.

Darkness crept over half the sky as Elisa's water passageway moved over the Omni Portal. What wasn't blotted out by the proceeding darkness was warped in appearance. Any light that fell upon Elisa's creation, bent and fractured under the pull of gravity, succumbed until the darkness eclipsed the Omni Portal and Elisa herself. Their images elongated as they were consumed. Finally, the darkness lifted and the tower of water retreated into the sea.

It is widely believed that to be consumed by a black hole is to be torn apart. Elisa, despite her power, would be subject to this same fate. For several long moments, the sisters stood in silence.

After giving her sisters a comforting hug, Cil said, "Come on. Let's finish up. Call Mavis over to see about Deborah."

Sarah turned off the fireworks. At that moment, she so wanted to revert fully to human so she might cry and feel the snow on her face, there was still work to be done. Such was the price of her gift and her glorified state.

As the four sisters went about the business of riding the island of any remaining demons and monsters, Ruth came upon Big Mike kneeling in the snow in front of a stone statue. Ruth was puzzled at first. She walked around towards the front of the stone object and covered her mouth in horror. Gabby had been turned to stone by Isadora's sorcery. Ruth immediately ran to the stone statue and embraced it screaming for Gabby to awaken. She collapsed into the snow alongside Big Mike and wept.

Ruth stood up and stared up into the heavens, calling "Lord, Lord…Please."

Ruth she stumbled around in the snow and her pleas became shouts as she screamed into the sky above. Sarah, who had taken to the air searching for stray combatants, landed beside her sister. Sarah embraced her. She simply held her until Ruth's wailing subsided.

When she calmed down, Ruth wrapped Gabriella in a blue shell and carried her with Big Mike back to the staging area where the sisters first landed. There, she and Sarah found Cil, and Deborah. Upon seeing Gabriella, the two older sisters gasped. The four of them consoled each other and Big Mike as best they could.

Moments later they were interrupted by armed services personnel wanting to debrief. A tearful Cil explained to the officers that she and her sisters still had one more task. The sisters had a warrant to capture Isadora and a decree to intern her permanently. The problem with executing either was that Isadora had escaped back to her own realm. Since time does not flow evenly between her world and ours, Isadora had what would equate to weeks to prepare for the sisters arrival. She knew they'd come after her.

For Ruth, Gabriella's death and the pursuit of her killer was transformative. It was as if Gabriella was her alter ego who could be strong when she couldn't. With Gabriella gone, Ruth took on the mantle that Gabriella had tried all those years to place on her. She stood in silence waiting for Cil to open a portal from which they could enter Isadora's kingdom. Ruth's face displayed absolute resolve that had not been seen before.

As Cil twirled her staff to open the dimensional doorway, the communications officer asked Cil, "Ms. Johnson, the admiral wants to know what you intend to do about this dragon sitting on his flight deck?"

Cil, looking back over her shoulder, answered quickly, "Tell him, that we'll take care of it as soon as we get back."

The portal opened and the sisters stepped through it. The glowing rip in time and space disappeared. The handful of service men standing there looked at each other in quiet bewilderment wondering what to do next.

# SACRIFICES • Alan D. Jones

# 23
# OBLIVION

*Isadora's Particular Corner of Hell.*

Four Angels fell from the sky into the pit of darkness. Each landed separate from the others in a corner of her own.

Cil, the oldest, realized immediately that their nemesis Isadora, Queen of the Dead, had managed to separate the sisters as they exited the portal into her world. Cil had opened the portal so they could come to the dimension of the damned. The sisters came to this world to capture the soul thief so that she could no longer visit her special brand of evil upon the living or the dead.

Being dropped in the middle of nowhere, separated from her sisters, was not part of the plan. Yet, Cil was not lost. Her sixth sense always lead her to her objective. Finding Isadora's palace would not be a problem for her. However, notifying her sisters of her whereabouts and how to find Isadora's palace would be a challenge.

Death was all around Cil. Isadora's hell hounds perpetually gnawed on the remains of corpses that were piled into enormous heaps. Cil crossed a valley of wailing souls to a blood-drenched road. Those wailing were the not-yet-dead souls Isadora had snatched. She fed off their suffering as they passed their last days in her realm. She relished in their despair. There are countless evils in the universe of which we are mercifully unaware. Tomorrow there will be more than today. But, Cil vowed that she would make sure that Isadora was no longer in that number.

The hell hounds caught Cil's scent and descended from the hills of rotting flesh to pursue a fresh kill. Cil allowed them to draw close, close enough for her to smell their putrid breath. When they pounced, Cil struck each one down with a quickness only the blessed would understand. She'd have to slay many more before she reached Isadora's palace, but she didn't mind. The long, hard road allowed her to leave a trail that her sisters could easily follow. She took two bones from the hounds and rubbed them together hard and fast enough to set one of the piles of flesh ablaze. This was her first marker.

Deborah descended into this nightmare world in the midst of chaos and madness, just as she had during her troubled days in the waking world. Many days in the psych ward on Grady Hospital's eighth floor, she knew with all her heart that God had forsaken her. Those days of inconsolable sadness and weariness when she wanted to abandon this life had prepared her for this day. And yet, she was unprepared for this.

"Deborah," the voice said.

"Mama? What are you doing here?"

"Baby, I fought it as long as I could, but I was bound for this hell from the day I was born, just as much as you are," said the whispery Lola Few, twenty years gone.

"Mama, I got to go. I've got things to do."

"What and leave me here alone?"

"Mama, you have haunted me for twenty years and for twenty years I have allowed it. But you never cared for me or any of us, for that matter. You never cooked for us, never wiped a nose or a single tear. The only time you ever came around was when you needed something. We all knew to hide our piggybanks whenever you were in town. Cil, Sarah and I figured you out for the most part, but poor little Ruth would still run to you despite how mean you'd been to her the time before. It was sickening. And, what's worse is that I used to blame Daddy for not being able to make you love him. But I realize now, that the only person you have ever loved has been yourself. So, it ends today – the guilt, the 'what could have beens, and the sadness. I know that the pain will remain with me in different ways, but it will transition in time and life will fill the void that you have caused. Your madness will not be my madness. You made your choices and now I'm making mine. I couldn't carry you in life. So, why would I dare try to carry you in death? Goodbye, Mama."

"I just wanted someone to love me. Is that so wrong?"

"That's right, Mama. Turn it around. You're a real piece of work. Even in death, you're still the master manipulator. My poor daddy."

"Baby, how can you say such things to me?"

"Yes, that's been my question to you for my whole life. And now it's your turn to ask the questions."

Deborah walked out from the shadow into which she had materialized and into a smoky plain filled with all manner of demonic beast. She could have cloaked herself in invisibility but, at that moment, she felt like fighting. She's always been a fighter. Now, she accepted it like never before. She cried as she fought. She released her pain into the darkness of her enemies. Her innate intuition showed her the way she must go and the pillars of smoke rising from the fires Cil lit confirmed the way and the truth she'd found.

Hopeless souls cried out as far as the eye could see. In the middle of them it all, at the bottom of that pit Ruth Ann was buried beneath countless number of bodies struggling against one another for higher ground. Their hands grabbed and pulled at Ruth as though she was the last life boat on a sinking ship. Perhaps, she was. The bodies were densely packed that Ruth found it hard to breathe. She was so deeply immersed in that sea of longing that she could barely tell up from down. What started out as a panic attack quickly became something worse. At the bottom of the lightless pit, buried beneath agonizing hopeless loss, Ruth thought for a moment how easy it would be to simply give up and join those who had gone before her. In the midst of her despair, she heard a whisper in her ear.

It was Gabriella's voice, "Get up." Ruth's body began to glow and the light within her illuminated all that which was around her. A blue shield formed around her and then, slowly, she began to move that blue cylinder upwards. She gained more and more speed as she rose.

When she reached the top of the heap, Ruth saw that The Pit was far beneath the surface. She refused to leave these lost souls clawing and scratching against one another in eternal torment. This was not of their creator's plan for them. Yet, they found themselves in this living hell created by a demigod who'd set herself up as God in this forsaken land. Ruth closed her eyes for a moment to focus her energy. When she opened them again, they blazed with a bright blue light.

Ruth stretched out her arms. The ground shook and the caverns rumbled. A bead of sweat formed on her forehead. Her eyes flickered and desperate hands fell from the pit walls. Isadora's entire hellhole began to elevate. Ruth spun around slowly with her face turned skyward as she'd done so often as a little girl, and sometimes still as a grown woman. Ruth spun and the whole world of these forsaken ones spun with her and slowly ascended with her. After several rotations, Ruth's ark broke through the ground above. Ruth gently turned the mountain-sized bowl she'd raised from the grave on its side. The prisoners stumbled out and dashed in every direction. Not one stopped to thank her. Ruth shed a tear, not for herself, but for those lost souls. Ruth took a deep breath. She thought, "At least these were finally free from pain for a little while."

Ruth did not possess the intuition, but she did know her sisters. While she was airborne she'd noticed a pattern: a line of fires burning in a straight line. They seemed to be pointing towards a mountain in the distance. She decided to follow the fire and smoke. Just as she'd resolved to move in that direction, a flaming yellow arrow rose from the East. It was from Deborah's bow. Ruth flew off in the direction the arrow came from until she found a second arrow rising from the ground.

Ruth called out, "Deborah!"

Deborah walked over smiling and crying at the same time. She grabbed Ruth and hugged her hard. Then, she revealed the reason for her tears, "I'm glad you're okay. I saw Mama here. She's one of the lost souls wondering around here."

Ruth shook her head, "So, where is she now?"

"I would have thought that she would have gone to see you next. But, maybe she took my tongue lashing to heart?" Deborah wondered, "Come, let's catch up with Cil. She's got a big head start on us."

"And, what about Sarah?" Ruth asked.

Deborah rolled her eyes and gave Ruth a hard gaze, "Now you know, they ain't got nothing here that can hold her. Think about it."

Ruth smirked and grabbed her sister's hand. She lifted them both skywards to follow Cil's markers.

Sarah emerged from the portal upon a mountaintop. She saw lush vegetation in every direction. There were cattle and vineyards in every valley and upon every hilltop.

Sarah heard someone speaking to her in a soft voice, "It can all be yours, a world of your own."

Sarah turned to see a ghostly image of Isadora standing behind her.

Sarah's eyes blazed.

"Soul Drinker, why do you send your shade to do a demon's work?"

"Sweet Sarah, I'm confident in my abilities, but I'm not fool enough to meet you in an open space like this alone. I know what you are. Besides, as I'm sure your eyes reveal to you, that what you see here is an illusion. But, you know full well that I can make it a reality for you and your sisters, as real as Elisa's paradise was to her. The war is over. You won. Leave this life and enjoy your immortality in peace. Surely you see this for the folly that it is? With your gifts, you could live forever. Yet, you risk your life, and that of your sisters, for these damned ones? Your sister Cil's a fanatic and the three of you have followed her into hell."

The demon looked around removing the illusion of paradise, so that Sarah might see Oblivion for what it was.

"But, you see clearly don't you? And, if you do succeed here? If you free them from me, then what? They are still turned away from this love you claim. Destroy me and they will suffer under some different Hell, but Hell nonetheless. What's the point?"

Sarah replied, "Even if your words were true, I would still not be inclined to allow you to continue your obscenities upon these souls unchecked."

"And, what of your mother? What if I released her to you?"

"You mean the woman who bore me? The one who abandoned us? The one who mocked my father and pierced my sister Ruth's soul repeatedly with such delight? The wicked dig their own graves."

"Yes, and yet, she still belongs to you. And, perhaps you could offer her another opportunity at redemption."

"You do, indeed, take me for a fool. Don't you?"

"Well, yes, I do. I take most of your lot as fools. But, if you're fool enough to come here after me when you have nothing to gain of it, perhaps, you're fool enough to try and save your mother."

The image of Isadora vanished. A legion of foot soldiers took her place. Each was armed to the teeth and their weapons were trained on Sarah as she stood alone on the mountaintop. An instant before they fired on her, she smiled.

High atop a mountain was a large plateau where a castle as large as a modern city stood. The residents could go a thousand years and never encounter an uninvited guest. Well before reaching the mountaintop, the screaming, crying, pleading and agony of thousands of lost souls would turn any such visitor away. A moat, a black river at least 40 miles in circumference, encircled the castle. Anything that fell into that water was never found again. The outer stone wall looked inviting because it had no gate. It needed no gate to protect the compound. The wall lived off the flesh of anyone who touched it. Queen Isadora herself had to create an opening to pass through it. The carnivorous wall only fed from its sides, so all manner of winged beasts perched on top of the wall. Even more terrifying creatures lay inside the walls of the compound.

Cil reached the mountain first. She reasoned that Isadora had warped time in her home world causing the sisters to be separated by time as well as distance. Since she was the first one to enter the portal, she arrived first in this hideous world. Deborah entered the portal merely one step behind her, but likely didn't materialize in Isadora's world until an hour later, perhaps longer. Cil surveyed the target from the foot of the mountain and weighed her options. Finally, it came to her. She would tunnel underneath the castle city and enter behind its walls and outer defenses. Cil twirled her staff faster and faster as she did when she opened portals between worlds. This time, instead of warping time and space, she moved dirt. It was a relatively simple task for one such as her.

Ruth flew towards the damned city from the western sky, drawing volley after volley of fire from Isadora's forces lined atop the city's walls. Unbeknownst to her attackers Deborah, invisible and silent, was already inside the city walls. Deborah took the time to knock a few unsuspecting guards off their posts along the top of the city wall. She didn't do it because Ruth needed the help. She was just being Deborah. It was funny to her. Ruth did not have Sarah's extra-sharp vision, but she could see a progression of guards along a certain portion of the wall mysteriously become airborne. She smiled.

Ruth maintained her distance from the city. She floated close enough to be seen and returned fire whenever it began appeared to her that she did not have the full attention of Isadora's troops. She worked at drawing their fire while Deborah commandeered transportation to Isadora's palace. Ruth assumed Cil was somewhere doing the same thing. The more resources they brought to bear on Ruth, the better for her sisters. Ruth would launch a more sincere attack if she witnessed any of the regiments disengaging and heading back to the palace towards her older sisters or until Sarah showed up, whichever came first.

Ruth didn't have to wait long. In the distance to the north, the sky lit up as Sarah began her assault on the northwestern wall. Ruth then launched force beams into the hungry wall lining the city and into the structures beyond it causing anything combustible to explode. Sarah sent a fireball up into the heavens in acknowledgement. Ruth Ann adjusted the pink lock across her forehead, stuffing it beneath a well-placed clip and began the task of destroying Isadora's forces in earnest.

Sarah was hammering Isadora's forces. She was, indeed, meant for this. Nonetheless, she kept a look out for Ruth. Sarah's concern for her was much greater than her desire to get Isadora. The Queen of the Dead's offer of a paradise of their own had been insufficient. What Sarah really longed for wasn't physical freedom, but emotional freedom. As long as those who had pursued them for so many years were free, the sisters never would be. Thus, capturing Isadora and all of their enemies was all a part of a bigger goal – a chance to live something close to a normal life, free of this battle between saints and sinners.

Sarah landed in front of the wall. Staring at that wall, she could see the souls it had consumed on Isadora's behalf. It sickened her to her core. Still ablaze, Sarah stretched out her hand and touched the wall. The wall burst into flames. The wall's many tongues flailed about. With each movement a tormented soul was released. Sarah did not know what awaited them, but they were free of this prison. In minutes, the hungry wall that lined the city would be ash. As Sarah walked through the flames and departing souls, the demons in the courtyard scattered like vermin before the light of day.

Beneath the city, Cil worked her way towards the palace. She stumbled upon on one of Isadora's many maze-like tombs. Most people would have been hopelessly lost within the complex paths. Cil, however, was never in doubt. She moved rapidly, turn after turn, toward the palace throne room.

Down one corridor, yellow eyes glowed. The lone torch on wall revealed only five of the fifty demons Cil knew were there in the darkness. The spirit-thirsty beasts were not used to resistance from their targets. As Cil began to twirl her staff, each of them sensed that this day would be different from any they'd known before. All at once, they charged Cil, but only two or three of them at a time could attack due to the narrowness of the tombs. Cil cut through them like a lawnmower through dry grass and was soon running through the darkness again.

Deborah hopped onto one of the transportation sleds that Isadora's guards used to scurry back and forth. Instantly, she knew how to operate it. Deborah made her way towards the city's heart shielded in invisibility. Her doppelgangers operated and were apparently slaughtered all around the city. As each replica met her fate, Deborah felt a pang in heart. She was diminished a bit. Deborah rode past acts of unfathomable cruelty and torture as she moved closer to Isadora. She wanted to stop and, if she had Ruth's sensibilities, she probably would have. But, Deborah knew the best thing she could do for the tormented souls all around her would be to cut off the serpent's head.

At last, Deborah reached the Isadora's palace. Deborah remained invisible as she stepped off of her ride and was greeted by a legion of armed spirits who appeared as ghostly vapors. By their reaction it was clear to Deborah that they could see her.

Their leader said, "Hello, Deborah. We've been waiting for you so that we might slay you for our Queen. The living have no place here!"

Deborah removed her sword, "So, you're not the welcoming committee? Well, if this is the day that I should die, so be it. But if I were you, I wouldn't bet on it."

Deborah raised the sword she and her sisters crafted for her and kissed it softly.

"Come get some," she said.

Cil lifted the floor grate and climbed into the palace pantry. That pantry was unlike any pantry mortal eyes had ever seen. There were shrunken souls captured in jars like fireflies. They were once just as mortal as Cil; now, they were misshapen, warped. Cil encountered sadness upon sadness but she pushed on. Cil crept through the corridors to Isadora's throne room. The main door was guarded by two large stone gargoyles. As Cil ran towards them, they drew their weapons down to engage her. Their speed seemed to match Cil's and their skin was an unearthly stone that did not yield to Cil's blows when she did land them. Slightly bruised with several cuts on her arms and legs, Cil reestablished herself five meters in front of them. Her eyes turned black and she began to swirl her staff. She swung it faster and faster until the fabric of time and space began to warp. Cil was in Gatekeeper mode and, as such, her will was unforgiving and unyielding unto the stone beings. Both gargoyles were consumed and cast into The Pit for all eternity.

Her path now clear, Cil spun and kicked the double doors leading to the throne room faster than the human eye could capture. The lock on the door buckled. Cil slowly pushed the huge doors open.    Isadora clapped as Cil entered the humongous gold-lined room.

Isadore said, "Well done, mortal. You've found your way to your own death. You might think that me versus you would be a fair fight, but you should know by now that I don't fight fair."

Isadora lifted her scepter. The dust on the floor began to swirl into several pillars. Each pillar then took shape into beings in godly attire.

Isadora laughed, "I know it's politically unwise to raise one's rivals from the grave, but desperate times call for desperate measures. I present to you the old gods of Egypt, Osiris, Set, Isis and Ra."

Cil responded, "Those who came before me vanquished them once before and, if the Lord of Light should allow it, so it shall be again. Thus, it matters not how many gods you raise, what shall be, shall be."

Osiris sighed, "Ah, the young one has raised us from the dead. So, I guess she's not as dumb as we thought and has come to understand the old ways. But what is this new harsh language she speaks. It sounds so argumentative even when there is nothing to debate."

Isis responded, "My love, it is the language of the ruling class in this day. Thus, it is fitting that we use it, so that this new world might understand our instructions and praise us accordingly. Isadora, who is this woman?"

Isadora addressed her elders, "This one is a demigod from the age of man. She is a descendant from one of the half-breeds who vanquished the old gods."

Set chimed in, "Yes, her stench does foul the air in a familiar way and she is a gatekeeper. Thus, I cannot wait to taste her flesh. But, another enters the room who is like her. One who is also part Nightwalker."

"I guess y'all been dead for so long you just come back saying anything."

Deborah made herself visible as she made her way to her older sister's side.

Isadora said to Cil in a thundering voice, "If the two of you bow before me now, I will allow you to serve me in death. Hesitate at your own peril."

Deborah laughed, "Really? You weren't talking that big back on the island, were you?"

Isadora, feeling the gaze of the old ones, hesitated, "I…"

"Yeah, that's what I thought," Deborah mocked.

Isadora quickly pivoted, "Forefathers, execute your vengeance on the prodigy of your enemies!"

The Old Ones smirked at Isadora's request but abided nonetheless. These were the descendants of those who drove out the old gods across the globe within a thousand years. While Isadora had only just resurrected the four of them, they felt as confident in their abilities as ever. Lightening erupted from Set's fingertips and into Cil's staff. She withstood the charge and sent it back at him. Set laughed.

Set's laughter was cut short by sound of the west wall of the throne room caving in. They watched Ruth descend in a glowing blue orb. Just as the Egyptian gods took in the new combatant, a blinding light came from their right as Sarah blazed through the north wall melting the stone in the process. Ra nodded towards Sarah.

"Yes, Ra, an opponent worthy of you," Isadora confirmed.

Ra took to the air to engage Sarah.

The sisters were at a numerical disadvantage, but they didn't have to worry about collateral damage.

As Set charged toward Deborah, he called, "Come here, you of the shadows. Let me show you what real darkness is."

Deborah's eyes narrowed, "My pleasure, wicked beast. I have picked out a special blade for you."

Set beat a mighty wind with his wings seeking to knock Deborah off balance. Like a cat, she landed on her feet. Set nodded in appreciation of her skill but, still, he had little doubt that he would be victorious. Osiris, too, believed he would be victorious in his battle with Cil. His power was superior to hers, but he sensed her natural talent.

Osiris thought, "This one has knowledge beyond anyone else here. Thus, I will slay her first and the others shall wither."

Osiris was a mighty warrior who had never been defeated except by treachery.

He proclaimed, "You've slain many a demon, but, now, you face a true god."

Cil replied, "Who are you to speak such things to me? I am as you, and they are as me. Yet, we are all the same to the most high."

Isis set her sights on Ruth. She called to the rubble created by Ruth's entry and immediately the stones sprung arms legs and teeth. Worse yet, they began to multiply as they attacked Ruth. Ruth responded by rolling her arms from the outside inward, sweeping up the deadly stone critters into a glowing blue bubble which she quickly launched out the hole in the wall to places unknown. Isis lifted a brow in recognition that she did indeed have a fight on her hands.

Isadora tried to hide behind her throne. These old gods prided themselves on being warriors, but Isadora always saw herself as more of a manager. Ruth, however, had no intent of allowing her to skip this battle. Ruth intended to quickly dispatch Isis so that she could focus on Isadora. She had to pay for turning Gabriella into stone. Ruth fired a force beam towards the throne driving it and Isadora into the back wall. Ruth knocked Isis into the opposite wall then walked briskly towards Isadora. Isadora struggled to push the large ornate thrown seat off of her. Isadora saw Ruth approaching and cast a spell. It was the same one she'd used on Gabriella. But, the spell could not penetrate Ruth's personal shield. Instead, it ricocheted and turned a golden basin to stone. Ruth grabbed Isadora by the collar with her left hand and repeatedly punched her in the face with her right hand.

Isis came up behind Ruth and tried to wrap a whip around her neck. Ruth easily dislodged the goddess by flying the two of them backwards into a wall.

Ra struggled to hang on to Sarah. Her fire was hot, even to his touch. He attempted to pare her with his sharp, unforgiving tongue, but she repeatedly squirmed free of his grasp. Yet, his speed surprised her, as did his power. Still, the white hot beams from his eyes did not kill Sarah as intended. His rays did, however, slow Sarah down enough for Ra to regain his advantage. Sarah wasn't sure exactly what would happen if that long knife he used as a tongue were to make contact, but she didn't plan to find out. Sarah emitted a series of fireballs from her own mouth, which pursued Ra like guided missiles. They landed on him one after another to bind him. She doubted that they would hold him for long, and they didn't. They did allow her a couple of seconds to figure out her next approach.

"Why are you here, young one?" Osiris asked Cil as they sparred, "Surely, you know these were wicked ones long before they arrived here? This is a hell of their choosing. So, why do you come here to fight for those who will never know what you call heaven? Do you do this for some reward?"

"Heaven does not hate anyone, for our God loves all, even these. Those who love the light have returned to the Creator. And, those who have chosen darkness are damned wander in a hell of their own creation, but not of yours. For it is unfitting for any mortal to damn another. We serve the call on our own lives. We were born of light, we live in light and..."

Cil swung at Osiris, but her staff passed through him.

"...and to light you shall return. Yes, I know. When I was mortal, I believed in such foolish things too. Set revealed to me the error of my ways when he murdered me. I was reborn as god of the underworld."

Osiris waved his hand and Cil was thrown against a stone wall.

"A god who inflicts his will rather than a silent one who allows his subjects to do as they please."

Smiling, Cil regained her feet and began to twirl her staff faster and faster before Osiris.

"So, once again power corrupts. It's an old story. Must it always be?"

Osiris nodded, "Yes, but it is also true that every hero who lives long enough will someday be a villain."

"Thus, the blessings of mortality."

The portal Cil created engulfed Osiris and took him to a level within The Pit that was reserved for demons. Cil knew that The Pit would not hold Osiris. He would reappear in moments. Cil quickly surveyed the scene and saw clearly that her sisters were struggling. Ra's speed was troubling for Sarah. Deborah was too crafty even for Set, but she didn't have the raw power needed to finish him. Ruth was more powerful than Isis, but she was contending with Isadora as well. Cil knew that with her own speed and tricks she could find an opening to defeat Osiris.

She'd defeated others like him in the past, but that would take time. In that time, she could well lose Sarah or Deborah, or both. So, she made the call.

Osiris was enraged when he returned from The Pit.

Cil said into the atmosphere, "Let everything which has breath..." before she whistled and then shouted, "Sarah, shut it down! Ruth and Deborah, grab that heifer!"

Cil twirled her staff to open another portal on the other side of the room beneath the throne. Ruth created a protective blue sphere.

Osiris protested, "Woman, there is nowhere that you can send me from which I cannot return."

"This door isn't for you," Cil replied.

One by one the old gods looked up to see Sarah's aura change from day to night. Her skin darkened as an eclipse over the Sun. With her eyes rolled back and her arms stretched out, Sarah began the process of bringing an end to time. Her opponents didn't fully understand what was happening, but they soon would. Cil rushed over to the battered and bruised Isadora who was being held by Deborah and Ruth. Cil clocked Isadora with an uppercut knocking her out for the trip home.

As the room began to spin and time warp, Ruth touched Cil's arm and said, "Here. You take Isadora. I'm staying with Sarah. I can't leave her here alone."

Cil nodded and tugged at Deborah's arm. Together they took an unconscious Isadora through the portal Cil had created.

The old gods could feel their world shifting beneath them and sought to restrain Sarah. Ra, the mightiest of them, attempted to grab her. As her black fire touched him, it spread up his arm quickly consuming him. The other gods realized this was no longer a fight for their world or their legacy, but rather, a fight for survival. Osiris sent forth a burst of energy that obliterated the ceiling. The throne room opened to the sky so that they might escape. Before the sister's entered Isadora's hell, the sky had been a hellish red. Now, it was now pitch black with tornados of black flames descending from the sky consuming all they touched. Isis covered her mouth in horror. Each of the gods realized that their brief resurrection would be coming to an end in moments.

At last, the tortured souls and the screams of the old gods were gone. There was nothing left, save Sarah, Ruth, and the fading portal Cil had created. Sarah had the appearance of a human nebula. What humanity remained in Sarah motioned for Ruth to go away. Ruth was under pressure to literally hold her own atoms together.

She sighed, "Sister, I can't live without you."

Even in her altered state, Sarah comprehended Ruth's words. She tried to let go of the destruction flowing through her body. Ruth took her sister's hand and pulled her close enough to wrap her arms around her. Sarah shook and shivered to revert back to something close to human and Ruth pulled both of them towards the fading portal.

At the portal's entrance, Ruth hesitated. She looked one last time into Sarah's face searching for her best friend in the darkness. Not seeing the assurance she so wanted, she started to allow the worm hole back to Earth and away from this collapsing existence to dissipate. Then, she saw the slightest hint of a smile on Sarah's face and she knew that beneath it all her sister was coming back. Ruth returned her smile and pulled them both through the portal and back to life.

# 24
# REPAST

*July, 1981 - North Hudson Bay, Canada*

*The truth of this life is that we should be less concerned about how long we live, more concerned about how we live.*

About ten seconds after the sisters disappeared, a light appeared in the middle of the group of service men the sisters had left on the beach. That light became a glowing disk which Cil and Deborah stepped through. Cil carried the bruised, limp body of Isadora with her. She tossed Isadora into the snow.

Big Mike asked, "Is she dead?"

Cil replied, "No, but if we kill this body, she will just claim another. If she does that, we'll have to wait until she pops her head up again to find her."

"We would appreciate it if you guys would take Isadora. Just keep her on ice in a saline solution and she'll be fine for transport. We'll keep Matasis at our place," Deborah added.

The Circle Knights had purchased, on the sisters' behalf, an old mansion in the Garden District of New Orleans which the sisters would use to imprison some evil spirits. The plan was devised as an alternative to sending them back into The Pit where they were often conjured up by wayward mortals.

A beaten and defeated Isadora muttered, "It's all gone, it's all gone..." as Big Mike's crew her into the cryogenic chamber for transport.

Cil instructed the servicemen to back away from the portal that was still open. A blue, almost blinding light began to shine through the opening. The service men saw Ruth and Sarah as they stood between two worlds. Ruth held onto Sarah, but this

Sarah did not appear as she did when she first went into the portal. She was the very embodiment of darkness, soaking in light of every hue. Looking at her was like staring into a starry night in some empty corner of the universe. She and Ruth were cloaked in a blue sphere of Ruth's creation to protect the others, as Ruth continued to talk Sarah.

Ruth kept calling her name, "Sarah, Sarah…" and tried to maintain eye contact with her younger sister.

By going dark and releasing her full destructive capacity on Isadora's realm, Sarah became a unique celestial anomaly. Ruth Ann and Sarah stood in the balance between worlds.

Ruth and Sarah had a special bond. Gabriella had sought to bring Ruth out of her shell so that she might reach her full potential. Sarah had become a surrogate mother to Ruth in her adulthood despite the fact that she was the younger sibling. It was a division of the labor of love. Cil focused on keeping Deborah between the yellow lines and filling her with her own spirit, while Sarah looked after Ruth. As a child, Ruth leaned on Gabriella. As an adult, she shared her darkest thoughts with Sarah. Ruth didn't know what she'd do the next time she got the blues if Sarah wasn't there to comfort her. Ruth had never actually hurt herself, as Deborah had done, but she had thought about it often.

Ruth continued, "Let go, breathe, release…"

Ruth smiled, held Sarah close, and began to sing softly into her ear. Sarah laughed at Ruth's singing and closed her eyes. Finally, the surface of her body began to show traces of something resembling human flesh. A few moments later, she stood as Eve did in the garden. Ruth covered her with glowing blue bands so that the two of them could step through the portal and onto the frozen tundra. The portal closed. Deborah took off her white cape and wrapped it around Sarah.

Deborah whispered, "Nice job, little sis."

The four sisters climbed atop the bluff to view the battlefield. The four of them stood shoulder to shoulder with their arms interwoven next to the still fluttering crimson family banners.

They called the names of the fallen into the mist and softly falling snow, "Uncle Jorge, Auntie Alejanda, Miss Elizabeth, Gabriella, Grandma Elisa, Grandpa Rob, Ashe."

This was the first time they'd ever dared to refer to Elisa and Rob as their grandparents. Elisa had telepathically conveyed the truth to them soon after they arrived in Mexico to live with Jorge's family, but had sworn each to a secrecy so severe that they dare not utter the truth. After calling out the names, the sisters sang the "Hallelujah" chorus of a song called "Total Praise" as they reflected on all that they had lost.

Cil looked out over the landscape and said, "It is done. This season of loss is over for us and the season of growth is upon us. Let's wrap up here so that we can get on with it." As the sisters turned away, images of The Elders appeared in the distance around the island like hours on a clock. The twelve Circle Elders were present. The Elders were pleased with them and had compassion for their losses.

The sisters joined Big Mike and his team on the watercraft that was ferrying Isadora and Gabriella's remains back to the Navy cruiser. Gabriella's stone body lay on the floor of the vessel. Ruth sat beside her on the floor stroking her face. Sarah sat next to Ruth and rubbed her hand across Ruth's pulled-back hair.

The Communications officer who was sitting across from the sisters timidly leaned forward to speak to Cil, "Excuse me, ma'am, I hate to interrupt, but about that dragon?"

# 25
# A KIND OF PEACE

*Late July, 1981 - Salvador, Brazil*

*"I have my doubts if my existence is conducive to life. The rain, the clouds and the emptiness beyond, all testify against me." said Sarah Johnson in a rare moment of uncertainty.*

Cil, Deborah, Ruth, and Sarah sat side by side on an isolated beach just outside of Salvador in northern Brazil. As young women, they spent time in the Brazilian state of Bahia where Salvador was located. They returned whenever they could. Life was beautifully simple there and they loved it. The four women braided one another's hair and discussed recent events and what their next steps should be.

Ruth asked, "So, we're giving the Destry a couple of days to build up their defenses before we attack?"

Cil responded, "Yes, we want all of their assets in play so that we can destroy them all while we're there. Because they know we're coming, I'm willing to bet that any Destry from off world is scurrying back to be a part of this battle. Their complex is located underground in an isolated part of the rainforest. So, we don't have to hold back much once we get inside."

The sisters all nodded in recognition that working without constraint would be to their advantage.

"And, what about the space gods?" my mother asked.

Cil looked out across the water for a moment and then replied, "They know what happened to Poseidon. They should know by now what happened to Isadora's world and her elders. So, they should understand the price of crossing us. Yet, they will come after us. When they do, we will have to pay their star systems a visit and demonstrate to them, planet by planet, why they should leave our planet alone."

This thought weighed heavy on the sisters as they listening to the tide wash across the sand. They each tried to process what their big sister was saying. The words were particularly for Sarah to hear, but as usual she hid her true feelings for the sake of the cause. The sisters leaned in to share a collective hug and each one reached out to touch Deborah's growing belly which pocked out prominently in her bathing suit.

Cil looked lovingly at her sisters and proclaimed, "It's time to eat."

The four rose and dusted the sand from their bottoms and legs. During this process, Deborah acknowledged the fresh tattoo Ruth was sporting.

"Nice tattoo," she said.

The tattoo spelled out "Gabby."

"Yeah? And, what you got to say about it?" Ruth asked. She was expecting criticism from Deborah.

"Oh, no, I think it's very nice and well done. I just question the placement. I mean what if you want to wear something low cut? People are going to see that. That's all I'm saying."

"Deborah," Sarah said in an exasperated tone.

Deborah replied, "What? Y'all know I been wanting to ask her about that tattoo all day, ever since we hit the beach. Y'all know me and my condition. And, for me to hold my tongue this long is something."

Deborah's sisters, including Ruth Ann, acknowledged her point and nodded in agreement.

While folding their blankets Ruth asked, "What about Willy?" The sisters had thrown a bag over Willy's head and tossed him through the portal to Elisa's paradise.

"What about him?" Deborah asked.

"Are we just gonna leave him there?" Ruth followed.

Deborah, replied as Cil and Sarah looked off, "He's in paradise, what else do we need to do for him? I'm carrying his children. That's more than enough."

Sarah wrapped her arm around Ruth's shoulder, "We'll get him, but he needs to stew for a little while and reflect on a couple of things." When they did retrieve Willy, they allowed him to believe that he's been abducted by aliens. It was a light sentence for his crimes, they all agreed

As they walked back towards the road carrying their blankets, Ruth Ann asked Sarah, "So, were you sick again this morning?"

To which Sarah replied, "Yes, I was, just a little bit."

Overhearing this Deborah stopped in her tracks and said loudly, "What?"

# 26
# REVELATION

*September, 2001 - Atlanta, GA*

*Every day we call into the abyss, but one day it will answer.*

The day of Aunt Cil's funeral was a particularly sad day. She had not died in battle as many who truly knew her had expected. According to the coroner, she died of natural causes. Since she was only fifty-one years old when she died, the coroner's conclusion was hard to accept. Cil relinquished the gift of not aging when she accepted the role of Gatekeeper. Still, such and early death of natural causes sounded dubious to all.

The various branches of the Few family from New Orleans to Atlanta gathered like seldom seen before. Many of the older women in the family business gathered in the kitchen to prepare the dishes for the repast. The young people conversed outside the window in the backyard. Sarah, Deborah and Ruth walked into the kitchen to thank each of the women for their efforts during their time of grief. Only women who were a part of this calling worked the kitchen during the repast of a fallen warrior.

One of the older women, Samantha from New Orleans, picked up a clean towel to dry the dishes she'd just washed.

She asked Sarah, "So, I take it since Cil is gone now, you're going to pack up your son and move to the west coast?"

"No, not right away, I want him to finish school first and I want to make sure that my sisters are okay before I go. But, how did you know that? Can you read minds and just haven't told anyone yet?"

"Child, please, I don't have to be able to read minds to know what's on your mind and in your spirit. Everyone has known since you were sixteen that you'd leave this life as soon as you got a chance. And, this is a good breaking point, a good time get away from this... all of this, isn't it?" Sam glanced over her shoulder towards Deborah and Ruth.

Taking Sarah's silence as acceptance, Sam peaked out through the thin white cotton drapes at the young folks basking in the fading summer warmth.

"Besides Reggie, none of them really have full understanding of what we do, do they, much less the burden of it all?"

"No, Auntie Sam, they don't and my son, Michael, knows nothing, at all."

Samantha was Sarah's great aunt. She was over four hundred years old although she didn't look a day over seventy and was the de-facto family historian. She wasn't gifted in the same way as the sisters, but she definitely had a gift. She had an insight that few could match. Some call this the gift of discernment.

"Yes, we are all sometimes kept blissfully unaware, aren't we?" Sam said as she washed out another bowl. Then she continued, "I been meaning to ask you something since the viewing yesterday. I noticed that the little steel cross you gave Cil was missing, the one that she always wore around her neck under her clothing. I know her husband doesn't have it."

A shocked Sarah replied, "How did you know about that?"

"Oh, I'm sorry. I know it was supposed to be a secret between you and Cil, but for some reason she told me about it back in eighty-one, right before y'all took on Matasis and his lot. Anyhow, you don't think the mortuary staff took it, do you?"

"No, they didn't bother her watch or her wedding set, so I can't see why they'd take just the cross. It was a simple thing that I made for her when I was a child."

"But she treasured it, didn't she? It meant so much to her. I can't imagine her taking it off."

Sam shook out the dish rag she'd been using and laid it out on the counter to dry before turning to assist the other ladies in placing the leftovers in the refrigerator for Cil's husband, Joe.

Sarah stood there at the sink processing what Sam had just shared with her. Then, she lowered her eyes and thought about the clues she'd missed. Still, she needed to be sure. Sarah walked over to her sisters who were still chatting with the other women.

Sarah was brief, "Hey, I need to run an errand. Ruth, can you make sure that Michael gets home safely? He's outside with the other young folks."

"Sure," Ruth said. She wondered what was driving Sarah into the street at this moment.

Deborah, who was lost in her own thoughts, simply grabbed a quick hug from Sarah and continuing sobbing.

Sarah quickly drove into the countryside. She found the secluded patch of woods where she occasionally hid her car. She quickly changed into her flame-resistant flying/battle outfit. Then, she took to the northern sky. She headed back to where they'd had their first great battle. The sensor-covered island appeared otherwise to be just as it was before that fateful day nearly twenty years earlier. Sarah landed on the shore beneath the high bluff wall where Cil and Deborah had battled Chase.

Sarah paced back and forth until she was sure of where she wanted to dig. She unleashed a steady stream of heat and microwave energies to melt away the ice that had built up over the years. Aided by her unique powers of perception, she saw Chase's body as she had expected. But, beneath his body was another.

Sarah rushed over and began melting away the ice from this body with her hands. She was ever so careful. Sarah kneeled in the snow and ice and pulled the body into her lap. When she turned the body over, she saw Cil's face and the cross she'd given her over thirty years earlier. Sarah leaned back and let out a loud cry. She caressed Cil's cold face as she rocked back and forth and the pieces came together in her own mind. Cil had not been resurrected or even healed by Deborah. Rather, she had been spontaneously recreated.

Cil had spent so much time counseling Deborah and sharing insights with her all those years prior to the battle. Cil was filling Deborah with her own spirit so that Deborah would know completely who she was. But, there was one thing about Cil that Deborah did not know about – the cross. The little comments people had made about Cil since their time on the island now made perfect sense. Sarah realized that all those years prior to her death here, Cil could, indeed, see the future. The new Cil had been more like Chase. She could assimilate numerous factors and weigh them fairly to predict an outcome. That is not the same as actually seeing the future.

Sarah remembered the story Deborah told about the day she tried to kill herself. She claimed that a woman who looked just like Cil, older and slightly taller, had rescued her; but, Cil had been with Sarah all day.

"What if Deborah was right? That would mean that Cil had been in two places at the same time," Sarah whispered to herself.

In an instant, she knew. Cil had traveled back in time to save Deborah. And, she knew that, in doing so, she would change history and forfeit her own life. Cil had found a way to move the very stars in heaven.

As the pieces fell together, a terrible reality fell upon Sarah. Her beloved sister Cil had been stabbed and tossed from the bluff to die alone in a powdery snow drift. She thought that they could have at least been there during her transition if not saved her life by rushing Mavis over to heal her.

As she wept, a calm came over Sarah.

She said to herself what Cil would have said to her in that moment, "It's time, Sarah."

Sarah removed the cross from Cil's neck and placed it on her own. She stood up, held the cross in her hand, looked towards the heavens, and said, "Yes, yes, yes, I will follow."

# Addendum
## THE SECRET SORROW OF SAINTS

*Uncertain*

I have seen Elisa's dreams enough to know that this meeting took place, but I cannot tell you if it happened a week before she died or three hundred years prior. Nor can I tell you if the parties met in person or via some as yet unknown gift of Elisa's to psychically convene disparate parties across time and space in some form of virtual reality. I do know that the scene took place on the same corner where Elisa, Henri, Chase, and Zi often met to break bread and drink wine. While the details of this dream are different each time it comes to me, what follows is the most coherent summation I can derive.

Henri and Chase stood up as Elisa arrived at the table. Zi nodded at her mentor with the sly smile she saved for her friends which were few and far between.

Henri poured Elisa a glass of wine, "Madam."

"Thank you, Henri."

Elisa took a sip before speaking again, "I guess we all know why we are here and, certainly, I may be out of line for doing this, but I just wanted to give you two the opportunity to walk away now."

For a moment there was silence before a boiling Chase erupted, "How might I do that? This is me. This is what I've become. This is what I have lived for the last three hundred years. I know nothing else. I am nothing else."

Elisa said softly to him reaching out to touch his hand, "Surely you realize that you won't survive this regardless of how this works out. There is no happy ending here for you."

"Was there ever?" a tearful Chase replied.

"And, your love would not want you to go on…?" Henri asked

"My love would understand that I have no choice," Chase replied.

Elisa squeezed Chase's hand before turning to Zi.

"Darling, are you sure you want to do this?"

"Yes," Zi answered before continuing, "Every way I turn I see evil. When I look upon the Elders, who seek blood and profane love, I see evil. And, when I look in the mirror, I see evil, for in my struggles I have become the very thing I despise. It has to stop."

Elisa stared deeply into Zi's eyes trying, out of respect for her, to resist the temptation to read her mind.

Again, she asked her protégé, "Do you really want to go through with this? You're not doing all of this just to support Chase because he helped you, are you?"

In the years after Elisa was cast into The Pit, Henri and the Nightwalkers also worked to keep Zi hidden from the Elders, but it was Chase who shed blood on her behalf. As the Elders dispatched Circle Knights to apprehend Zi, Chase often fought at her side. In the early years after Elisa left, he worked to protect Zi as she came into her own power.

Chase's face took on a look of concern before Zi answered, "Perhaps, at first, but after considering how I have been literally stripped of everyone and everything I loved, isn't that reason enough? And, what about you? Hundreds of years in The Pit suffering on some level of Hell that most could not imagine in their worst nightmares and, still, you are here holding up the cause? I don't understand how you can still believe that this battle is worth fighting. If Armageddon is inevitable, why go through all of this to preserve this wicked age if it will still all be ash one day anyway? Why not work instead to usher in that day?"

Elisa realized that the years of isolation while she was on the run had taken a toll on Zi's mental stability.

She decided to try once more to reason with her, "Zi, do you remember paradise where I keep my dragon?"

"Of course, I do. Who could forget that?"

"What if you could live there forever? Would you forget all of this and go? In fact, I'll give you that whole world and throw in the dragon, too, if you'll just walk away from all of this today."

For a moment, the woman was a little girl again. She fought back a smile. She looked at her hands and thought about the blood, innocent blood she had shed to pave this path in her life. Zi shook her head no.

Elisa suggested, "If it's the Elders you're worried about, I'll ask them to leave you alone. I think they'll listen. They will owe me for what I am about to do."

Zi saw the Elders as an inflexible, unforgiving lot and simply could not accept what she believed to be false hope. Tears filled Elisa and Zi's eyes. So, too, did water pool in Henri's eyes. He had known Chase well before he ever met Elisa or Zi.

Henri stretched out his hand towards Chase and simply asked, "Brother?"

Chase took Zi's hand in his own and said to the others, "I think we're done here."

## SACRIFICES • *Alan D. Jones*

# Epilogue
## ETERNAL PRAYERS

*We are an echo, resounding through the darkness, lest any of us think we are our own creation.*

Every day, they come. Every day they come looking for healing. Every day they come here looking for some kind of miracle. Although my ability to transmute matter does aid me in caring for the sick and dying, I am no healer. I am certainly no healer of a war-torn and crumbling world. The hospital wards of alien worlds are much like those on my beloved Earth, full of hope and suffering. The smoke-filled-skies blot out their sun. Their land has not yielded a harvest in years. Their failing food factories designed to recycle waste into sustenance lie in ruins as do all of their institutions beyond armies and hospitals. Through my gift, I am able to turn much of the debris here into a sort of manna. I spend my days tending to the injured and feeding the hungry. There are so many now that they lay in the streets surrounding the hospital waiting for me to come outside and bless them with something to eat regardless how crude it might be.

Now this day, one of the few remaining, is done and I am alone again in my quarters save my memories scattered around me. A picture of my mother brings back so many pleasant memories. Though she lived into her three hundred and thirty-second year, I still mourn that she was taken so soon. Like me, she appeared to be thirty-two until the day she died. Factually, she was undone by treachery. But in truth, she was undone by a weariness of life, her life. After Deborah died, Sarah's role of keeping her safe died, too. My mother's other role was that of an avenging angel. It was a mantle she never wanted. Yet, she wore that heavy crown with as much grace as anyone could hope. Still, when I was alone with her, I saw the growing despair behind her beautiful eyes. With each battle and every life she took, her spirit diminished. She had sacrificed her humanity for the rest of us. She died physically two years after Aunt Deborah, but her spirit died a little with every drop of blood she shed.

Uncle Joe and some of the men from the community, including the one who discovered my mother, found the guys who attacked my mother and exacted some small measure of justice. I'm just fine with that.

Deborah battled the demons of mental illness all her life, like her mother. On more than one occasion, her sisters pulled her back from the abyss of self-destruction, even when she fell into witchcraft. Still, she lived a life of grace. She should have been dead at fourteen as all the stars in heaven would attest. Each day that she lived was a new mercy for those who loved her. While Deborah walked the Earth, she performed many miracles. Strangely, Deborah was oblivious to the fact that many of her illusions were reality. But with the assistance of her sisters, Deborah did a number of good things, most of which the world will never know. She died the death she always wanted – a good death, on the battlefield defending the living, without regret. I will always remember the stories Aunt Deborah told. Her sisters had been hesitant to share the details of their exploits. Deborah relished sharing the tales. My favorite story was the one about how they toppled Olympus and walked upon the dust. When Aunt Deborah neared the end of telling the story, she'd pull a small vial from around her neck. It contained a thimbleful of Olympic dust. In the darkness, it glowed and twinkled like a star.

Aunt Deborah never mentioned her dealings with the Nightwalkers. Seeing her dreams clearly like I do, I know many of those events well. Their members were sworn to secrecy. Now that they are all gone, perhaps I will share some of Deborah's adventures with that clan.

At this writing Auntie Ruth is still alive and living on Earth. She still defends mortals from external threats. The Elders have asked her to join them multiple times. She has refused each time. Ruth has no interest in status, managing others, or meting out punishment. Her only desire is to protect and serve. Oh, how I love my Auntie Ruth. Ruth lives on an island encased by one of her bubbles. She and the few who reside there with her are the failsafe of human existence. My remaining cousins and I visit when we can. When we get weary in this battle against the darkness, we go see Auntie Ruth.

Elisa fought the good fight, but as she said, "It's hard to walk through Hell without developing a stench."

Rob, after many years serving the very Elders who imprisoned his secret wife, became a Gatekeeper so that he might free her. I can hardly imagine how it pained him to serve them, to earn their trust, to endure so for hundreds of years, just for his beloved's freedom. And in the end, he forsook his immortality and gained the ire of the Elders to rescue Elisa.

Elisa was so damaged by her time in The Pit that she lost her will to live. Throughout their years back on this side of existence, Elisa would visit her husband secretly at night. She did this for his happiness, not her own. Often Elisa saw happiness as a delusionary state between harsh realities. Rob tried to help her work through her experiences in The Pit. At most, he helped her develop a sense of purpose: to protect their grandbabies.

Many days in The Pit, Elisa prayed for death. For nearly three hundred years, her prayers went unanswered. While there she saw friends and loved ones suffer and perish. She was so hopeless that even after she was delivered from The Pit, a bit of it stayed with her all of her remaining days. She inflicted pain upon herself to quell the voices in her head. She hid the scars of her self-mutilation until her last day in the world. In the end, she witnessed one last unbearable act, one last sacrifice she must push down and hide, before leaving this world. She nearly lost control of herself when she saw Chase drive his blade into Cil.

Aunt Cil hid her dreams from me, or so it seems. The glimpses of her dream life that I have seen have been of her praying. In her prayers she asks for nothing, she's simply content to sit and be with God. She was like a feather caught up in the current of the Spirit. Certainly, that tells me a great deal about who she was, but little of her story, as she saw it. Thus, I know her better by her deeds and by how those around her loved her. I know that she knew the future and understood time in a way that I shall never know. She knew a truth well that only a select few know only in part. She knew that Deborah would not have survived without her intervention. She knew the price would be her own life. That was Aunt Cil. The replacement Cil only died when Deborah was ready to let go of Cil. On a subconscious level, Deborah knew that Cil died. She just couldn't accept it until some twenty years later. Yes, Aunt Cil was a fanatic. She was a fanatic about love. At every turn, she denied herself for the sake of others. Her hidden sacrifice still rings loudly through the ages to those of us who knew her and through those whom we love. I know, given that her dreams were of things of heaven, that it was for my own good that she took measures to largely hide them from me. I'm sure that even that act, had a price.

One thing Aunt Cil said stayed with me all of these centuries later: "Often times when we say God did it. We mean that God did it through us or, through another, for it is God's Spirit in us which crosses the sea, climbs the mountain, frees the captives, and conquers all – even death.

In the end, it's not about your creation story, your political affiliation, your gender, or your race. It's about how authentic your love is. It's about whether or not you will place someone else's needs before your own. It's about sacrifice. I came to this war-torn world knowing that it might well be my last mission. In saying that, I did not come here to preach or to proselytize. I'll leave that to others. I came here simply to serve those in need and to share with them the love that has been given to me. With my gifts or through my teleporting cousin, Akina, I could have left this world long ago. Even now, if I really wanted to leave, I could. I chose to stay here and walk with them as they enter the valley of death. They see me as this alien of questionable sanity for remaining with them when I could leave. A few dare to ask me why. That is when I share what I believe. Within that moment, this love is truly shared with them and placed upon their hearts.

"What good does it do to share such a love with those doomed to die so soon?" you ask.

"What better time?" I reply.

This love that empowers them to help each other in this darkest of days, this love that pushes away the night, this love that death cannot hold is not bound by the hands of time. This is eternal love.

There is much more to tell. The third act of this particular tale weighs heavy on my heart, but time is short. I may not be the one to tell it. Let me close with this. It is unwise to compare one sacrifice with another. Each gift is weighed on a scale none of us can balance. Public sacrifices are intended to correct the path of another, rather than to set our own. However, it is the silent sacrifice that echoes within our souls and denotes the true path of our hearts. At the end of day, this life is about what we were willing to give for the benefit of others. The measure of our love is found in the weight of our sacrifice.

Made in the USA
Charleston, SC
15 November 2013